CW00430076

THE SUNRISE RAIDERS

Spitfire Mavericks Thrillers
Book Four

D. R. Bailey

SAPERE
BOOKS

THE SUNRISE RAIDERS

Published by Sapere Books.

24 Trafalgar Road, Ilkley, LS29 8HH

saperebooks.com

Copyright © D. R. Bailey, 2024

D. R. Bailey has asserted his right to be identified as the author of this work.
All rights reserved.

No part of this publication may be reproduced, stored in any retrieval system, or transmitted, in any form, or by any means, electronic, mechanical, photocopying, recording, or otherwise, without the prior written permission of the publishers.
This book is a work of fiction. Names, characters, businesses, organisations, places and events, other than those clearly in the public domain, are either the product of the author's imagination, or are used fictitiously.
Any resemblances to actual persons, living or dead, events or locales are purely coincidental.

ISBN: 978-0-85495-225-0

I would like to dedicate this book to my friend Susanne Winterstein-Smith. I've known Susanne for nearly twenty years, and we've always been very good friends. She has become one of my biggest fans. So, this dedication is my way of saying thanks for being there, being my friend and one of my cheerleaders.

CHAPTER ONE

The North Sea, 1941

I lay in the dinghy, shading my eyes against the sun. Dawn had finally broken after a long night. I was adrift in the North Sea somewhere between England and Holland; I had no idea where. It wasn't a pleasant place to be. I had a raging thirst and nothing to drink. My hopes of an early rescue had been dashed after being shot down on a sortie the night before.

It hadn't been an auspicious mission in the first place. The three of us, Pilot Officer Willie Cooper, Pilot Officer Jonty Butterworth, and me, Flying Officer Angus Mackennelly, had been sent out on a patrol. There was a shroud of cloud cover above us, which was never a good thing to be flying in. Bandits could remain concealed until the last moment, when they attacked.

We crossed the water just after Clacton and headed towards the coast of Belgium. We would patrol northward up the middle of the sea between the two countries. It was one of those times when you got the feeling something wasn't right.

"I don't like this, Skipper," said Jonty over the radio, as we turned to fly our patrol up towards the north.

It was unlike Jonty to be pessimistic. He was normally an incurable optimist. If he didn't like it, then there was definitely something amiss.

"What's the matter?" Willie teased him. "No ballads in the offing?"

Jonty's propensity to burst into song was a bone of contention between them. He had a knack for composing ballads out of everything and anything, to Willie's annoyance. The two of them were, nevertheless, the best of chums.

"No," said Jonty. "No, there's something in the air and I don't like it."

Willie left off baiting him and we anxiously scanned the skies above and to the rear. If there was going to be a place Jerry would attack from, this would be it. After twenty minutes or so, I decided we'd had enough and should head for home. That should make Squadron Leader Richard Bentley, CO of Squadron 696, the Mavericks, happy at least. We'd have done our patrol and returned safely.

I was just about to give the order to return to base when Willie cried out in alarm.

"Bandits, bandits coming in fast, two o'clock high."

"I told you! I told you this would happen," said Jonty.

"Break, break now!" I said frantically, seeing the incoming planes for myself.

"There's only two of them," said Jonty, half relieved.

We had split up and were circling in to meet their attack.

"Wait a minute," said Willie. "Those aren't ME109s."

"Well, what the hell are they?" I said, noting the absence of the familiar yellow nose.

"Damned if I know, but let's take them anyhow. How hard can it be?"

Never were there more famous last words. We tried to fly in a pincer movement, but these newcomers were quick. They flipped out and away before any of us could fire.

"What the deuce?" I said.

"He's on your tail, Jonty! Watch out!" Willie turned to help Jonty, who had one of the bandits right behind him.

Jonty was twisting this way and that, but the newcomer stuck to him like glue.

"The usual stuff isn't working!" he yelled. "What do you suggest?"

"Shooting him down would be good," Willie retorted, closing in.

"Yes, well, that's what I'm trying to do, but I can't shake him off!"

I had no time to answer because the second plane had decided that I was his prime target. I immediately pulled up into a climb and then tried to loop over, but he just kept coming.

I could see now why Jonty was having a problem. I attempted various tricks to get away from the attacking Jerry, but he was far quicker. The adrenaline was pumping now, as I realised I was up against a superior foe and I was damned if I knew what to do about it.

To the left of me, Willie's guns sprang to life.

"Got him! Got the blighter," he said.

I flicked a quick glance to see that the first Jerry was diving towards the sea with a smoking engine. As agile as these planes were, they were no match for two Spitfires. But that was all the time I had. As I tried once more to bank out of the way, the one on my tail opened fire. I heard bullets ripping into the fuselage behind me.

"He's hit me!" I shouted. "I'm hit."

"Hang on, Skipper, I'm coming — hold on."

"Easier said than done," I replied, trying to turn away from the incoming fire once more.

Another round of tracers hit my engine. It stuttered and died.

"Now I'm in the basket, chaps," I said as the plane lurched downwards. I struggled to control it, wondering if my time had come. I was a sitting duck, and a lame one at that. Was he coming in for the kill?

"It's all right, Skipper. We're on him."

Jonty's guns chattered while I tried desperately to level out my kite.

"Oh blast," said Jonty, sounding annoyed.

"He's doing a runner," said Willie.

"Leave him," I said. "Get back to base. I'll be all right."

"You damn well won't be, Skipper, not until we've seen you safely down."

I was too preoccupied with trying to glide down onto the water to argue with Jonty. I had managed to level my Spitfire off and she was losing height at a steady rate. Fortunately, the sea was relatively calm.

"I've got it, I think … yes… I've got it under control," I said.

"Easy does it, Scottish. You'll make it," said Willie.

My plane hit the water with a splash and skimmed along the surface before coming to a stop. I breathed a sigh of relief. That was the worst part of the landing over. Knowing I would not have very long before the Spitfire began to sink, I pulled open the canopy and climbed out onto the wing. I inflated the life raft and eased myself into it.

Jonty and Willie buzzed over me and dipped their wings. Then they headed for Blighty. I watched their planes until they were small specks in the distance, while my plane slowly sank into the ocean. Finally, I was alone, with just my thoughts for company.

My thoughts were not very pleasant. What were the chances of me being found? I didn't like the odds. I thought of Sergeant Angelica Kensley, to whom I was engaged. What would she be thinking? She would know I went down, having been listening in on the comms. Most of my thoughts were of her and how she would feel if I did not come back. This thought kept me going. I needed to survive, for her.

Sleep eventually claimed me, and then I woke with the dawn. I had not been rescued, which was hardly surprising since I would be harder to spot at night. My hopes were renewed with daybreak, in spite of the hunger and the thirst. Jonty and Willie would have let them know my position, and Squadron Leader Bentley would move heaven and earth to get me back. Surely someone would find me?

I sat up and took a look around. I could not see land in any direction. Had I drifted north? The further north I went, the less likely I was to be picked up. It wasn't a pleasant notion. Hopefully, the Navy would be out looking for me.

Suddenly there were a lot of waves. They were not from the wind but looked like the kind of waves that were made a vessel. Except there were no boats to be seen.

A submarine started to break the surface. This was all I needed. I hunkered down and peered over the edge of the dinghy. Just my luck. It was a U-boat. Hoping they might ignore me, I kept my head down and waited.

After a few moments, there was a lot of shouting. It got closer, then the dinghy started to bump against the hull of the submarine. I looked up and there was a German sailor, pointing a rifle at me.

"*Hände hoch, hände hoch,*" he said.

I didn't speak German, but even I knew that meant I should put my hands up. I sat up in the boat and did as he requested. For a few moments, we stared at each other. He did not drop his rifle. I was wondering what to do next when he was joined by another man, who I assumed from his insignia was an officer. In fact, he was most likely the captain.

"English?" he said.

"Yes."

There was no point in trying to prevaricate; it was perfectly obvious from my RAF uniform.

"Pilot?"

"Yes," I replied again.

"Get up onto here," he said, holding out his hand.

I took it, since there was nothing else for it, and let him haul me up onto the deck of the submarine.

"So, you were ... shot down?" he asked affably.

"By one of yours, yes."

"Bad luck," he smiled. He took a packet of cigarettes from his pocket and offered one to me.

"Thanks, but I don't smoke," I said politely.

He looked surprised. With a shrug, he lit one up himself, then puffed on it contentedly. He seemed in no hurry to do anything about me, but then if I'd been cooped up in the nautical equivalent of a tin can for days, I'd probably feel the same.

"So, what happens now?" I asked him when he did not volunteer anything further.

"What happens? You are our prisoner. You will come back to Germany," he said.

"I'd rather not, if it's all the same to you," I quipped.

He laughed. "Ah, you British, always with a sense of humour. But I'm sorry, I cannot let you go. You will need to come with us."

"Right. I see."

I contemplated the odds of simply diving off the side and going under. It didn't seem like a good plan. Firstly, I would not be able to stay underwater for long enough, and secondly, they would shoot me when I surfaced.

"We will kill you if you jump," the captain said conversationally, perhaps divining my thoughts.

"I know," I said.

It was pointless. It really seemed as if luck had run out for me this time. I had survived being shot down in France and got home in one piece. But everyone's card is marked and at some point, fate outplays us.

"One more cigarette and then we go," the captain said. "You can get some food and a drink."

He threw his spent cigarette into the water and lit up another. I suspected that he could not smoke in the U-boat, and thanked providence for a few more minutes of freedom. The food and beverage did sound rather good just the same. If I had to be captured, then at least it had started off reasonably well. I wasn't looking forward to travelling in a submarine; it seemed rather claustrophobic. I had never been attracted to serving in the Navy for that reason.

As his cigarette burnt down to nothing, the captain surveyed the horizon with practised ease. I knew there was less than a minute or two before I would finally have to go into the depths. Just when hope was gone, however, something turned up.

There was shouting from the conning tower of the submarine, and I heard the drone of several aircraft.

"*Achtung!*" shouted one of the sailors. I turned to look. Three Spitfires were heading towards us at speed. The gunner on the submarine opened fire, and everyone's attention was on the Spits.

"Come on!" shouted the captain. "Let's go!"

He indicated to me that I should run for the turret. I hesitated.

"Come on!" he shouted again and drew his Luger, aiming it at me to force me to comply.

Just as he did so, the Spitfires opened fire and bullets strafed along the surface of the water. I figured at this rate I was going to die either way, so I launched myself from the submarine and into the drink.

I hit the water and swam under. Above me and to my rear I could see the hulk of the sub, and the noise of the aircraft was deafening as they flew over.

I bobbed up briefly and saw the planes circling back around while the U-boat crew was running for the conning tower, including the captain. I was forgotten for the moment. I started to swim away from the submarine as fast as I could in all my gear.

The planes came in on the attack once more and strafed the deck. They might make one more pass, but that would be it; they would be out of ammo and by then the U-boat would have dived. The captain was still climbing the ladder of the conning tower when there was a tremendous splash and then another. Some large projectiles, which I immediately assumed were shells, had impacted the sea on either side of the U-boat.

I looked over to my left and saw a British Navy destroyer, which had suddenly appeared from nowhere. Its guns were trained on the U-boat. The German captain frantically tried to get down the hatch, but this time it was his luck that had run out. A direct hit on his submarine caused a massive explosion. I dived under the water again as debris hit the surface all around me. When I came up for air, I saw that the U-boat was listing to one side. There was no sign of the captain, but there were a couple of bodies floating in the water. Another shell slammed into the U-boat and I went under once more.

The next time I surfaced, the U-boat was slowly sinking and leaking black oil, which was spreading in its wake. I swam away to avoid getting sucked under as the sub went down. Then I started to wave and shout for help, hoping the crew on the destroyer would see me.

It began to steam towards me. I breathed a sigh of relief. The cards had fallen in my favour after all.

Not long afterwards I was ensconced in the officers' mess wearing some overalls leant to me by one of the crew, since my uniform was soaked through. I sipped a glass of whisky and pushed away my empty plate. The cook had whipped me up some eggs and bacon, and a cup of tea, after which I'd been offered a very welcome tot of single malt.

"You're lucky we spotted you," said the Navy lieutenant, whose name was Christian Jones.

"I'll say. I was almost a Jerry prisoner," I said. "You chaps came in the nick of time."

"We've been hunting that bloody U-boat for weeks. It was a lucky strike. Your Spitfire chaps radioed it in and we happened to be a short distance away."

I had an inkling of who the Spitfire chaps might have been, and assumed Bentley would have let them go up to look for me. I made a mental note to thank him, if it was indeed the case.

"You'll have to stay with us until we get to Portsmouth, I'm afraid," said Jones. "We'll find you a cabin and sort out your uniform, if that's all right?"

It was more than all right. I was eternally grateful that I wasn't under the sea in that blasted U-boat.

"Absolutely."

"You'll get to your squadron soon enough."

"Thank you."

"Don't mention it. Officers' mess tonight — Commander Marley is keen to meet you."

"I'll be happy to meet him," I said, "and to thank him for his prompt action."

"Not at all. It's another feather in our caps."

I nodded and finished the whisky.

It took us a couple of days to reach Portsmouth, not because we couldn't get there sooner, but because the Navy's duty took precedence over returning a downed Air Force pilot. It turned out that Commander Marley was a jovial man with an excellent sense of humour. Various jokes were made at the Air Force's expense, but I was on Naval territory so had to wear it.

A telegram was delivered to me during this short sojourn from the Mavericks. I was delighted to find it was from Angelica.

So glad you're safe darling STOP, it read. *I can't wait to see you STOP I love you STOP.*

I folded it and put it in my pocket, receiving a sympathetic look from the radio officer.

"Your young lady?" he asked me.

"My fiancée."

"Is she pretty?"

"She's more than just pretty."

She certainly was. I recalled Angelica's face at once, wishing she was there in front of me — her brown eyes, her perfect lips, her black hair. I sent back a suitable reply and said I couldn't wait to see her either.

The Navy very kindly had a car drive me up to Banley. It was going on for late afternoon when we finally rolled up at the airfield.

I had hardly bade my driver goodbye when a familiar figure came hurtling towards me. Since I was now used to Angelica's boisterous nature, I braced myself for the impact.

"Oof," I said as she jumped into my arms full tilt.

"Oh, Angus, Angus, you stupid man!" she said, before kissing me soundly. Since this activity usually left me bereft of thought, I said no more for quite a while. I was as glad to have her in my arms as she was to be there.

"You promised me you wouldn't get shot down," she said as we pulled apart. "And there you were, ditching in the sea! I might have guessed you'd do something silly like that."

Since it was just like her to tease me for coming off worst in a dogfight, I took it in good part. Besides, I was overjoyed to see her.

"I couldn't exactly help it," I replied, smiling.

"Well, you should have!"

"You are probably the most unreasonable woman I have ever met," I told her.

"Oh, and have you met many unreasonable women? Don't answer that. I know already."

She wasn't wrong. I'd had a bad run with women in the past, and that was part of the reason I had been posted to the Mavericks in the first place. On the other hand, had I not been, I would never have met Angelica. Every cloud had a silver lining.

I laughed, and so did she. Our relationship was on the sparky side at times, but we both secretly enjoyed the repartee.

"I'm so relieved and happy to see you, darling. You need to come and tell me all about it," she said, taking hold of my hand.

"I'd love to, though I think I'm going to have to tell Bentley first."

I spied Section Officer Audrey Wilmington heading straight for us, and as she was Bentley's adjutant it was bound to be on his account.

She saluted as she came up to us, and I returned the salute. We kept up protocols in company although we had become friends, and she was Angelica's bosom buddy.

"Bentley…" she began.

"Wants to see me?" I finished it for her.

"Yes, yes, he does."

"Well, lead on. I don't suppose he'll mind if I bring Angelica?" I asked.

"I'm sure not, particularly under the circumstances," she said.

Bentley was fairly benign in this regard, and often informal. He had encouraged me to become engaged to Angelica in order to "cure me of my wayward activities" as he once put it. Besides which, he seemed to give me more latitude than others, which was partly due to his lining me up to lead the flight if the current flight leader, Flight Lieutenant Brent Judd, was shot down and killed. Thankfully, Judd seemed to bear a charmed life and I had so far been spared that duty.

We reached Bentley's office and Audrey ushered us in. It was quite plain inside, with a desk for Bentley and another one for Audrey. The walls were a shade of light blue, with a grey carpet and Bentley was sitting behind his desk, fiddling with his pipe.

He stood up as soon as he saw us enter, and said, "Ah, Flying Officer Mackennelly, come in, come in, and Sergeant Kensley too."

"Thank you, sir," I said saluting. Angelica did likewise.

"Sit down, Angus. Sergeant, I'm mighty glad to see you."

"I'm glad to be here, sir."

"You seem to have had your fair share of lucky escapes, Angus," he mused.

We then watched him go through the ritual of replenishing his pipe. We had learned that this sacred operation was not to be interrupted. It consisted of emptying the used tobacco, scraping out the bowl, filling and tamping in the new tobacco and finally lighting it. This could take a while and almost seemed a meditative process. One of the benefits of it was that it seemed to calm Bentley down, which was very useful when he had become somewhat irate. I couldn't see many other benefits, particularly since I did not smoke and the pipe kicked out quite a stink, not to mention filling the room with a smog that could rival that of London on a particularly bad day. I had secretly dubbed it the 'pipe of doom'.

When the CO had quite finished and was puffing away contentedly, he said, "What happened out there?"

"It was a new kind of plane," I said. "Not an ME109. I'd never seen it before, and it was bloody quick. I wasn't able to evade it, and I paid the price for that."

"Yes, Cooper and Butterworth said much the same. And then?"

"I managed to land on the water and got into the dinghy. Then I was almost taken prisoner by a U-boat."

"What?" Bentley spluttered.

It appeared Bentley wasn't aware of this, so I recounted the tale for his benefit. He listened intently and then pointed his pipe at me in an accusatory fashion.

"Only you could get captured by a U-boat," he said crossly. "Always getting into damn scrapes, you and those reprobates Butterworth and Cooper. I sent those blighters out there to find you — they never said you were on a blasted U-boat. What will you get up to next?"

Angelica shot me a triumphant look, as if Bentley had just clinched her argument.

"Well, I could hardly help it that a U-boat was in the vicinity," I replied, slightly put out by these aspersions. It was almost as if I had deliberately requested a German submarine to come and pick me up.

"Trouble seems to find *you*, Angus — that's the problem. How am I supposed to make you flight leader when you keep getting yourself into these damnable situations?"

"I thought that was only if Judd bought it, sir," I shot back, somewhat aggrieved by the unfairness of his remarks.

"Yes, well ... fortunately he hasn't ... yet." The CO eyed me somewhat irascibly and took several more puffs of his pipe. "Anyway, never mind all that. What's done is done."

I waited, wondering if there was more.

Bentley sighed heavily, as if the troubles of the world weighed on him. "We've heard reports of a new German plane, a new fighter."

"The ones we encountered?"

"No doubt," he said. "No doubt. It's a Focke-Wulf Fw 190, apparently. Blasted plane is wreaking havoc with our fighters. We've nothing to touch it."

"I see," I said. This was grave news indeed. Obviously, air superiority was vital. If we didn't have that and the Germans decided to invade again, then we were definitely in the basket.

"Yes, it's a rum do and no mistake." He returned to his pipe, seemingly in no hurry to tell us to leave.

"So what do we do about it?" I asked him.

"What do we do? A damn good question, and damned if I know. We're still going to have to continue to fly against them, no matter what the odds are, until the War Office works something out."

"Right."

This wasn't good news and Angelica's face fell. She often worried that I would be killed in action, and now with this new fighter, it certainly seemed as if the cards were stacking up against me, and all the other pilots in the squadron.

"We will need to work out some tactics to counter it, if we can. In the meantime, we might get a short respite from the bloody Circuses and so on."

The Circus was a codename for a joint bomber fighter incursion into France. The idea was to drop bombs, lure out the Luftwaffe and shoot down their planes. With this new turn of events they'd be more than happy to come out and decimate ours, I mused. It was a depressing thought. The Circuses had not been a great success in any case, in spite of what Fighter Command might want the War Office to believe. On top of that we'd had Rodeos, which were fighter sweeps, and Rhubarbs, which were two-aircraft stealth incursions. It was a Rhubarb that had seen me get shot down in France, and I wasn't enamoured of these either.

"Let's hope we can come up with a plane to beat it," I said.

"All well and good, but the time it will take to refine and manufacture something won't be short," said Bentley. "Our best bet is to see if we can modify the Spitfire designs we already have. I'm sure they'll be working on it, but it's just a damn shame we haven't got one of these new planes to examine."

"Chance would be a fine thing," I snorted. Getting our hands on one was about as likely as Hitler voluntarily deciding to end the war.

"Yes, well … for the moment, we have to do what we have to do," said Bentley with an air of finality.

I nodded.

"Go on, get off, the pair of you. I'm sure you've got some catching up to do. Take a couple of days' leave."

"Yes, sir, thank you, sir," I said gratefully.

"And when are you two going to tie the knot?" he asked as we stood up.

This rather caught me on the hop, as I had not discussed it with Angelica. She had been most reluctant to get engaged for some time, and I didn't want to rock the boat.

"We'll talk about it," said Angelica. "We haven't decided yet, sir."

"Right, well…"

He left the rest of it unsaid, but his meaning was obvious. I sighed inwardly. I was going to have to broach the subject with Angelica and I wasn't looking forward to it. Our track record regarding marriage had been a little awkward, to say the least. Angelica shot me a mischievous look. We saluted and left the room.

"I'll make arrangements," she said.

"For what?"

My mind was still on the issue of getting married, but hers moved far faster than that.

"Our leave, silly."

"Oh, yes, of course."

"Go and see your chaps, and then I'll get Fred to drive us somewhere. We might as well enjoy our leave."

"Good idea."

Fred was the general nickname for Sergeant Bruce Gordon, who was batman to myself and several other officers billeted at Amberly Manor. He and I had formed a friendship due to the various escapades I'd been involved in. Gordon seemed to know everything that went on in the squadron and was quite a philosopher to boot. He gave me fatherly advice at times, which had been most welcome. Naturally, Angelica fell informally under his remit now that she was attached to me.

She kissed me softly and danced away to organise our leave. I headed for the pilots' hut to see Jonty and Willie.

"What-ho, Skipper," said Jonty, who had been sitting outside the hut having a brew with Willie. In spite of their frequent disputes, they spent most of their time together.

"Glad to see you, Scottish." Willie came up and put an arm around me.

"I'm bloody glad to be here. I thought I'd bought it for sure when that U-boat surfaced."

"Ah, yes…" said Jonty with a wry smile.

"So it *was* you," I said.

"It was us all right — me, Willie and Tomas. When I saw that blasted German captain trying to force you to go with him, I saw red!"

"We practically begged Bentley to let us run more patrols to find you," said Willie.

"It's a good job you did, or I'd be languishing in some Jerry POW camp by now."

"That's your second lucky escape, Skipper," said Jonty.

"Bentley said much the same thing."

We laughed and Flying Officer Tomas Jezek joined us. He and I had got into a few adventures of late to do with spies in the squadron.

"Come on, Scottish, come on. How many lives do you have, eh?"

"If it's as many as a cat, then I'm still in credit," I joked.

We talked for a few moments about my recent escapade, and then our conversation turned to the more serious matter of the new German fighter.

"This new plane," said Tomas. "It's a problem, no?"

"Yes, the Focke-Wulf," I said. "Bentley says it's been causing problems for several squadrons."

"I think I got a lucky break shooting that one down," said Willie, becoming serious.

"Probably because he was too busy chasing Jonty."

"Damn blighter," added Jonty. "Couldn't shake him off. Willie got him in the nick of time."

"So, what do we do?" said Tomas.

"We fight on," I said. It was a lame response, but I had no other answer. What could we do? The Germans had produced a superior aircraft to ours, but we still had to go into combat. We fell silent. The war, which sometimes seemed further away for those of us stationed in Blighty, now moved a little closer.

"Let's have a cup of tea." Tomas was a great believer in the British panacea for all ills — tea.

"Good idea, and then I've got to get off for a couple of days. Bentley's given me and Angelica leave."

"See, it was worth getting shot down after all, Skipper," said Jonty, who always liked to make a silk purse out of a sow's ear if he could. "But before you go, you must hear 'The Ballad of the Downed Pilot', which I have composed in your honour."

"He must not," said Willie at once.

"I say he must."

"It's the last thing he needs before going off with his lady."

"I should have thought it was just the ticket."

"Well, it's not!"

Tomas shot me an amused glance. Their disputes over Jonty's ballads were well known. We followed them into the dispersal hut while they continued to argue amicably over the proposed recitation, and I shook my head. They would never change, and for that matter, nor would I want them to.

Angelica had arranged a stay at a hotel not far away. We'd sojourned there more than once and they assumed we were married, which we practically were. I had lost any compunction about us becoming intimate long ago. The war did that to you, and having a new enemy plane to deal with brought the immediacy of it home once more.

Gordon was pleased with my reappearance and said so as he picked us up in the jeep.

"Good to see you, sir," he said. "I'm mighty glad you made it back."

"Likewise, Fred. I thought I was going to end up as a POW."

"Really, sir? Do tell."

He had not heard the story, which surprised me, since he knew almost everything that occurred in the squadron. I related the tale once more on the drive to the hotel, where he left us, promising to return in a couple of days.

At dinner, Angelica seemed to be toying with her food.

"What's wrong? It's not like you to lose your appetite," I said gently. I had certainly not lost mine. It was probably all the adrenaline of recent events.

"I just can't help worrying," she said with a sigh. "About this new plane, and what it might mean for us."

"What might it mean for us?" I enquired, knowing full well what was coming.

"You're going to die, I just know it," she said dramatically.

"I'm glad you have such confidence in me," I said with a wry smile.

"I can't help it. Every time you go up I'm scared to death, and now this Focke-Wulf thing… I know you're a good pilot, but sometimes I just can't bear it … and I do try not to worry."

A tear trickled down her cheek and I moved around to comfort her. She shot me a tremulous smile and I kissed her.

"Better?" I asked her.

"Not really, but thank you for asking," she sniffed.

"Why don't you try to finish your food?" I suggested.

This was rather unromantic of me, but now we were at war it was ingrained in us all not to waste rations.

She managed to eat it while I stayed beside her, holding her hand between mouthfuls.

Later that night we lay together in the rather cosy room. It was a warm night and the passion had been hot. I could tell Angelica was brooding a little, probably about the plane. I wished I could take away her fear, but it was impossible. Afterwards, she lay in my arms and sighed contentedly.

"I wish we could just lie here together, like this, forever," she whispered. "Forget the war and everything about it."

"I should think you'd get quite tired of lying in bed after a while," I replied.

"Oh, why must you be so prosaic?"

"Because it makes you laugh when I tease you."

"I'll show you teasing," she said, her lips once more close to mine.

"Haven't you had enough for one evening?"

"Never…"

The two days passed pleasantly enough. Angelica and I were inseparable, and we both tried to forget about the war for a while. We went for walks, ate lunch at the local pub, and otherwise spent the time in our room. These interludes were few and far between, so we made the most of each other while we could.

Angelica seemed a little more relaxed by the evening of the second night, so I decided to broach the subject of marriage. Since Bentley had mentioned it, I felt it was incumbent on me to at least have a discussion with Angelica about it.

"What do you think?" I said tentatively as we lay once more in bed after a particularly passionate bout of lovemaking.

"About what?"

"Us … getting married … you know…"

She was silent for a few moments, which didn't bode well for her answer. If she had to think about it, then it probably wasn't something she was keen on.

"We will … in due course…"

"In due course?"

This was not the response I had hoped for. Although I wasn't in a hurry to get married either, it still irked me that she would be reluctant. After all, we had got engaged with that intention, so why wouldn't she want to follow it through?

"Yes … when it's time."

"And when will that be?"

"I don't know. Could you try to be patient, darling, please?"

She had said the very same thing when I had first asked to kiss her. Angelica very much dictated the terms of engagement between us, to put it in military terms. I was irritated but let it lie for the moment.

"In which case," I said, "it's time for something else."

"Oh?"

She was smiling, and I could see her eyes twinkling suggestively in the half-light. I kissed her and was hopelessly lost, as always. I pushed the idea of marriage to the back of my mind as she started to command my full attention in other more pressing ways.

CHAPTER TWO

Gordon picked us up and returned us to the base after our two days away. Angelica's mood had seemed a little forced at breakfast that morning. The prospect of me flying again was preying on her mind.

"You know you can't die," she said suddenly as we packed our things in the room. "You know that, don't you? I know you have your duty to the Air Force, but even so..." She smiled at me a little tremulously.

"Well, I'll try my hardest not to," I replied, somewhat amused.

"No, you can't, you see, because if you do, well, I will never forgive you."

I stopped what I was doing and took her in my arms. "You're completely adorable and I love you, and if this is a ploy to get me to kiss you, it's working," I told her.

We kissed for what seemed an age and then reluctantly we left off to finish packing. We went downstairs to wait for Gordon.

"Good break, sir?" he said affably as we drove back to Banley.

"It was marvellous, Fred, thank you," Angelica chimed in.

"What she said," I replied, and we all laughed.

"There's a briefing scheduled — you should both be in time for it," said Gordon, moving on to more mundane matters.

"From Bentley?"

"I believe so, sir, yes."

I had a shrewd idea as to what this would be about, and I wasn't far off the mark. We assembled in the main hangar where Bentley often liked to give briefings when it was more than just the pilots. The fact the tech crew and others were present meant it would be something significant.

Angelica and I sat together with Jonty, Willie and Tomas at the front.

"How was your leave, Skipper?" said Jonty as we took our seats.

"It was very good," I replied.

"Good show, Skipper. Things have been terribly quiet here for the past couple of days."

"You haven't been up?"

"No, not since you left," said Willie.

None of us were under any illusion this hiatus in flying would pertain for long, but we forbore to say anything further. Besides, at that moment, Bentley strode up to the front in his usual brisk fashion. We all stood to attention, but he waved us back into our seats.

Then, right on cue, the pipe of doom was produced, and the CO proceeded to empty it. We waited patiently for him to refill it, tamp it and light it. Then it emitted several clouds of smoke while he puffed on it, simultaneously surveying us all. Audrey stood patiently beside him, and I was glad I didn't have to be quite so close to his smokestack of a pipe.

"Now," he said. "I've called you all here today because we've got a bit of a problem." He paused for a puff or two before continuing. "I am sure you are all aware that Jerry has a new plane. But if not, then I can tell you our intelligence sources confirm it's definitely a new kind of fighter called the Focke-Wulf Fw 190. We've already nearly lost a pilot to it. Other squadrons have not been so lucky."

There was silence at this disclosure, not because it was unexpected, but more because it was immensely unwelcome news. Angelica glanced at me.

"It's unlikely that Jerry will have them in droves as yet, but we have to be prepared. No doubt we will still be going up against ME109s, but we're going to see more of these Focke-Wulfs and there's nothing we can do about it. After all, if the boot was on the other foot I'm sure we'd be producing them as fast as we could."

He had a point, and Bentley was nothing if not pragmatic in his outlook. He took a few more pulls on his pipe before pointing the stem at us in an accusatory way, as was his habit when he wanted to emphasise a point.

"Regardless of this new hazard, we cannot allow the Air Force to be grounded just because Jerry has a more lethal toy than we do. No, by Jove, we cannot!"

Glances were exchanged at this. The punchline was about to be delivered.

"We have to get out there and do our duty, no matter what the cost. These planes may be better, faster, and more manoeuvrable, but they are not invincible, and we shall prevail regardless."

This was beginning to sound rather Churchillian, but I supposed this is what had to be said, particularly when the odds were stacking up against us.

"We've been ordered to run some fighter sweeps up towards the North Sea and along the south coast over the next few days. There are various convoys and suchlike crossing the Channel, it's the RAF's job to ride shotgun. So, get out there, watch each other's backs, and try to get back safely. Understood?"

There was a chorus of agreement at this, since what could one do but simply agree?

"Well, good luck — you'll get your operational orders in due course. Dismissed."

Bentley strode away rapidly, perhaps not wanting to hang around. I was fully aware that command hung heavily on his shoulders. He had revealed as much to me in past conversations. It was one of the reasons I was reluctant to become the flight leader. However, this new turn of events only made the prospect more likely. Judd was a damn good pilot, but as I had discovered, none of us were bulletproof.

As everyone filed out, Angelica stayed until we were alone. The others left us to it. She put her arms around my neck and pulled me in close.

"I've got to get on post," she told me softly. "Take care out there."

"I will do my very best," I told her.

"Just try not to get killed while you're doing your best…"

She kissed me before I could reply. In any case, I had nothing cogent to say. She pulled out of my embrace, put a finger to her lips and then pressed it to mine. I watched her go before walking down to the dispersal hut.

Jonty and Willie were standing outside, drinking tea. Beside them was a fresh-faced youth of around nineteen years of age. He was tall, with black hair and brown eyes. He had the look of every new pilot, a little eager and less jaded than the rest of us.

"What-ho, Skipper, this is Pilot Officer Phillip Charlton," said Jonty by way of greeting.

Phillip snapped a crisp salute, and I returned it perfunctorily.

"At ease," I said. I knew he would soon drop most of the protocols, as we all tended to within the flight.

"Call me, Phil, sir," he said. "Everybody does."

"Oh aye," I replied. "And where do you hail from, Phil?"

"Sussex born and bred. Hailsham, actually."

I could tell from his accent that he was a southerner.

"Ah, yes, I've been to Hailsham — dreadfully dull place," said Jonty at once.

"You're not wrong!" Phillip laughed.

"So, what brings you to the Mavericks?" I asked him.

It wasn't usually polite to ask why someone had been assigned to our squadron. We all had our reasons for joining the motley band of pilots none of the other RAF squadrons wanted. Most of the time we let it lie, but Phillip seemed very young to be relegated to our misfit crew.

"I ... I did something rather regretful," he said bashfully.

"Oh? Do tell." Jonty regarded him with interest.

Phillip didn't seem reticent at all. "Yes, well, I, er ... I buzzed the CO's office on my solo flight, and he wasn't best pleased."

Jonty let out a crack of laughter. "Really? That was brave of you."

"Oh, not brave," Phillip demurred. "It was a bet I had with one of the WAAFs on the base. She bet me I wouldn't do it for a kiss. Of course ... I had to."

"That's more like it," said Jonty with approval.

"It didn't help that she was his niece..."

"Oh," I said cottoning on. "Oh, I see."

"Still, it seems a bit harsh, sending you here just for buzzing his office," said Willie, digesting this.

"Well, there was a bit more to it."

"Isn't there always?" Jonty chuckled.

"I was caught *in flagrante delicto* with the same young lady."

"I see," I said. Indiscretion had been my downfall, and so I had some sympathy with Phillip on that score.

"The CO told me at the passing out parade that he'd see to it I never got to fly with any of the decent squadrons in the Air Force."

"I say," said Jonty, most put out. "That's a bit damn rich! This is one of the best squadrons there is."

"Sorry... I didn't mean..." said Phillip at once, wondering if he'd committed some terrible solecism.

"It's fine," I told him. "We are not regarded as the finest squadron there is, certainly not by the top brass, in spite of the excellent job we do."

"Don't ever intimate that to Bentley," said Willie sagely.

"He'll have your guts for garters," said Jonty. "He's had mine several times over."

"Yes, and whatever you do, don't emulate this reprobate."

"I say!" Jonty protested.

"You'll end up on Bentley's carpet quicker than you can say Jack Robinson," Willie continued.

"That part is true," Jonty conceded.

Phillip stayed chewing the fat with us for the rest of the afternoon. It turned out he was a likeable fellow for all his youth. Tomas joined us and regaled Phillip with stories of his time in Czechoslovakia, which kept us all amused.

As twilight approached, Phillip said, "Oh well, I've got to go. I've got a date for the pictures."

"Oh?" said Jonty at once. "Who's the lucky lady?"

"Her name's Audrey."

There was a stunned silence at this admission.

"What? Section Officer Audrey Wilmington?" said Willie.

"Yes, that's her."

"Bentley's adjutant?" said Jonty.

Phillip's face fell. "Oh crumbs, is she?"

"I'm afraid she is, old chum," Jonty said sympathetically.

"I mean, should I … ought I…?"

"To cry off?" I finished for him. "On no account — she'd not be amused."

I knew Audrey quite well by now, and being stood up would not put him in her good books. Not that I blamed him — I had considered asking her out myself before Angelica had appeared on the scene. I was surprised she'd let someone quite so young ask her out, but there was no accounting for these things, as bitter experience had taught me.

"You're a fast worker, I'll give you that," said Willie.

"And a brave one too; Bentley's adjutant … well, I'm blowed," said Jonty, mightily impressed.

"Look, I didn't know that. I just thought she was … nice," said Phillip, looking from one to the other.

"Leave off teasing him," I admonished them. "If you've got a date, you'd best get off and don't keep her waiting. Audrey is nice, I can vouch for it."

"Good luck, old chap," said Jonty as Phillip hurried away.

"He's a live one," said Willie.

"Let's hope he is once he gets into combat," I said.

There was something about Phillip that bothered me slightly, but I could not put my finger on it. Was it bravado, perhaps? Buzzing a CO's office was one thing, but going into combat was quite another. Time would soon tell.

I told Angelica about it as we ate fish and chips sitting on the nearby village green. It was something we had done since we first started seeing each other.

"Really? Audrey is going on a date with that new pilot?" she said.

"Oh, so you've noticed him as well?" I said acerbically.

"Well, he is rather dashing…" She sneaked a playful glance at me.

"Is he?"

"Yes, all the girls think so."

"Apparently he's quite a ladies' man," I said and then related the reason he had been sent to the Mavericks.

"Well, he's in good company then," she shot back when I finished.

"Touché," I said. "I suppose I'm never going to live it down as far as you're concerned."

"Only when it suits me," she informed me, adopting a teasing tone. "Anyway, I shall find out all about it from Audrey, never fear."

"That's exactly what I do fear," I retorted.

Angelica caught my meaning at once. "Oh, I don't tell her *everything*."

"I'm sure there's more than enough latitude in that statement," I said.

She bundled up the empty wrappers and put them in the bin nearby. Then she snuggled close and looked up at me.

"Kiss me."

I obliged her at once, unable ever to resist her, as she knew only too well.

The following day, we arrived at Banley to be greeted by Flight Lieutenant Brent Judd.

"We're going up at ten hundred hours," he said. "The full squadron will be running a patrol up from Southend, and returning once we reach Cromer. Orders are to engage the enemy if sighted."

"Here we go, Scottish," said Tomas as we grabbed a final brew before it was time to leave.

"Yes indeed," I said.

The route was very similar to the one where we had previously encountered the Focke-Wulfs and I had been shot down on. I was very much hoping there would not be a repeat performance.

Ten o'clock rolled around and I was about to head for my plane. I felt a light touch on my arm and found Angelica beside me.

"Fly safely," she said in a small voice.

"I will."

"Come back to me, darling. I'll be waiting."

I embraced her and kissed her to catcalls from the rest of the squadron as they made their way to their Spitfires.

I pulled away reluctantly. She held my hand until the last moment and watched me go.

As we took off I could see her standing there still, and I knew she'd be waiting when we returned. If we returned. I chided myself roundly at the thought. I had to stop thinking like that. *No matter what the cost*, Bentley had said. I hoped the cost would not be too high.

We took up formation in our sections. Jonty was on one of my wings and Willie on the other. Red Section had become quite the flying team, watching each other's backs like hawks. I had more than once been grateful for Willie's intervention in a dogfight or with a Jerry on my tail. The new pilot, Phillip, was in Green Section over on the other side of the flight. I hoped he would fare well.

Judd gave us the bearing once we arrived on station over the Channel, and we wheeled northwards as one. Down below us the waves were flecked with white, and it looked pretty choppy all told. Not a day to go down in the drink.

"Keep your eyes peeled for bandits," Judd cautioned us over the radio as we made our way up the Channel towards the North Sea.

There was an unusual quiet about the squadron, as if we were all expecting something to happen. There was no banter and very little chatter, not even from Jonty. We were wary of what might come at us and wondering if it would be the new planes: it was a clear day, so we would see them for miles if they came at all.

Down below we passed over several Navy ships and I wondered if one of them was the destroyer which had rescued me. I was very glad to be above the sea and not on it.

Time passed slowly until, finally, we were almost level with Cromer and ready to turn back. I was on the point of breathing a sigh of relief when the cry went up.

"Bandits, bandits at three o'clock!" yelled Jonty.

Sure enough, over to the right was a squadron of enemy planes coming in from the coast.

"Break, break, engage," said Judd at once, and then we were in it.

The German planes closed rapidly with us, and I noticed the distinctive yellow noses. They were ME109s. Those we could deal with. As they too broke formation, I selected one for a mark and went after it.

The Jerry immediately soared up into a climb and I gave chase. I heard the chatter of machine-gun fire as the fight began between our planes and theirs. The 109 pilot I picked was evidently experienced, levelling off and taking a zig-zag course. I tried to draw a bead on him and missed after firing off a couple of quick bursts. He dived again steeply and I followed, hoping to catch him the next time. The G-forces kicked in quite hard, but he kept going. Just as I was gaining on him, an urgent plea from Phillip came over the radio.

"He's behind me. I can't shake him off. I can't…"

I could see his plane off to my right with a Jerry right on his tail. He would very likely get caught. I was nearest and the 109 I was chasing was still diving. I broke off my attack and turned sharply towards Phillip and his pursuer.

The Jerry fired at Phillip once, twice, and by some miracle, he wasn't hit. I could tell it was only a matter of time before the German got him. Phillip was inexperienced, and his reactions were just that bit slower.

The Jerry hadn't seen me, though, so I flew at him from the side. I fired once, twice. The salvos hit home and his engine began to smoke. The 109 pitched forwards and dived seawards.

"You're safe, Green Two," I told Phillip, turning away.

"Thanks, Red Leader," he said. His voice sounded shaky.

I had no time to ponder it, as tracers whipped past my canopy. The 109 I had been chasing had turned back and now I was the hunted, not the hunter.

I swore under my breath, pulling to the left and steeply diving. He followed, and I pulled up suddenly, banking sharply. As I throttled back, he shot past me. He hadn't been expecting that. I pushed the throttle forward once more. As I made use of the Spitfire's ability to turn very tightly, for a split second he was in my sights.

I fired on instinct, and the bullets shredded his tail. His plane went into a spin. I left off pursuing him further, knowing he was probably a goner. Around me, the fight was almost over.

"Disengage, let's reform," said Judd as the remaining 109s fled the scene. The plane I had hit managed to level off and started limping towards the Dutch coast. As much as I would have liked to finish him off, I knew Judd wouldn't wear it so I let it go.

"Let's head for home," said Judd.

We turned for Cromer once more, and when we were over the town, we headed for Banley.

"I say, *that* was fun," said Jonty, who seemed to have recovered his *joie de vivre*.

"Be grateful they weren't those new planes," said Willie.

"Yes, by Jove, that was a stroke of luck!"

"I know what you're thinking, and don't," Willie continued in admonishing tones.

"Oh, what was I thinking?" Jonty shot back at once.

"Just don't."

"A ballad? Is that what you mean?"

"God preserve us ... why did I even mention it?" Willie groaned.

"A wizard idea it is too. Let's see ... oh, the Battle of Cromer had begun, but by the Mavericks the day was won," sang Jonty.

"Why? Why?" wailed Willie in tragic tones.

For once Judd didn't intervene and we were all treated to Jonty's ballad on the way home.

We landed, taxied to our standings, and I jumped down from my kite. Angelica was waiting, and as soon as she saw me she ran to me, hurling herself into my arms as usual.

"Oof! I'm glad you're pleased to see me," I said, kissing her roundly.

"I'm glad it wasn't those horrid new planes," she said.

"No, we were lucky."

I was about to say more when I noticed Phillip standing alone at the boundary fence with his back to us. I wondered if something was amiss. Perhaps it was just a hunch, but I felt that I should go and talk to him.

"Darling, would you mind? It's the new pilot. I just…"

She glanced over to where Phillip was and picked up my meaning at once.

"Yes, of course. Go and see how he is. I'll wait here."

I walked over to him, and when I got close enough, I said, "Phillip, are you all right?"

He didn't answer, so I tried again.

"Phil?"

He turned to me and I could see the fear in his eyes. His hands were shaking and his face was pale. The recent combat encounter must have affected him badly.

"What's the matter?" I asked him, concerned.

"I can't…" he said. "I can't do it. I can't."

"Can't what?"

"I can't fly. I can't do that… I…"

He seemed genuinely in distress, and I wanted to help. After all, he would not be the first pilot to suffer an attack of nerves after a close encounter.

"Come over here and sit down," I said, indicating the bench where Angelica and I had also had some difficult conversations. Today seemed like it would be one of those days.

He followed me wordlessly and sat down, staring out into the distance. I took a seat beside him. In my peripheral vision, I saw Angelica draw nearer to us, out of sight of Phillip.

"What do you mean you can't fly?" I asked him gently.

"I … I thought I could… I thought I could do it … but then … up there…"

"Have you never been in combat before?" I asked him.

He shook his head. I cursed inwardly. We had all been in his position and I tried to reassure him.

"Look, we all feel like that to start with, but it'll pass," I began.

"It won't," he said, looking at me straight. "It won't. I know it won't. I don't think I can go up again."

I was nonplussed. Angelica noticed my hesitation. She came and sat on the bench on the other of side Phillip. She was very empathetic by nature, and I did not object to her intervention.

"Phillip," she said, taking hold of his hand. "Can I call you Phil?"

"Yes, all right," he said.

"Was it ... very bad up there?"

He shook his head as if to clear it. "It was terrible, worse than I could have imagined. I just never thought ... when I signed up..."

"Thought what it would be like in combat?" she asked gently.

"Yes, being shot at, pursued by the enemy. It was nothing like I imagined."

She tried to reassure him, talking softly. "It will pass," she said. "You're a brave man, I'm sure. It will pass."

"Will it?" he asked her.

"I'm sure of it. We all feel afraid at times — it's much worse for you pilots — but we're counting on you, you see. You do see that, don't you?"

"That's exactly what my father said when he made me join the Air Force." Phillip let out a sob, and his shoulders shook for a while.

"Is that why you joined up, because your father made you?" Angelica asked him.

"Yes, yes, he was a pilot, and my brother is a pilot — he said I had to... I had to..."

He couldn't finish and Angelica put her hand on his shoulder sympathetically.

"But you're here now. You made it through training, and through your first combat. It'll get easier, I promise you, it will."

"She's right," I added. "You'll find it gets easier the more sorties you fly."

"Will it? Are you sure?" he said, brightening up a tad.

"I'm sure. You'll be all right. Honestly, we've all been through it," I said.

This seemed to mollify him a little. He lost the fearful look which he'd had before.

"I hope you're right," he said, standing up. "Sorry ... sorry to make such a spectacle of myself."

"It's quite all right," Angelica told him.

"Thank you," he said. "I'll be fine now."

I watched him go with some trepidation. Was he really fine? He seemed to be reassured, but what if it happened again?

"Do you think he'll be all right?" Angelica asked me after he had left.

"I don't know," I said. "It's hard to say. I've never seen anyone react quite like that after a sortie."

"But what can you do?"

I thought for a moment. There was only one thing to do.

"I'll try and talk to Bentley, in confidence, perhaps."

"What will he say, do you think?"

"I don't know."

I genuinely didn't, but I felt I had to at least make him aware. After all, the squadron was his responsibility. If one of the pilots was a little shaky, to say the least, he ought to be informed. The trouble with Bentley, however, was you never quite knew how he might take things.

I decided to go and speak to Bentley at once. Angelica accompanied me to his office and left me outside the door, departing with a kiss. Still in two minds about the wisdom of what I was doing, I knocked and waited until Audrey answered.

"It's Flying Officer Mackennelly, sir," she said to Bentley while I waited.

"Well, show him in. Don't leave him standing there," the CO said testily.

Audrey rolled her eyes at me, which I took to mean he wasn't in the best of moods. This did not augur well at all for our discussion. It would very likely not improve his temper. Nevertheless, now I was there I resolved to try.

I entered and saluted.

"Sit down, Angus, sit down," he said.

Bentley had a weary look about him as he picked up his pipe. I waited while he scraped it out, refilled it and lit it. Smoking seemed to improve his temper. Audrey returned to her seat and got on with her work. She would certainly be listening, however, and this was about Phillip. On balance, I felt it would be better if she knew.

"Nothing like a good pipeful of tobacco," Bentley said.

"Sir," I replied.

"Balm to the soul, Angus, balm to the soul."

He seemed content just to sit there and keep me hanging. After a few more moments, he said, "Well, what brings you here?"

"I wanted to talk to you, sir, in confidence."

This got his attention at once.

"Oh? Something amiss, is it? How did the sortie go? I thought it went well by all accounts."

"It did, sir, pretty well to be honest. We were lucky to meet some 109s, and I never thought I'd be saying something like *that*."

"Ah, yes, indeed … bloody Jerries and their new planes, hmm. But if it's not the sortie, what is it?"

He looked at me a tad suspiciously. I took a deep breath, wondering exactly how to phrase things.

"It's the new pilot, sir."

"Which new pilot?"

"Pilot Officer Charlton, sir."

"What about him?"

Bentley started to puff on his pipe a little quicker, a sure sign of agitation. I wanted to cut and run but now I'd brought it up, I would have to explain myself. I flicked a glance at Audrey, but her expression revealed nothing.

"I'm concerned, sir, about his reaction to the recent sortie, and I wanted to bring it to your attention, in confidence."

"Go on," he said.

"After we landed, sir, I saw him over by the fence. He seemed distressed…" I told the story as accurately as I could. Audrey must have schooled her reactions to things she heard in Bentley's office extremely well, as she showed no sign of being affected by what I had said.

"I see," Bentley said, while continuing to puff on his pipe for several long minutes. Then, finally, he took it out of his mouth and pointed the stem at me. This was a bad sign.

"And what do you want me to do about it?"

Of all the reactions I was expecting, that was not it. A frown crossed Audrey's brow, but she kept her head firmly down over her typewriter.

"I was wondering if he should be flying, sir, if I'm being honest."

He regarded me for a moment as if I had lost my mind. "Not Fly? What are you talking about? Of course he has to fly!"

"But, sir, he seemed genuinely affected. Surely it would be better for all of us if —"

Bentley cut me off. "He's here on the same terms as the rest of us — do or die, no exceptions."

"I understand that, sir, but —"

I was disposed to argue not just for Phillip's sake but out of concern for the squadron as a whole. The frown on Audrey's brow deepened, but only for a second.

"Angus! What would you have me do? Charlton signed up as a pilot of his own free will. He's been trained at great expense, and he will fly into combat regardless of his reaction."

I was surprised that he was being so emphatic about it. Normally Bentley would show at least a modicum of concern for the wellbeing of the pilots under his command.

"Well then, I hope you're right, sir, about him," I said.

This was perhaps unwise and could have amounted to insubordination. It probably did. However, Bentley's response was to begin another ritual with the pipe of doom. He carefully scraped the bowl once more, filled it, tamped it, and lit it. I knew the whole routine well, having witnessed it on so many occasions.

"Angus," he said at length, having now filled the entire room with tobacco smoke. "Let me tell you a story."

"Sir?" I coughed. I wasn't sure where this was leading.

"The story of, let's say, an Air Vice-Marshal with a son who is already a distinguished pilot. With me so far?"

"I think so, sir, yes," I said.

"Good. So now imagine he's got another son. Let's just say that son was reluctant to become a pilot, but this nameless Air Vice-Marshal insisted on it. So, the reluctant son does the training, gets his wings, and then after various pranks and indiscretions he gets posted to this squadron, the Mavericks. Another misfit, hmm?"

I was beginning to catch his drift and I nodded.

"Let's also say that orders, very strict orders, were issued that this pilot must fly on every possible sortie into combat, no matter what — orders from the Air Vice-Marshal endorsed by, for argument's sake, even higher authorities in Fighter Command."

"I see…" I began, at which Bentley jumped out of his chair and began to pace the room in a most irate manner.

"No you don't see, nobody does. I'm trying to fight a war here, but in the meantime I've got bloody Fighter Command telling me how to run my show whenever they damn well feel like it just because one of them has a son who is in the bloody Air Force even though he doesn't want to be!"

He paused but seemed to still be in full flow, so I said nothing further for the moment.

"And then let's suppose, along comes another pilot — a Flying Officer, for argument's sake — to inform me that this pilot, the son of a blasted Air Vice-Marshal, looks as if he cannot handle being in combat… Do you get the picture?"

"Loud and clear, sir," I said, understanding his dilemma.

"Then you see there is very little I can do, even if I wanted to." Bentley gave a heavy sigh and resumed his seat.

"What if he jeopardises the rest of us?"

I had to ask the question because now I had the full story, there were ramifications beyond just Phillip's reluctance to fly.

"Then you'll just have to manage the risk, Angus, won't you?"

I should have expected that response, I supposed.

"And it goes without saying that this little story I told you is not something the squadron can be privy to, understood?"

"Understood, sir, yes."

"Good, so now that we understand each other, is there anything else?"

"No, sir, not at present."

He took a few meditative puffs of his pipe. "You know, when I got to be squadron leader, I thought it was a jolly good show. Made something of myself. Then I was made CO of the Mavericks. I was rather pleased at the time." He smiled in recollection. "That was before I realised what a bloody thankless task it is."

I didn't reply. What could one say to that?

"You and all the others are what makes it all worthwhile, not those blasted Johnnies upstairs, no, by Jove! So don't forget it. I'm counting on you, Angus. And try to keep an eye on that young lad for me, won't you?"

A faint smile crossed Audrey's lips on hearing this.

"Yes, sir," I said, realising that I had done Bentley a disservice by believing he had no compassion. He did care, a great deal, but it was tempered by orders from top brass.

"Dismissed."

I left Bentley's office in a thoughtful frame of mind. I had some inkling of the pressures he was under, but he naturally did not share the bulk of his burden with us. It weighed heavily with him at times, that much was certain. Since there was now no other choice, I resolved to try to watch Phillip's back and keep him out of trouble, if I could.

CHAPTER THREE

"Good God," said Angelica when I had told her the tale.

There were few secrets between us, and her security clearance exceeded mine by a very high margin. Since we'd been through so much together, we had become used to sharing things. I treated her as a best friend and confidante.

"How did Audrey's date go?" I asked her. I was interested now, since Phillip had gone out with her the previous night. Audrey had also been privy to the intelligence about him from Bentley, although she probably already knew as she would have seen the orders.

"She liked him; she said he was jolly good fun," Angelica replied.

"Just good fun?" I said, raising an eyebrow.

"That would be telling."

Angelica laughed and I decided it would be better not to enquire further.

"How does she feel about, you know, all this?"

"I don't know — I'll have to ask her tomorrow. I will report back, never fear."

"I'm still concerned about Phillip flying. What if he does something stupid?" I said, becoming serious once more.

She touched my arm. "Don't put yourself in danger, not on his account. I need you and you can't save everyone, especially not from their own folly."

I didn't argue. In any case, I could not imagine not wanting to fly. I had wanted nothing else from a very young age.

The following day we were sent out once again on a sweep over the Channel. We were to follow the same route as the day before.

"Hey ho," said Jonty as we left the dispersal hut. "Here we go again."

"Yes," I replied, with some misgivings. We'd been lucky last time. I wasn't convinced our luck would hold.

Angelica came to see me off just as she always did. I turned to face her and she put her arms around my neck.

"Take care," she said. "Don't do anything foolish."

"Like?" I smiled.

"Like protecting other pilots from their own rash decisions."

"I'll try not to," I said.

"I love you."

"I love you too."

We kissed with all the passion we could muster. Each goodbye might be our last, and we both knew it. Then we parted company. She stood watching me leave while I caught up with Phillip, who was walking to his plane.

"Okay?" I asked him, wanting to gauge his mood before we flew.

"Yes, yes, I'll be all right," he said, sounding more confident than the previous day.

I wondered if he really was, but there was nothing further I could do. Even if he was still afraid, his father was part of the top brass and had insisted he flew.

I climbed into my own kite while Leading Aircraftman Dominic Redwood helped me strap in.

"All right and tight, sir," he said, making sure everything was secure.

"Thanks, Techie," I said.

I spun up the prop and took off with the rest of the squadron. Angelica's familiar lone figure stood at the side of the runway, watching us go. It was a fair day, and reasonably warm. It felt rather nice to be up in the blue yonder. There were a few fluffy clouds but nothing to worry about. Nothing for the Jerries to hide in, at least. One had to be thankful for small mercies.

We were soon over the water, leaving Southend behind us, and then we headed northwards once more.

"Watch out for bandits," said Judd over the radio, but it was an unnecessary warning. We were already scanning the skies around us.

It wasn't long before my fears were justified, and this time it was Pilot Officer Jean Tarbon who spotted the German planes.

"Bandits, coming in fast, three o'clock!" he shouted.

"Break, break," Judd told us and once again we peeled off left and right.

"They're those Fockes," said Willie, who was quicker at identifying the enemy than most of us.

My heart sank. Even though we'd been expecting this, it was still a daunting prospect.

"Damn!"

"Steady, steady," said Judd.

It was all well and good for him to say that, but the aircraft's reputation preceded them. It could not have escaped the Luftwaffe's notice that their Focke-Wulfs were superior to anything we had. There were six to our twelve, which should have evened the odds. However, I had a feeling it would not. It felt almost like they were thumbing their noses at us by sending half a squadron.

They closed with us rapidly and came in on the attack. It really did feel as if we were on the back foot, and almost immediately there was one flying straight for me. I cursed inwardly, wondering why they always picked on me. There wasn't time to ponder, and instead I banked sharply. I noticed that he anticipated me and was quicker. Damn those planes! As I started to evade him, he matched my every move and was far more agile. It was taking every ounce of skill I had to keep out of his way.

He was soon in pursuit, no matter what I tried to do to turn the tables. His guns fired, once, twice. Fortunately, the bullets passed me by. I was damned if I'd go down a second time.

The radio chatter reached a crescendo as dogfights occurred all around me.

"Bank left, left."

"He's on me, he's on me."

"Watch your back! Watch your bloody back!"

I was conscious of planes wheeling and turning in my peripheral vision, but I only had time to avoid the Jerry on my tail. In desperation, I tried a dive, which sometimes worked, but he followed me swiftly. I'd done a similar stunt before, heading straight for the sea then pulling up at the last moment. Hoping it might work again, I kept going in spite of the G-forces, but he stuck to me like glue. I swore, but now I was committed.

Focusing my attention, I pulled out of the dive with only feet to spare. I could see the wave flecks underneath me. I flattened off, almost skimming the waves, and then made a tight turn. Checking my mirror, I saw he was still there. I was running out of options. Was I really going to get shot down again? Just then, Jonty came to the rescue.

To my relief, he flew in from the side unseen by my pursuer and fired off a salvo. The Focke pitched upwards quickly and turned away. I didn't know if he was hit, but I turned too. This was not an opportunity to miss. Now the two of us were hunting him. We might even beat the odds.

"Tally-ho, Skipper," said Jonty, in high spirits as we tried to chase him down.

Alas, Jerry was still too quick, even for both of us. Nevertheless, he thought better of taking on both of us at once. He started to head for the Belgian coastline.

"Shall we get after him, Skipper?" said Jonty, still eager for action.

"No, let him go," I replied.

"Oh blast!"

"Disengage," said Judd at that moment. "Reform."

Over to the right of us, six specs disappeared into the horizon. I quickly counted our planes and found we had not lost any, which was a minor miracle. I had no idea how Phillip had fared as we headed back to Banley, but fervently hoped he felt better than the previous day.

"Well done, Mavericks," said Judd.

I wasn't so sure. Was it well done? Or were we just lucky this time? Perhaps the Jerries were just probing us, assessing our capabilities while trying out their own. One thing was certain: they would be back.

The encounter had been fast and furious. Nobody spoke as we flew towards Banley. Even Jonty, for once, wasn't singing. Perhaps they all felt as I did. This time the cards had fallen in our favour; next time they might not.

We landed, and after I alighted from my plane, I went over to where Phillip was just leaving his own kite.

"How was it?" I asked him.

He looked at me and seemed calm enough. "Not too bad," he said. "I managed to get some shots in, but missed."

"Good, good to hear."

"Thanks," he said with a tight smile.

He didn't say anything more but walked onwards to the hut. I watched him go. Was he really all right? Or was it just a front? It was hard to tell.

The next moment, Tomas was at my elbow.

"He's a nervous one," he said, jerking his head in Phillip's direction.

"Is he?"

He rolled his eyes at me. "Come on, Scottish, come on. I watched him; he is afraid. He doesn't fight with his heart. That is what I'm saying."

I stopped and put out my hand gently to prevent him from going past me. I needed to nip this in the bud.

"Well, if it's all the same to you, can you refrain from saying so too loudly?"

He looked at me in a considered way, then shrugged. "Sure, okay, if this is what you want."

"It's not what I want," I told him. "It's what's best for the squadron."

The last thing we needed was a pilot being singled out by the others, particularly considering what I knew about him. I could not tell Tomas directly what was amiss, but he was very good at guessing.

"So…" he said. "Perhaps this Phil, he has some connections in the Air Force, hmm?"

"Connections?"

"Someone who is wanting him to be a pilot."

"How on earth do you figure that?"

He was right on the button, of course, but I wondered where he'd got the information. Tomas put a finger to the side of his nose.

"Ah, I keep my ears open, and my eyes too, Scottish. I know... I know."

"Well, whatever you know, keep it to yourself," I repeated, not wanting to discuss it any further. I wouldn't put it past him to try and get the full story out of me.

"I see how it is, Scottish, I see. You can count on me," he said, lowering his voice.

Tomas could be quite blunt at times, but one thing I did know was that he could be trusted. Perhaps that was why he had come to express his reservations directly to me.

"Yes, well..."

"Come on, Scottish, it's me, Tomas. Have I ever let you down?"

"Well ... no..."

"There, you see!"

Just then I spied Angelica walking briskly towards me. I was more than happy to be extracted from the awkward conversation I was having. Tomas and I had shared many confidences, but Bentley had expressly asked me not to talk about Phillip. In this case, I was obligated to stick to my word.

"Go on, see your lucky lady," Tomas laughed and made his way to the hut.

I breathed a sigh of relief.

"You're back," Angelica said happily, once more winding her arms around my neck.

"As you see."

She kissed me passionately as always, and I thanked my lucky stars for having found her.

"What are you thinking?" she said as our lips parted.

"That I'm a lucky man."

"Yes, yes, you are."

She took my hand and led me towards our bench at the edge of the field. I wondered if there was something particular she wanted to say to me. I hoped it was nothing bad. Previous occasions like this had made me wary.

As if reading my thoughts, Angelica flashed me a smile. "I just want to tell you about Audrey, silly," she said.

"All right."

Naturally, I was interested to hear what Audrey thought of Phillip. As we sat looking out at the fields, she said, "Audrey really likes Phillip, in spite of ... you know."

It appeared that the incident I'd related to Bentley in Audrey's presence had not altered her opinion.

"So the date went well then?"

"Yes, and they're going on another."

"Right, well, that's good ... I suppose."

She laughed and patted my arm affectionately. "Oh, you. Of course it is. Audrey needs someone ... you know ... to distract her."

"Does she?"

"Yes, she does. She is becoming far too maudlin."

"If you say so."

"Anway," she continued, "how was Phillip on the sortie?"

I shrugged. "I don't really know. I was a little too preoccupied to notice. But afterwards, I asked him and he said he was all right."

"And was he?"

"I don't know — perhaps. It's hard to tell."

Angelica sighed and tucked her hand in my arm. Since we seemed so in accord, I decided to broach the subject of marriage again.

"Have you thought any more about..."

"About what?"

"Well, you know, what we talked about the other day."

I was wary of saying it more directly, but she got my meaning at once.

"I told you, it isn't time," she snapped, withdrawing her arm at once.

I was a little taken aback by this sudden change of mood. Angelica could be quite mercurial on certain topics, and this was turning out to be one of them. The things that should have been quite simple to resolve between us never were.

"It was just a question," I said, trying to mollify her. I was not disposed to argue; whenever we did, I usually lost in any case.

She softened her tone and put a hand up to my cheek. "I just... I can't..." She stopped. "It's just not time."

I put my hand up to cover hers, and she smiled. Then she tilted up her face to be kissed and I obliged her.

I said no more, but it left me wondering even more than before why she was reluctant to get married. Was it me? Something I had said? I resolved to talk to Gordon at the first opportunity. If anyone would have some advice on the subject, it would be he.

I had precious little time to buttonhole Gordon for a couple of days, partly because if I wasn't flying, Angelica was always with me. For a couple who weren't yet wed, we were constantly together. The irony wasn't lost on me. As luck would have it, we were stood down one afternoon and I slipped away while Angelica wasn't about.

"Something amiss, sir?" asked Gordon as I found him enjoying a cigarette in his jeep.

"I just wondered if we could..." I didn't finish the sentence, but he caught my drift.

"Tea and crumpets?" he asked perceptively.

"Splendid."

It had almost become a code between us. Annie's Kitchen was a tearoom where we went to talk. Gordon was full of good advice and privy to the many ups and downs of my relationship with Angelica.

Once ensconced in the cosy atmosphere of Annie's, who we both agreed served the best crumpets we had ever tasted, I broached the subject of my marital issues.

"You've probably guessed that this is about me and Angelica..." I began.

"I had surmised as much, sir, yes."

I was sure it came as no surprise to him that I was seeking his advice once again.

"Have you ever been married?" I asked him.

He laughed. "I've never had the pleasure, no. Though some may see it differently ... as a hardship."

I laughed too. He was often as sardonic as he was wise.

"Oh, well, the thing is, I would rather like to get married to Angelica. We are now engaged, after all, and you know what a thing that was."

"Yes, sir, I do," he said, no doubt reflecting on the elaborate subterfuge it had required to get to the point of proposal.

Annie brought tea, crumpets, jam and butter. She informed us it was homemade strawberry jam, and I had a feeling she had probably kept some aside, especially for Gordon. No more was said while we reverently ate a crumpet each, lavishly spread with jam and a little bit of butter. Having paid suitable homage to Annie's cooking, I sipped my tea.

"Well, the thing is," I said, "you would imagine that after all that, the getting married part would be easy."

"And it's not?"

"No, it's not easy," I continued rather hotly. "It's becoming bloody difficult."

"I see," he said and thought for a moment while he drank his tea. "Doesn't she want to get married?"

"I don't precisely know. Each time I've mentioned it, she tells me it isn't time…" I trailed off, noting the faint smile playing on his lips. "Do you know something I don't?" I demanded.

"Not at all, sir, no. But 'the time's not right' is unfortunately a coded phrase for 'I don't really want to do this' and also 'I don't really want to discuss my reasons'."

"Really? Oh blast!" I said, although I should have guessed as much.

"Yes, I'm afraid so."

I finished my tea and started on the second crumpet while Gordon replenished the cups.

"So, what should I do?" I asked him between mouthfuls.

"It's hard to say," he said. "If she doesn't want to get married, then there is probably some deep-seated reason for it that she doesn't want to tell you."

"What?" I couldn't keep the alarm out of my voice.

He laughed again. "No, no, nothing like you're thinking. It doesn't mean she doesn't love you."

"What does it mean then?" I demanded.

"Love isn't about marriage, sir. I'm sure you know that much. I'm sure her feelings are as steadfast as they always have been."

"Oh, right, I see," I said, feeling a little mollified. I wished I was a little wiser in the ways of women in love, but I had never been in love myself until I had met Angelica. It was all new to me and I found it hard to fathom at times.

"Marriage has implications, you see," he said.

"Implications?"

"It means that you are no longer quite your own person, completely independent, if you get my meaning. Particularly if you are a woman."

I was much struck by this line of reasoning, and I finished my crumpet while I considered it.

"So what does that mean as far as Angelica is concerned?"

He shrugged. "Perhaps she's just not ready for that … sacrifice."

"What sacrifice?"

"Her autonomy, sir. That's what I mean."

"But I wouldn't — I mean, I don't… I mean…"

"It's not you, sir; it's how society is generally, as regards the female sex."

I didn't quite understand him, but then I had never probed things like this too deeply. Of the two of us, he was the philosopher, which was why I so often sought out his advice. I had grown up in a man's world, and I supposed I did not particularly put myself in the shoes of the opposite sex. I had not seen this as a failing on my part, but love, as I was discovering, had the capacity to change one's thinking.

"So what am I to do? Settle for never getting married at all?"

"Hardly that, sir," he replied. "Just give her the time she needs."

"How much time is that?"

"Now that," he laughed, "is a question no man has ever answered."

I laughed too. As far as Angelica was concerned, he was probably right on the money. I couldn't help thinking about Barbara, Lady Amberly, with whom I had had an affair before starting a serious relationship with Angelica. Barbara would have married me at the drop of a hat. But I didn't love her.

Instead, it was my lot to have fallen hopelessly in love with the most stubborn woman in the Air Force.

"Don't be too hard on yourself," said Gordon, getting up to pay. "Things have a habit of working themselves out, in the end."

I had to concede he was right. I let him pay; it was his turn. It was an unspoken rule that I didn't try to pull rank on him over it. He was a proud man, and I wasn't one to take that pride away from him by insisting on paying every time just because I was the officer.

The talk had been helpful, but it had settled nothing at all. I could see that Angelica and I would not be getting married any time soon. What Bentley would have to say about that, I didn't like to think.

"I missed you, this afternoon," Angelica said as we sat together, eating a dinner of fish and chips on the village green.

"I was with Fred," I said.

"Oh, I see … man talk?" She flashed me a smile and popped a chip in her mouth.

"You have Audrey, I have Fred," I said defensively.

"I don't mind, darling, really I don't," she replied disarmingly.

I was glad she did not enquire further into the topic of my conversation with Gordon, since I would have had to prevaricate and dissembling wasn't really my forte.

"All right, but I hope that I'm your very *best* friend," she said, tilting her head to one side in the endearing way she had.

"You will always be that."

It was true. We were best friends. She was the one I wanted to share things with, and I was sure it was the same for her.

"Anyway," said Angelica changing the subject, "Audrey seems quite smitten with Phillip."

"Oh?"

"Yes, she's a fair way to being in love with him already," she said, scrunching up her wrapper, and taking mine to do the same.

"But they've only just met," I protested.

"And what?" she shot back. "I loved you from the moment I saw you, don't you know that?"

"I…"

"Silly goose," she said softly. "Look what I went through just to get you."

"And now you have."

"Yes."

Nothing more was said for a while, as we kissed passionately. We had become so tender with each other. I supposed it was part of being in love, getting used to being two instead of one, becoming in tune like two violins in an orchestra.

"Well," I said as we pulled apart a little, recalling our earlier topic of conversation. "I hope for her sake he can continue to handle the sorties."

"Don't you think he can?" she asked, looking concerned.

"I don't know. Tomas doesn't seem to think so; he told me that Phillip's heart is not in it. He's often right about things like this."

She shrugged and took my hand. "Well, perhaps going out with Audrey will settle him. Love makes you brave."

"Does it?"

"Oh yes, I'm with *you* after all," she teased at once, her eyes dancing.

"You really are quite…"

"Incorrigible?"

"That's the word I'm looking for, yes."

"And what else?"

"Beautiful, wonderful, charming…"

She cut me off by putting her lips on mine. I wondered if this passion would last a lifetime, and if I'd ever get to know. The war was ever present, like a spectre hanging over us. I hoped she was right about Phillip. Mettles were sorely tested when it came to matters of life and death. What would happen when Phillip was really tested in combat? I just didn't know.

As luck — or perhaps misfortune — would have it, I was about to discover whether Tomas was right or wrong about Phillip. We were sent out on yet another sweep up the Channel, as if we were the only squadron available to do it.

"I think Fighter Command wants to bore us all to death," complained Jonty when Judd gave us the orders.

"Hardly," I said. "So far we've encountered bandits almost every time."

"Yes, those blasted Focke-Wulfs!"

"It's not just us," I replied. "Jerry is deploying them as fast as they can make them by all accounts."

"Give me a 109 any day," said Jonty.

"I bet you never thought you'd be saying *that*!" Willie chimed in.

"No, and what are our chaps doing to counter it?" Jonty demanded.

"I'm sure they are working on something," I told him.

Naturally, I had no idea, but I couldn't imagine that this development would go unchallenged. What the aircraft boffins could do about it was another matter. One of the problems was that they didn't know enough about the new plane. It was much easier to counter something if you knew exactly what you were up against.

"Time to go," said Willie, and we started off towards the field.

Angelica was by my side in an instant. I had become used to her sudden appearances by now, and simply turned to embrace her.

"Come back safe," she whispered, her lips on mine.

"I will," I replied, before kissing her softly.

We said the same things every time, as if it were a ritual. I got into my kite and waved to Angelica while Redwood strapped me in. Once ready, I fired up the Spitfire and taxied to my position. We took off in formation and flew once more towards Southend.

"If I have to see that blasted pier one more time..." said Jonty.

"I'm sure you'll be seeing it plenty more times," said Willie with what sounded like glee.

"Don't rub it in!" Jonty groaned.

The pier had, in any case, been taken over by the Navy as a base of operations and control centre for the Thames Estuary. We dipped our wings as we flew over. Below I could see some of our Navy chaps waving. Once out to sea we turned northwards again, and started on the now familiar route up as far as Cromer.

"Watch out for bandits," said Judd over the radio.

There really was no need to remind us. All of us were on high alert, as if we were courting trouble by continually running these patrols. However, part of the reason for them was ostensibly to deter the enemy from attacking our naval convoys. Instead, our patrols appeared to be acting as a magnet for the Focke-Wulf squadrons the Luftwaffe was forming.

We passed over a fair few vessels below us, some of which were headed for the icy waters up north. It always made me glad I had not joined the Navy. Volunteering had meant I had had a choice, instead of being conscripted. Flying was in my blood, so I had joined up the first chance I got.

We made it almost as far as Cromer without incident, and I thought it was going to be our lucky day. It wasn't.

"Bandits, bandits, four o'clock!" Tomas sent up the cry.

"Here they come, break, break," said Judd.

We peeled off immediately and turned to meet our foe. The lack of yellow noses told us all we needed to know. A full squadron of Focke-Wulfs was on the attack. My heart sank; this was going to be a fight and a half.

I decided to try some new tactics. I flew skywards, intending to attack them from above if I could. Jonty and Willie followed me, divining my intention. The Fockes did not give chase, but instead became engaged with the remaining Mavericks. Had they not noticed us? I hoped not.

Below us, our planes and theirs were engaged in a duel of death. While they were preoccupied, I thought perhaps the three of us might manage to bag one of them at least.

"Tally-ho," said Jonty, who seemed to maintain his fighting spirit no matter what.

We bore down on one lone Focke, which was chasing Jean Tarbon.

"Get off me!" he shouted irritably to nobody in particular, weaving this way and that.

"We've got you," I said, pressing the fire button.

Though the three of us fired a salvo, the Focke simply evaded it all and flitted away with ease.

"Damn it!" Jonty said.

The tactic had failed and now we were on the same terms as the rest.

"Break, Red Section, let's get amongst it."

I didn't have long to wait before I was engaged by another Focke-Wulf. In an even match these planes were getting the better of us, there were no two ways about it. I was glad of all my combat experience, which had honed my reflexes. I was soon pulling tight turns, and tried a couple of loops without success. When I did get a shot in myself, it went wide as he easily avoided me.

Over on the left, I saw a Spitfire go down in a ball of flames. I wondered who had bought it this time. There was no time to reflect on it with the Focke-Wulf on my tail. Guns chattered behind me, and I heard Jonty's voice.

"Tally-ho, Skipper — got that blighter!"

He had too. The Focke-Wulf spiralled away with smoke coming from the engine.

"Thanks, Jonty," I said.

"Don't mention it."

He wheeled back into the fray, and so did I. I managed to get another Jerry in my sights more by good luck than judgement. He hadn't seen me coming. I fired and was rewarded by seeing his plane starting to pitch and yaw. He turned and ran for the mainland. I was about to give chase, when another shout went up.

"He's on me! I can't shake him — I can't..."

The voice was Phillip's, and I saw his plane being hotly pursued by another Jerry.

"Get him off me! Get him off!" he screamed in panic.

His aircraft was banking violently left and right with jerky movements. I didn't hesitate and turned in on the attack.

"Hold on, Green Two. I'm coming," I said. "On my way."

"I can't do it. I just can't," said Phillip, whose plane now seemed to be rapidly going out of control.

Needing to do something quickly, I fired at the Jerry, though I was possibly too far away to get him. Tracers whipped past his canopy, and I saw him glance over to me, then bank steeply away. I started to give chase, to keep him at bay.

"It's all right — you're out of danger. Get yourself under control, Green Two."

It was Judd, watching the whole thing play out from somewhere in the vicinity.

"No, no, I can't! I can't do this anymore!" shouted Phillip.

The Jerry I was chasing turned tail and left the scene, along with his compatriots. However, my attention was forced back to the sight of Phillip's plane rapidly heading for the English coastline.

"Green Two, get back in formation!" ordered Judd.

"I can't. I'm sorry, it's no good… I just can't do this anymore," said Phillip, not altering course at all.

"Mavericks, disengage and form up," Judd commanded the rest of us.

As we did so, Phillip's plane continued to disappear into the distance.

"Green Two, return to formation, form up — that's an order!" thundered Judd.

Phillip didn't answer.

"Green Two, I order you to return to your position! Can you hear me, Green Two? Green Two!" Judd had now become exasperated and all of us could tell.

After a few moments of radio silence, Judd said with a heavy sigh, "Mavericks, let's go home. The patrol is over."

We headed back in silence. We were all shocked by what had just occurred. Phillip had turned and run from the enemy. No doubt it had happened in other forces, but I had never encountered it in the Air Force, certainly never in the Mavericks. One of our own had committed an act of cowardice, and now the die was cast I wondered what would ensue.

We crossed the coastline and continued on to Banley. Phillip's plane had long since vanished from view. What was going to happen to him when he landed? The incident would have been picked up by comms and no doubt already reported to Bentley.

I landed in a sombre mood, and I was sure the others felt the same. As I alighted from my plane, I saw that Phillip was standing alone, flanked by four ground personnel carrying rifles. He was looking at the ground. Bentley was waiting for Judd, with Audrey at his side.

We gathered in a group while Judd walked over to confer with Bentley in hushed tones. The airfield, which was usually a buzz of activity and noise, was strangely quiet.

"It's a rum do, Skipper," said Jonty quietly.

"Hush," said Willie.

Angelica was standing a little way off from us and didn't run to me. It was as if time stood still, waiting for something to happen.

After speaking with Judd, Bentley strode over to where Phillip was standing. We heard his words clearly.

"Pilot Officer Charlton, you have committed an act of cowardice in the face of the enemy. I am arresting you and you will be detained until such time as a proper investigation is held, and then a court-martial may be convened. Do you understand?"

"Sir, yes, sir," said Phillip, saluting at once.

"Take him away," said Bentley to his escort. "And lock him up."

The men saluted, and the sergeant in charge gave out the orders.

"Prisoner will left turn! Escort, forward march!"

I watched them taking Phillip away with mixed feelings. On the one hand, I felt there was nothing else Bentley could do. On the other hand, Phillip was still a fellow pilot and it was a damn shame.

Bentley left directly, walking in the direction of the main building. Audrey was left standing on her own. I started to walk towards her, but Angelica was quicker than me and at her side in a flash. She took Audrey in her arms, and Audrey broke into sobs. Angelica shot me an anguished look and waved me away.

I left them to it and caught up with the other pilots, who were talking about the shocking turn of events.

"It's a rotten show," Jonty was saying. "A bloody rotten show."

"I never would have believed it," said Pilot Officer Colin Bridgewater.

"Well, he's a bloody coward and he should take the consequences," interjected Pilot Officer Gerald Haliday.

"I say," said Jonty. "Innocent until proven guilty, old chap!"

He was always one to defend the underdog.

"Nonsense, we all saw him run," said Gerald.

"Why don't we leave it?" Jean suggested as voices started to get louder.

I stepped away, not wishing to become embroiled in bitter words. It was true that Phillip had been cowardly, but didn't he at least have the right to a fair trial?

"I told you," said Tomas, who had detached himself from the group on seeing me. "I said his heart wasn't in it."

"It seems you were right," I said.

"I'm right, I know!" Tomas smiled. "What do you think will happen to him?"

"I don't know," I said.

"In my country, we would just shoot him."

I stared at Tomas, who broke into a grin.

"I know, I know, this is England... You do things a different way..." He trailed off.

The truth was I didn't know what the consequences were, but the idea of Phillip being shot for cowardice impinged itself forcefully on my mind. I determined to go and see Bentley forthwith.

"I will see you later," said Tomas. "I'm going for some tea. Life goes on, eh?"

I nodded and turned away. I could see Angelica sitting with Audrey on our bench. They would no doubt be there for a while. I started off for Bentley's office.

CHAPTER FOUR

"Come!" barked Bentley when I knocked on the door.

He was in the act of cleaning out his pipe, and I waited while he did so. He completed his routine and lit it, then motioned me to sit down.

"Angus. What can I do for you?" he said with a world-weary air. "No, don't tell me — you're here about Charlton."

The CO was often rather perspicacious, but it wouldn't have been hard to work out why I had come to see him so quickly after the incident.

"Yes, sir, I am," I said without prevarication.

He puffed on his pipe for a moment, savouring the flavour of the smoke with evident satisfaction.

"Well?"

"I just wondered, sir, what's going to happen to him?"

"What's going to happen to him? A court-martial is what's going to happen to him."

"Yes, but what then?"

Bentley tapped his pipe on the desk to settle the tobacco and took a few more puffs.

"I've just been on the phone with the Air Vice-Marshal, his father, who has informed me that I must throw the book at him, no quarter given," he said with a look of disgust on his face. "His own father said that, yes indeed."

"Oh, I say —"

He continued, cutting me off. "So, I will formally examine him, as the procedure tells me I have to do, and then convene a court-martial. He will be tried, and there's no doubt of the outcome, I would suggest, considering the number of witnesses."

I nodded. This was no more than expected. The trial would be a formality at best.

"And then?"

"If, or rather when, he's found guilty, you mean?"

"Yes."

"Hmm, well…"

In the most irritating fashion possible, Bentley decided to refill his infernal pipe. He had smoked the contents in moments. He was obviously exceptionally put out by the proceedings. I waited somewhat impatiently. After all, for all I knew, it could be a matter of life and death.

"I suppose," he said at length, "you think he'll be shot."

"I —"

"Well, you can rest easy on that score," he said, to my immense relief. "We don't shoot people in the RAF. He'll most likely be stripped of his rank and wings and drummed out of the force."

"Oh, I see," I said. This didn't sound too bad on the face of it.

"Unfortunately, that's not the end of it. His employment record will carry the stain of his cowardice and he'll find it difficult to find another job."

This seemed grossly unfair. Particularly in wartime, it would mean nobody would want him. He'd be an outcast.

"I'm afraid there is absolutely nothing I can do," said Bentley. "And since he did what he did so publicly, there is virtually nothing that will mitigate his actions … besides which, I've received explicit orders from on high…"

I said nothing. The reaction of Phillip's father was entirely predictable. His father who had precipitated the situation in the first place.

"I don't like this any more than you do. I won't be in charge of the court-martial, to ensure impartiality. He'll have a fair trial."

"Will he, though? Will he be allowed to tell the court his side of it, why he did it?"

Bentley regarded me with interest. "I imagine it depends on who is going to defend him, and I doubt there will be many takers."

"He should be entitled to fair treatment," I said. "No matter what he's done."

"He'll get it, in as far as I am able to obtain it for him," said Bentley, taking up his pipe once more.

While he puffed on it, I was struck by an idea. I have an innate sense of justice, no matter how much my own behaviour may have crossed lines in the past.

"I'll represent him," I said.

"What? Are you sure?" He raised his eyebrows.

"I will defend him, sir, if I may. He's entitled to a decent defence, at least."

Bentley put his pipe down on the desk with care whilst he considered my request. He treated his pipe with a certain reverence, as if it were a religious artefact.

"Very well," he said at last. "You can do that if you wish. In fact, it's a good notion, since it will perhaps prevent some of your colleagues from becoming too partisan. I'm sure you'll treat it with the seriousness it deserves."

"I shall do my best," I said.

"You know it won't change the outcome, don't you?" he said. I supposed he wanted me to be sure of what I was getting into.

"I know, but I'd rather see justice done properly than not at all."

"Spoken like a lawyer already."

He smiled and so did I.

"Very well, in which case you'll have access to the prisoner, naturally, to help you to prepare his case. He'll be treated well while in custody, I'll see to that. In fact, I shall probably address the squadron on the issue, since I do not want this becoming a bun fight."

"Thank you, sir," I said.

"You may not thank me afterwards, but chalk it up to experience if nothing else."

"Yes, sir."

He was silent once more, toying with his pipe. In the end, thankfully, he elected not to refill it a third time.

"I gather we lost a pilot today," he said, almost as an afterthought.

"Yes."

"We're lucky it wasn't more, I suppose."

I knew exactly what he meant. He was talking about the Focke-Wulfs. It was a topic which preyed on all of our minds of late.

"Those planes are causing us a headache for sure," I said.

"Don't I know it, Angus, don't I know it."

He dismissed me with a nod of his head, and I left his office in a pensive mood. What would Angelica think of this latest turn of events? I hoped she wouldn't castigate me for taking on Phillip's defence. Some part of me felt for him: he had been forced to do something he didn't want to, and now it had all gone for a burton he was going to pay a heavy price. No doubt his father would disown him, and what would he do then? His future was bleak.

"There you are," said Angelica. "I was looking for you."

"Well, now you've found me," I replied.

"And where were you?" she smiled playfully. Whatever had passed between her and Audrey had not affected her composure.

"I was seeing Bentley," I said.

"Oh?"

"Yes, shall we walk?"

"If you're going to tell me what it was about?"

"Of course I am," I said.

She tucked her arm into mine and we strolled back across the field to our bench. As we sat down, I slipped my arm around her shoulder. She snuggled into me and sighed.

"Audrey was distraught about Phillip," she said.

"So I gathered."

"She's fallen in love with him and now this has happened. It's very sad."

It certainly was, but I couldn't see how she could form a relationship with a pilot who was about to be thrown out of the Air Force.

"What's she going to do?" I wondered.

"What can she do? He's going to be court-martialled."

"Yes, well, that's what I went to see Bentley about."

"About Phillip?" She sounded surprised.

"Yes, I wanted to know what would happen to him."

"And what will happen to him?"

I told her and she sat up straighter.

"So his whole life will be blighted from here on in?"

"Yes, I'm afraid so."

She pursed her lips but said nothing more, so I decided to tell her about my decision.

"I've offered to defend him," I said.

"You've what?" She pulled out of my arm and looked at me in surprise.

"I've offered to be his defending officer in the court-martial."

"But why?"

"I don't know. I just feel it's unfair. Everyone will be against him. I heard the chaps talking already. I know he's done perhaps an unforgivable thing, but he never wanted to fly. He was made to do it, and now he hasn't a friend in the world."

"But you hardly know him," Angelica protested.

"Audrey hardly knows him and she's in love with him."

"It's different," she shot back.

"Don't you want me to do it?" I asked her, even though we both knew I would do it anyway.

"No, it's not that, it's just … well, I was rather taken aback. I didn't think you were quite so … charitable."

"Well, perhaps you're seeing a new side to me."

"Then I'm proud of you, for standing up for what you believe in." She smiled at me.

"I believe in justice, but Phillip's not going to get it," I said.

She shook her head. "No."

"At least he will have someone to speak up for him."

"Have you asked him if he wants you to do it?" she asked gently.

"Not yet, but I intend to."

"I would want you to defend me," she said softly.

"Would you?"

"Yes, always."

She kissed me then. I was happy to have received her approval; it meant a lot. I had no idea what the point of my defending Phillip was, other than principle. I had never thought I was a man of great principle, but sometimes it takes another fellow's predicament to make you see it.

The following morning, Bentley convened a muster in the hangar. Virtually all of the squadron was there. I assumed it was the announcement he had intimated he would make regarding Phillip. If nothing else Bentley had a way of stamping his authority on the squadron, and he would do so quite ruthlessly whenever it was necessary.

I stood with Angelica at the front of the ranks, alongside Willie and Jonty. There were no seats provided this time, so the briefing was going to be short. I knew feelings were running high with some of my fellow pilots about what Phillip had done. However, I was sure Bentley was determined to nip this in the bud. Part of me was glad that Pilot Officer Lawrence Calver was no longer around, since I could imagine him being more than vociferously vocal on the subject.

Bentley strode into the hangar with Audrey by his side and everyone snapped to attention.

"At ease," he said, standing up on a podium placed there for his use. This put him up higher than us.

Before saying anything, he naturally decided to produce the pipe of doom from his pocket. I assumed he must have filled it earlier, since he didn't perform his usual ritual. Instead, he lit it and smoked it with evident satisfaction while surveying us through the awkward silence. Finally, he removed the pipe from his mouth and began to speak.

"Yesterday there was an unfortunate incident when the squadron went into combat on a routine patrol."

"I'll say," murmured Gerald a little too loudly. He had been very vocal on the subject the day before. All eyes turned to him momentarily.

"Did I ask you to speak, Pilot Officer Haliday?" said Bentley, at once fixing him with an irascible stare.

"No, sir," said Gerald, abashed.

"Then don't," said Bentley shortly, before continuing. "Yesterday, Pilot Officer Charlton fled the field of combat and disobeyed direct orders from a senior officer to return. Needless to say, this is conduct unbecoming of a member of this squadron, and of an officer in the Royal Air Force."

There was a shifting of feet while he paused and took a few puffs on his pipe.

"As a result of his actions a court-martial will be convened, justice will be done, and that will be the end of the matter. Whatever consequences Pilot Officer Charlton must face will be dictated by the court-martial and by nobody else. Do I make myself clear?"

This was a definite warning to any of the squadron who might be contemplating visiting their displeasure upon the unfortunate Phillip.

Bentley didn't wait for an answer. "Until such time as due process has taken place, Pilot Officer Charlton shall remain in custody and nobody other than those detaining him, and his defending counsel, is to have any contact with him whatsoever. I want that clearly understood!"

I glanced at Audrey and saw a flicker of grief at this statement. She would be hurting no matter how little she had known him. Love is love, and when it hits you, it drops you just as surely as a bullet. I knew that now for certain.

Bentley was in no hurry to get things over with, I could tell. He wanted his words to sink in. He took another pull on his pipe, sending out clouds of smoke.

"In the interests of fairness and impartiality," he said, "Flying Officer Mackennelly will conduct Pilot Officer Charlton's defence with my full approval. Never let it be said that this squadron does not do things by the book. We do and we will, and I won't hear a word against anyone involved in these very unfortunate proceedings. If I do, then mark my words: they will have me to deal with."

There were a few interested looks cast in my direction, but Bentley in his inimitable way had carried out a pre-emptive strike. I was fairly sure that whatever the other pilots thought of my actions they would, for the most part, keep it to themselves. Angelica squeezed my hand and smiled at me in reassurance.

"In the meantime," continued Bentley, "we've still got a war on. So put your attention and efforts in that direction. God knows that's enough for any of us." He scanned the assembled company one more time before saying, "Dismissed."

Then he left with Audrey as rapidly as he had come. There was a fair bit of murmuring as we broke up, but nobody spoke too loudly as we started to file out.

"Well played, Skipper," said Jonty.

"Do you think so?" I asked him.

"Yes, of course. Even the worst of fellows need someone to speak for them."

He smiled. I wondered if he really considered Phillip the 'worst of fellows' but I imagined not. Jonty was fair-minded.

"Thanks, Jonty."

"He's right, Scottish. Someone has to defend him regardless. You're a stalwart," said Willie, clapping me on the shoulder.

"In a way, it's better that you don't really know him: it will make you more impartial," said Jonty.

"I don't know how much good it will really do," I replied.

I decided, on balance, not to go back to the hut. The announcement would possibly not be greeted with equanimity by everyone, and it might be as well to let things simmer down. I was not one to shy away from confrontation, but sometimes discretion is the better part of valour. Instead, I went with Angelica to our bench once more and we sat in silence, looking out to the fields through the fencing.

However, a short time later, Audrey came up to us and stood by the bench.

"Hello," I said when I noticed her. "How are you faring?"

"As well as I can, I suppose. It's all been a shock," she said.

"What is it, Audrey?" asked Angelica with concern.

"I'm afraid I need Angus," she said.

"Oh?"

"There's two gentlemen to see you."

At these words, my heart sank. Two gentlemen could only mean one thing: the two chaps from MI6. After the last caper, I really hoped I had seen the back of them, but it seemed that was not to be.

"Is it…?" I began.

"The Marx Brothers, yes."

I had dubbed them the Marx Brothers, a nickname to which Audrey and Angelica were privy.

"What on earth can they want now?" said Angelica, sounding annoyed.

She had every right to be. The Marx Brothers had involved us in their madcap espionage schemes three times already. One of those could well have resulted in me and Angelica parting ways.

"I suppose I had better go and find out," I said, standing up.

"I'll see you afterwards?" said Angelica, walking with us.

"Yes, I'll find you."

"I'll find *you*," she laughed.

"You're good at that."

Audrey showed me into the familiar large room in which I'd met the Marx Brothers several times before. It had also served as our HQ during the recent secret mission I had been asked to lead.

The two agents were sitting at ease smoking cigarettes. Each was dressed in a similar dark suit, white shirt, and different-coloured ties — one red, one blue. Their fawn trench coats were draped over the back of a chair, and their hats rested on the table. They both had moustaches and were of a similar appearance. The real difference between them was the blue eyes of the one I'd dubbed Chico and the grey eyes of the one I had designated Harpo. I had no idea of their real names, and probably never would.

"Ah, Flying Officer Mackennelly," said Harpo, lazily getting up and holding out his hand.

I shook it, even though I was less than glad to see him or his companion.

"Nice to see you again," said Chico motioning me to sit.

I did so and waited, while they smoked in silence.

"He's not very pleased to see us," said Chico conversationally.

"No," agreed Harpo.

"Why would I be?" I said bluntly, taking the bait. "Every time you chaps turn up, I end up embroiled in some sort of damnable farrago."

"He's right," Harpo concurred.

"Indeed," said Chico.

"You're probably wondering why we're here," said Harpo, stating the obvious.

"The thought did cross my mind, yes," I said, becoming a little acidic.

"Well, wonder no more, because we are here to tell you."

I sighed inwardly. This conversation was heading the usual way, and I was perfectly certain I wasn't going to like what they were going to say.

Harpo stubbed out his cigarette and immediately lit up another. He took a long drag with evident satisfaction.

"How are things going in the squadron?" he asked me.

"Pretty much the same as usual," I replied. I was being non-committal until I knew what they wanted.

"No trouble in combat?"

I wasn't entirely sure what he was getting at, but surely they weren't here because of Phillip? I decided to ask.

"This isn't about Pilot Officer Charlton, is it?" I said suspiciously.

"The coward?" interjected Chico. "No, not him."

"Oh."

These two were uncompromising in their defence of the realm, I knew that much. So, a cowardly act such as the one perpetrated by Phillip wouldn't be looked on too kindly.

"Any *other* problems in combat?" asked Harpo.

I wished they would not talk in riddles, but this was their way. They liked to come at things obliquely; perhaps it was in the nature of being a spy.

"Well, there's the fact Jerry's got a blasted new plane, the Focke-Wulf, if that's what you mean," I said.

"Precisely," said Harpo with a smile, taking another pull on his cigarette. He blew out the smoke triumphantly.

"What about it?" I said.

"It's causing a headache for the Air Force, and naturally we can't have Jerry stealing a march on us like that," said Chico.

"As far as I can tell, there's precious little we can do about it," I shot back. "Not until the designers come up with something better."

"Exactly," said Harpo.

I was becoming, as I often did, exasperated by these cryptic utterances. They acted as if they were a pair of magicians conjuring up some fantastical scheme.

"Exactly what?" I asked somewhat tersely.

They were not at all fazed by my tone, and seemed impervious to snubs of any sort.

"The problem for the chaps who make the planes, is they don't really know what we're up against."

"No," I said, although this was rather stating the obvious.

"Yes, they don't know because they haven't got one," said Chico.

"I suppose they won't, because I doubt the Germans are going to hand one over for us to examine it," I said, becoming sarcastic once more.

"Not hand over, no — not willingly," said Harpo, smiling.

"So, what are we supposed to do?" I said. "Go over there and steal one?"

"Bingo!" said Chico at once.

"He's got it!" said Harpo with a grin.

I stood up and stared at them, aghast. "You've gone round the bend, both of you," I said. "You can't seriously be saying you want to steal one of Jerry's new planes."

"That's exactly what we're saying," said Harpo. "The War Office wants you, the Mavericks, to steal a Focke-Wulf."

"The War Office?" I repeated.

"Yes, that's right," said Harpo.

"The War Office wants us to steal a Focke-Wulf?" I had to repeat it because I wasn't sure I had heard them correctly.

"Yes, that is it in a nutshell," said Chico.

"You're mad," I said, starting to pace up and down in agitation.

"Not at all, old chum."

"I suppose we're just going to waltz over to France, get in one, and fly it back?" I said.

"Something like that, yes."

I sat down and they waited patiently while I absorbed the import of what they were asking.

"You realise that this is an insane idea, don't you?" I said at length.

"The best ones often are," said Harpo, offering his colleague another cigarette. They seemed to have increased their consumption of the damn things since I last saw them.

"If this is the best idea, then I would hate to hear the worst ones."

"We always enjoy your sense of humour, Flying Officer," said Chico.

"Yes, we do," agreed his colleague.

I gathered my wits, since they were deadly serious about the scheme.

"How do you propose we're going to pull off a stunt like that? And why have you picked the Mavericks yet again, when you could have the pick of any squadron in this country?" I demanded.

"So many questions," said Chico.

"All in good time," said Harpo.

This was typical. Everything was done on their terms.

"Well, have you thought this through?" I asked. "As to how it's going to work?"

"We've a rough plan, yes."

"And?"

I curbed my rising temper, since it wouldn't do any good to get annoyed. They were also completely undeterred by any kind of opposition, so it was pointless to argue anyway.

"Well, first let me answer your second question," Harpo continued.

"Go on."

"Your squadron undertook an immensely successful mission not long ago with that assassination caper."

I nodded. That part was true, although it had been exceptionally difficult all the same. I winced a little, recalling the necessity of shooting down another British pilot.

"And the War Office is very pleased with you, as is Fighter Command," said Chico.

I didn't like the way he said "*you*", and I had an inkling of what would come next.

"Yes," said Harpo, divining my thoughts. "You're the man to lead this mission."

I sighed. There wasn't going to be a choice and I knew it. In for a penny, in for a pound as they say.

"Well, then tell me how this mission is supposed to work."

"We are in the process of locating a suitable airfield," said Chico. "One with easy access to the new planes, using our contacts in France."

"And then?"

"You will fly your six-plane team in Spitfires to the airfield under cover of darkness. Simultaneously, a Lysander will drop a pilot to fly the Focke-Wulf near the airfield. Using our contacts in the resistance, he will make his way to the airfield perimeter."

"And then?"

"It will be timed so that you arrive just as dawn breaks. You will strafe the airfield, destroying all of the planes but one. In the pandemonium, the pilot will take the remaining Focke-Wulf and fly it back to Blighty."

"Bob's your uncle, we've got the plane," said Harpo.

I shook my head in wonder at what had to be one of the most hare-brained ideas I had heard in a while. However, since we were engaging in a serious discussion, I had some serious questions.

"Why can't you just get bombers to do this, rather than Spitfires?"

"Accuracy," said Harpo.

"Accuracy?"

"Yes, you can accurately destroy all the planes but the one we need, whereas the bombers may destroy them all, thus defeating the object of the mission."

He made it all sound so easy, yet accurate ground strafing under fire would be difficult in practice.

"It's a tall order," I said. "Even with us potentially being more accurate."

I emphasised the *potentially* part, since there were so many things that could go wrong.

"You will practise, beforehand," said Harpo. "With a set of dummy planes as targets."

Even with practice beforehand it still sounded like madness, but I continued with my next question.

"Will there be a ground attack, like last time?" I asked him.

"We can't guarantee that, no," he said.

I wasn't pleased to hear this, but on the other hand relying on a set of resistance fighters who for various reasons might not make the rendezvous was probably not wise either.

Regardless, the mission was fraught with potential failure points in my opinion, and I said so.

"You realise there are numerous things which could go wrong," I said.

"Yes, yes, we do, but this is a chance in a million and we've got to take it. It's up to you and, naturally, us to make sure nothing does go wrong."

The obvious question came next.

"And who is going to fly the Focke-Wulf?" I asked.

"We're locating a pilot," said Chico.

"I see."

A thought was forming in my mind, a thought that I should be the one to fly that plane home. I didn't voice it, however. Instead, I asked a more obvious question.

"Have you spoken to Bentley about this?"

"We will, but we wanted to speak to you first," said Harpo.

"Since you are the man of the hour," Chico added with a smile.

"I'm surprised to hear that, since two of the spies you wanted captured were shot during the other missions, one by me and one by Barbara," I reminded them.

They had not been best pleased at the time, but Chico dismissed the incidents with a wave of his hand.

"Well, you know, fortunes of war and all that."

"We let bygones be bygones," said Harpo. "Time to move on to bigger and better things."

This hardly qualified for either of those statements, although they had just given me a far bigger problem than the previous mission we had flown. It also brought Barbara to mind, whom

I had not seen for some time since. She had been recruited, by all accounts, into the Secret Service after the shooting incident.

"How is Barbara, by the way?" I asked them, more out of curiosity than anything else.

"Lady Amberly?" said Harpo.

"Yes."

"She's ... serving her country ... very well..." said Chico.

They wouldn't impart any further details, and I didn't really want to know. No doubt if she ever reappeared, she'd buttonhole me and regale me with an edited version of her exploits. However, perhaps she had finally discovered her forte.

"Have a think about the mission," said Harpo, returning to the matter at hand. "We'll give you some time and talk again. We've things to put in motion, in any case."

"So, I have a choice?" I asked him bluntly.

"We always have a choice, Flying Officer," said Chico in a tone that implied precisely the opposite.

"You won't be ordered to do it, if that's what you're asking," said Harpo. "But the king, your country and Winston Churchill will be exceedingly grateful if you would accept the assignment."

They knew full well that when they put it like that, I could not refuse. Who could? It put me in mind of Phillip; we were cast in different moulds. I needed to get on and see him, but at the same time, I would have to think about this mission.

"In the meantime, try not to get killed," said Chico.

"I'll do my best," I replied stiffly.

They seemed in no hurry to leave, so I stood up to go.

"If there's nothing else?"

"No, not just now. We'll see you in a couple of days," said Harpo.

"All right."

"Toodle pip," said Chico affably, and took another drag on his cigarette.

I nodded and left the room in a pensive mood. They had certainly set the cat amongst the pigeons.

CHAPTER FIVE

I had not taken too many steps from the main building before Angelica was at my side.

"Well?" she said at once.

"I see you found me," I replied.

"I will always find you, Flying Officer Mackennelly," she replied, tucking her arm into mine. "At least when I want to. Anyway, never mind that — what did they want? I'm dying to know."

This was no more than I expected from her and since her security clearance far exceeded mine, I would be able to tell her without compunction. She had also worked for the Marx Brothers — although that assignment had ended rather badly all told. Assuming the mission went ahead, she would certainly be the mission comms.

"Let's go where we can't be overheard then," I said.

"All right, but you need to kiss me first."

"Is that compulsory?" I asked her, noting the twinkle in her eyes.

"It most certainly is," she replied, putting her arms around my neck.

I was bereft of thought for some moments. I couldn't imagine how I'd ever contemplated being with anyone else, she had captured my heart so thoroughly.

Once we were back on the bench, I elaborated on the Marx Brothers' plan while Angelica listened quietly.

"Well?" I said when I had finished. "What do you think?"

"What do I think?" She smiled faintly. "It's insane is what I think, but I would expect nothing less from those two."

"My thoughts exactly."

She took my hand and looked at me with a serious expression on her face.

"Are you going to do it?" she asked.

"I don't feel as if I have a choice," I replied.

"No."

If I thought that was the end of it, I was wrong. Things had a habit of escalating quickly around Angelica.

"Who is going to fly the Focke-Wulf back?" she asked quietly.

I hesitated because I didn't want to tell her what was on my mind. "Well … I…"

"Don't tell me you're thinking of doing it yourself," she said at once with an edge to her voice.

"I…"

"Don't say it, please! Don't say you're contemplating *that*!"

She was determined to have it out with me before I'd even had it out with myself.

"Well, what if I'm the best person for the job?"

She snatched her hand away at once.

"I knew it! I knew as soon as you told me that you'd be thinking of risking your life yet again by putting your duty above everything. I know … I know that's what you're supposed to do, but sometimes…" She stopped, her eyes filled with tears, and she turned away. "I just wanted to hear it from your own lips, and now I have."

I heard her voice break a little and knew she was crying.

"I didn't exactly say I was going to do it…" I protested.

"You don't have to, because I know you; I know you will put the country first, like I did on that spying mission … and I regretted that so much. I just wish for once you'd think about the fact you don't have to do everything, always putting your life on the line. I know you think you should be a hero, but it's unnecessary and ... wasteful ... risking your life doing something so bloody dangerous — flying a plane you don't even know how to fly!"

"Angelica, I..."

I put my hand on her shoulder, and she shrugged it off.

"Don't touch me, Angus. I'm so angry."

I tried to be reasonable. "Look, I haven't even had a chance to think things through. I haven't..."

She cut off my efforts to explain. "You shouldn't need to think about it," she said, turning back to face me.

Why wouldn't I say what she wanted to hear? Was I really serious about piloting the Focke-Wulf? Why did I have to be so stubborn? I didn't know the answer to any of these questions, and the situation seemed to have spiralled out of control.

"I put up with the fact you fly out almost every day and you might never come back. I wear it because that's the war and that's your duty as a pilot in the Air Force. But this is putting your life on the line with so many things that could go wrong..."

"Well, I know, but..."

"No, you don't know! You can't know how much my heart breaks every single time you go out. How much it broke that time you were shot down in France, and then again over the Channel. I'm always wondering if the next time you take off will be the last time I ever see you again!"

She had never expressed herself quite so forcefully before, and I realised just how much she had been bottling up her feelings. I stared at her aghast, unable to move or say anything.

"But this ... this is beyond anything, and I won't endure it," she said.

"What difference does it make? It's just another plane," I said, knowing as soon as I had said it that it was the wrong thing to say.

"It's not just another plane! You've never even flown one before and you'll be on the ground — so many things will be out of your control. At least up there in your Spitfire, I feel as if you have a fighting chance."

"I'm sure I could work out how to fly it…"

I was digging a hole for myself, and it was getting deeper.

"Really? That's your answer? Well, if you're determined to do it, then you can do it without me," she said in a voice that was suddenly icy calm.

"But I didn't say…"

She wasn't listening. Instead, she stood up and pulled at the engagement ring on her left hand until she got it off.

"Here, you can take your bloody ring! I don't want it."

She flung the ring in my direction, turned on her heel and stalked away.

"Angelica!" I called after her, but she didn't turn around.

I could tell by the set of her shoulders that the last thing she wanted was me chasing after her like a fool. I bent down, picked up the ring and put it in my pocket. Then I sat for a very long time wondering what had just happened. It seemed I had fallen in love with the most volatile woman on earth, but even so, I couldn't bear the thought of being without her, not for a minute. I hoped for both our sakes she didn't really mean to break off our engagement. I went back to the pilots' hut only to find that we had been stood down for the day. Left to my own devices since I was currently *persona non grata* with the woman I loved, I sought out Gordon.

Ensconced once more at Annie's, with tea and crumpets, Gordon eyed me sympathetically.

"I assume, sir, something has gone awry," he said, sipping his tea.

"More than just awry, Fred..."

I took out the engagement ring and put it on the table. He contemplated it for a moment while buttering another crumpet.

"Oh dear."

"Yes, Fred, I don't know what to do."

"Might I ask what brought this about?"

He took a bite of his crumpet. I had hardly touched mine.

"I can't really tell you because it's classified, but it concerns something I was thinking about doing, which she really doesn't want me to do."

"I assume this ... thing involves putting yourself in some sort of jeopardy? Am I right?"

He had divined it perfectly. It seemed he was far more in tune with Angelica's feelings than I was.

"If you put it like that, yes."

"And would it be that you had a choice about whether you, erm ... put yourself in harm's way or not?"

"Yes, and the thing is I hadn't decided on it either..."

Gordon wasn't a fool. He probably knew that the Marx Brothers had been to visit Banley, since he knew virtually everything that went on at the airfield. It didn't take a genius to work out that they hadn't come just to pass the time of day.

He finished his second crumpet and poured himself another cup of tea.

"What did she say, sir, if I might at least ask that ... before she gave you back the ring?"

"She said I could do what it was I intended to do without her, and that I could have my bloody ring back, because she didn't want it."

"Ah, I see … right."

"That's bad, isn't it?" I prompted him.

"It's not good, sir."

Gordon had a way of understating things in that peculiarly British fashion where the deeper meaning was obvious, though not expressed.

"Damn," I said, having expected him to say no less.

"Do eat your crumpets, sir," he said gently. "Annie would be most disappointed if you left them."

"What? Oh yes."

I found my appetite after all and swiftly ate them both. I washed them down with tea and took another cup.

"Wouldn't be good to upset two women in one day," he observed.

We both laughed, and I felt somewhat restored.

"So, this thing you're deciding about is obviously fraught with danger," Gordon continued.

"Yes. In fact, it's one thing or another. Both are dangerous, but one is probably foolhardy at best," I admitted.

"And that's the one she doesn't want you to do," he said.

"In no uncertain terms," I told him.

"Indeed."

He thought for a moment. "Another round, sir, my shout?" he said.

"Why not? But isn't it my shout?"

"I'll pay, sir, I insist."

He smiled and I did not argue. I had regained my appetite in any case, and dinner would be a while. Gordon signalled to Annie, who disappeared into her kitchen. In a short while, more tea, crumpets, butter and jam appeared. We had sat in companionable silence while Gordon lit up a cigarette. I let him muse on things, since his advice was always worthwhile. I poured another cup of tea for each of us.

"You know, in Japan, the tea ceremony is almost akin to a religious rite," he said, watching me.

"Is it really? Have you been there?"

"I've been to a few places in my time, yes."

"I suppose the British might view drinking tea in the same way," I said.

"It's the cure for all ills, as my mother would say."

He smiled, buttered another crumpet and spread it with jam. Then, having taken a bite and consumed it, he evidently felt ready to express an opinion on the matter at hand.

"Sir, if I may say so, you don't have to be the hero every time. Sometimes it's better just to be the person who helps the hero succeed."

"I see," I said.

"It's rather like football, sir. The person who scores the goal often needs someone to set it up, you see, and their role is vitally important."

"Yes, that makes sense," I replied, taking a bite of my third crumpet with satisfaction. "So, discretion is the better part of valour, is that what you're saying?"

"That and don't spoil the ship for a ha'p'orth of tar."

"My prospective marriage, you mean?"

"Exactly."

He finished his crumpet and sipped his tea before continuing.

"Think about it this way: is it worth losing Angelica for the sake of one brave but possibly foolhardy moment? You have your entire life ahead of you, if you live to see it, and you can spend it all with her."

I laughed. "You think I'm being stubborn, just like she does, I suppose?"

He drained his cup and poured yet another. He declined to comment on what he thought of my actions. Instead, he adroitly suggested an alternative view.

"You're not the only person who can do whatever needs to be done, I'm sure of that."

Without knowing anything of the mission, he had, naturally, hit the nail on the head.

"You're right, of course," I said, unable to deny the truth of his statement.

"Better to lose gracefully than to win at the expense of two people's happiness, don't you think?"

I put my hands up in mock surrender. "I'm convinced. I'll tell Angelica ... assuming she gives me the chance to do so."

"That's the ticket."

Gordon smiled and so did I. He always knew the right thing to say, and he was, invariably, correct. I didn't need to fly the Focke-Wulf. Not just because Angelica was angry with me, but because she was also right. I had no idea about flying a German plane. It might be the same as a Spitfire, but it might be very different. There would be no time to work out how to fly a plane when you were trying to steal it under fire. You had to know what you were doing. The question was, who would the Marx Brothers find to fly the damn plane then?

We finished our crumpets, moving on to speak of other topics. Gordon paid and I resolved to ensure that I did so the next time.

We sat in the jeep and before setting off, he said, "Where to now, sir?"

Since the prospect of going back to Banley did not fill me with enthusiasm, I opted to return to Amberly Manor.

"Home, I guess, Fred. I don't think I'll be having supper with Angelica tonight."

He nodded. "Right you are, sir. Amberly it is."

After an indifferent night, I appeared at breakfast slightly bleary-eyed. I had taken dinner with the rest of the officers billeted there but had very little to say.

"What-ho, Skipper," said Jonty, who was tucking into his eggs on toast with a generous portion of baked beans. Apparently, baked beans were classed as an essential wartime food for rationing purposes. We certainly ate our fair share of them.

"Jonty," I said, taking my seat.

"What's up? You didn't say much last night at dinner," Jonty continued.

"Leave the man alone," said Willie at once. "He's obviously preoccupied."

Willie was quite perceptive where people were concerned, and also protective of me. I certainly had occasion to be grateful for that out in combat.

"And," Willie added, "he doesn't want one of your infernal ballads either."

"Well, have you asked him?" Jonty said, taking another bite of his breakfast.

"I don't need to ask him. Just look at him."

"I would have thought a ballad would cheer him up."

"It would not!" said Willie emphatically.

"Woah, woah, easy chaps," I said, laughing. "I'm in the room here, remember?"

"Sorry, Skipper," said Jonty at once.

"No ballads," said Willie.

"Enough," I protested as a plate of eggs on toast with a side of baked beans was placed in front of me. "Let me eat my breakfast in peace without you two arguing."

"I told you," said Willie triumphantly.

"No, you didn't, and it wasn't me who suggested a ballad."

"But you were thinking it…"

I shook my head and concentrated on my breakfast. I determined that I would seek out Angelica as soon as I got to the base. I wasn't going to allow something like this to come between us.

However, as luck would have it, Audrey intercepted me the moment I arrived.

"Bentley wants to see you, sir," she said.

"Oh, right." I could well imagine why.

As I made my way to Bentley's office with Audrey, she glanced at me.

"It's not worth the loss of the woman you love, you know."

She didn't have to say any more, and she probably knew about the mission since the Marx Brothers would have spoken to Bentley already.

"She talked to you?"

"She was incredibly distraught." Her tone was earnest and naturally full of concern for her friend.

"Oh damn. Really?"

"Yes."

I could have guessed this, of course, but it was different to hear it like that. I felt terrible that Angelica was distraught on my account. I needed to put things right as soon as I could. However, first I had Bentley to deal with.

We reached his office and Audrey ushered me in before taking her place at her desk. She busied herself with her work, though I knew she would be taking everything in just the same. Bentley glanced up at me and started to empty his pipe.

"Ah, Angus," he said after I saluted, motioning me to sit.

He said nothing further while completing his pipe of doom ritual. Then he took a few puffs before speaking.

"You've no doubt had a conversation with those blasted MI6 Johnnies about their damn fool scheme?" he said.

I knew he held no great opinion of the Marx Brothers. It was they who had pretended Lawrence Calver was dead when in fact he wasn't. This had later resulted in him stealing a Spitfire, which had to be shot down.

"Yes, sir, I have."

"Hmm," he said, puffing on his pipe. "What do you think of it?"

"It's a big risk, sir, if I'm honest."

I wasn't going to sugarcoat it. The entire operation was fraught with things that could go wrong.

"Yes, true. But, when you think about it, the rewards of getting hold of one of those planes…"

He didn't finish his sentence. We both knew that the risk was probably worth it.

"There is that."

He pointed the stem of his pipe at me. "Do you think you can pull it off? I want an honest answer before I sanction this tomfoolery."

I gave him a non-committal response, partly because I really did not know if we could do it or not.

"With careful planning and the right resources, it might work," I said.

He paused to take a few more puffs and added to the smoke already pervading the room.

"Yes, but the real question remains: when all's said and done, is it worth a try?"

He genuinely wanted my opinion, that much was clear. Unfortunately, there was only one answer I could give him.

"I suppose given what's at stake, yes."

He nodded. "Hmm, I see. I tend to concur…" He tapped the pipe stem smartly on the desk. "One thing, though."

"Sir?"

"You're not flying that bloody Focke-Wulf!"

This wasn't what I had been expecting him to say at all, and I was somewhat taken aback.

"I —"

He cut me off. "I know you, Angus. It would be the first thing you'd think of, and I'm not having it."

"Sir, I … I wasn't going to volunteer."

This was dissembling, since I'd only just decided not to after talking to Gordon, and Bentley wasn't buying it.

"Oh, really? You'll pardon me if I don't believe you."

I sighed. He could see right through me, and he wasn't wrong. I elected to own up after all. "All right, it was my initial thought, yes."

He shot me a triumphant smile. "I knew it! It's just the sort of damn fool hot-headed notion you would have."

"Sir."

Bentley probably knew me better than I knew myself, and as I'd already been raked over by Angelica, I took this with equanimity. However, Bentley wasn't finished.

"Well, I am ordering you not to do so under *any* circumstances, do you understand?"

"Yes, sir, understood."

"Good!"

He was probably satisfied he'd scotched any chance of me attempting to fly the Focke-Wulf; however, he continued to warm to his theme regardless.

"We'll find someone to fly it, someone who can fly German planes and who isn't my backup to my squadron flight leader. I need you leading this mission and seeing it through, not pulling some half-baked stunt trying to fly a plane you've never been in. Do I make myself clear?"

"Perfectly, sir," I said again, hoping he was satisfied, now he'd thoroughly rubbed my nose in it.

To my relief, he moved on to other matters. "Well, on that understanding, who do you want on the mission team?"

This was an easy question. It would be Jonty, Willie and Tomas, and Pilot Officers Arjun Sharma and Jean Tarbon.

"The same as last time, I think. It worked well before…"

"Good, good, and I presume you'd like your fiancée as comms?"

"Yes, sir."

I couldn't help pulling a face at this question, and he picked it up at once.

"Something amiss?"

"I'd rather not say at this juncture, sir, if you don't mind."

I didn't want to explain to the CO how Angelica had hurled her engagement ring at my feet; however, I didn't need to.

"Hmm, well, if you've fallen out with her, then you're a bigger fool than I take you for. I suggest you go and bloody well sort it out forthwith."

"Sir."

He nodded. "Good. What else do you need?"

"I think we'll need that Mosquito again for navigation."

"I'll see what I can do."

"We'll also need a Lysander to drop the pilot."

"Yes, those MI6 chaps mentioned it and said they would see to it. Let me know if there's any problem."

"Sir."

"Good. Get your team together and brief them. You'll need to practise for the mission. The good news is that I'll be able to get more pilots and probably planes out of Fighter Command. We'll use the mission planes we mothballed."

"It's a good job we didn't return them then, sir."

"Damn right. I wasn't going to give them back in any case."

He laughed. As much as Fighter Command was the bane of his life, he knew how to play the game.

"I'll speak to Redwood," I said.

"Jolly good. I will let those MI6 reprobates know forthwith."

I got up to go, but he hadn't finished.

"And Angus, don't forget your other duties."

"Sir?"

"You are the defending officer for Charlton. Get on and see him as soon as possible. I want to wrap up this damned court-martial as soon as I can."

I glanced at Audrey, who was steadfastly typing as if she had not heard. "Yes, sir, I will."

"You and your team will remain on active duty for the moment, so try not to get killed, all right?" he said.

"Sir."

I wondered how long that would pertain, but right now he did not have enough pilots. No doubt Fighter Command would give us some more once the mission was ratified.

"Dismissed," he said.

I left the CO's office and decided to seek out Angelica at once to put things right.

On a hunch, I walked to the edge of the airfield and saw the lone figure of Angelica sitting on our bench. She did not turn as I approached and sat down next to her. I said nothing, waiting for a sign from her.

At length, she turned to look at me. She had dark rings under her eyes, and I could tell she was miserable. I felt quite wretched that this was on my account.

"Well?" she said a little coldly. "I wasn't expecting to see you."

"Why ever not?" I replied, distracted from my purpose.

"You know why," she replied, with a mulish expression on her face.

"I'm not going to fly the Focke-Wulf. I just wanted to tell you," I said.

Her expression softened immediately. "Really?" she said, looking rather surprised.

"Yes, it's better that someone flies it who has more experience with German planes, and besides…"

"Besides?" she said.

"Bentley has ordered me not to do it."

"Well, at least somebody has some common sense," she said.

I edged closer. She did not demur, so I took her hands in mine.

"I realised that I don't have to always be the hero. I can be the person who helps the hero succeed." I borrowed the phrase from Gordon, knowing he would approve.

"Really?"

"Yes, really. I love you, more than anything, and I would never deliberately do anything to hurt you," I said.

"You know I would have accepted it, if … if it was the only way…" she said quietly.

"I know, but you were right, and so is Bentley."

"I missed you so much last night," she whispered.

Tears began to roll down her cheeks, and I took her in my arms and kissed her. We said no more for a few moments, happy to be reunited. When our lips parted, she didn't let go of me, but held me tight.

"I'm sorry," she said. "I was horrid and beastly to you."

"I probably deserved it," I replied, all too willing to wear the sackcloth and ashes.

"You didn't. You've got your duty. But it's just so hard — you don't understand how hard it is."

She buried her face in my shoulder and I stroked her hair. I was glad she had revealed to me just how much she worried. It brought home to me how much harder it was for the person left behind than the person going into combat. In combat, you had no time to think. In Angelica's position, you had all the time in the world to contemplate losing the person you love. I had perhaps been too insensitive in the past and resolved to do better by her.

"Sorry," she said, sitting up and smiling weakly. "Now I've made your jacket all wet."

"It doesn't matter, and I'm sorry too. I didn't understand what you've been going through."

"I tried to hide it from you. I really tried," she said.

"Well, you can stop hiding your feelings from me."

She shook her head, and both of us felt better. I reached into my pocket and brought out the ring.

"I was wondering if you still wanted to wear this?"

"Oh God, what must you have thought of me?" She shot me a stricken look.

"I was rather devastated, if I'm honest," I told her.

"I'm sorry, it was bad of me; of course I want it, more than anything else in the world."

She took the ring and put it back on her finger, showing it to me proudly.

"What else did Bentley say?" she asked me.

I told her what had transpired, and how the CO wasn't entirely enamoured of the scheme even though he was going along with it.

"Do you think it will work?" she asked me.

"I think there's a chance, and if there's a chance, we will have to take it."

"Yes," she nodded.

"Would you like dinner tonight, as usual?"

"Fish and chips?"

"Yes, absolutely."

"All right but ... kiss me first ... before you go back to the hut."

I did so, and just for a little while, all was right with the world.

CHAPTER SIX

I didn't intend to broach the mission with the others until I'd had the official go-ahead. This entailed waiting for another conversation with the Marx Brothers. They would no doubt appear without warning in due course.

In the meantime, I needed to speak to Phillip, plus there was the matter of yet another sortie. This time we had to patrol to the Seven Sisters, and then fly westward along the coastline before returning home. I was happy I had made it up with Angelica before flying again. Now it seemed the worst thing in the world would be if something happened to me and we'd fallen out with each other.

"Take care, darling," she said, holding me tightly before I started off for my Spitfire.

"I will."

She blew me a kiss while Redwood ensured I had strapped in, and then I fired up the kite. She remained watching us as always until we faded into the distance.

We headed south for the cliffs, and once there we'd sweep right. We had made similar sorties many times before, but now we'd have to be far more vigilant. Nevertheless, I wasn't convinced Jerry would come out looking for trouble as we flew over the water.

Then I spotted a large number of ships steaming out from Portsmouth. This could certainly be a potential target. We were only one squadron, though, and if the Germans came over with bombers and fighters, things were going to get rather difficult. Although it hadn't been their habit to do so on convoys this far south, there was always a first time.

As luck would have it no such attack was forthcoming, and we turned back towards home at Bournemouth. I can't say I was disappointed not to see any action. As we crossed over Southampton, I started to feel a little easier. Surely we should be safe enough well into British territory. The Jerries had not made a habit lately of coming inland. Unfortunately, no sooner had I thought we were home and dry when Willie shouted, "Bandits at six o'clock!"

My heart sank. Sure enough, there were Focke-Wulfs dropping out of the sky on top of us.

"What are they doing up here?" said Jonty, sounding most put out.

"Never mind *that*, break, Red Section, break," I said, banking left and peeling off from the main pack.

"Break, Mavericks, break," said Judd quite calmly, while the rest of the flight followed suit and split up.

We turned to face the enemy planes. I couldn't imagine what they were doing this far inland either, but there was no point second-guessing the Luftwaffe. There wasn't time, in any case.

A second later, I narrowly avoided a stream of tracers which streaked past my wing. Seeing them out of the corner of my eye, I flipped the joystick, and the shots went wide.

"Watch out, Skipper," said Jonty.

I pulled a tight turn and tried to draw a bead on the offending Focke-Wulf, but just like the others I'd encountered before, he was too fast and slipped out of reach. He was a little too far away from me to chase, so I left him.

At that instant, I had spied Willie with another Jerry on his tail. This was more urgent. I banked sharply and throttled up, flying towards them. I hoped to catch the Jerry off guard, but it was not to be. He saw me coming and turned quickly, out of range.

"Damn," I said under my breath. These new planes really were a menace. Also, this lot seemed more interested in taunting us than fighting us. What the hell had they come for?

"Come back here, blast you," said Colin, trying to chase down another.

The two of them twirled in the sky, as if in a waltz, while the German remained just out of reach.

We were still circling over Southampton, but unlike the usual dogfights we'd had, the gunfire was sparse. This was simply because we couldn't get any of the Jerries in range.

"If this goes on much longer, we'll be out of fuel," said Willie in frustration.

I flicked a glance at my gauge. He wasn't wrong. I became determined to put a stop to their games and picked a Focke-Wulf at random. If I shot one down, maybe they would either engage us properly or leave. Either option was better than this.

I flew straight at him and doggedly pursued him. For a change, I managed to keep up with his shenanigans. He flew higher, then dived down, but I stuck to him like glue. Sometimes when you've just had enough, things go right. In this case, they did; perhaps he had become overconfident during these manoeuvres. He turned one too many times and without warning slid momentarily into my sights. I fired on instinct, one burst and then another. They hit him amidships, and I watched his plane go into a spin with great satisfaction.

"So, you're not invincible after all," I said to myself, rather pleased.

The next moment, I heard a cry from Tomas.

"Judd's been hit, he's been hit!"

I banked around to see Judd's plane rapidly losing height but still in control. Behind him was another Focke-Wulf, looking to put paid to him for good. I wasn't having that.

I throttled up and headed directly for the pursuing German. He had not seen me, and I fired. The bullets went wide but he must have registered the danger he was in. Another second and I'd get in a killing shot.

However, I wasn't going to make two kills after all. He turned away and I saw that the rest of the Focke-Wulfs had thankfully finally given up.

"They're going," said Willie with relief.

"Thank God for that," said Jonty.

"Chaps, I'm going to try and land in that field," said Judd. "Angus, take over the flight. Get them home intact, will you?"

"Yes, sir," I said, but I was still concerned about whether he would make it down in one piece. "Willie, Jonty, escort him down."

I didn't want to risk the Focke-Wulfs changing their minds and coming back. I circled around while Judd coasted onto a field with Willie and Jonty guarding his flanks. When he had landed, I took one last look around.

The Focke-Wulfs had definitely gone, so I said, "Mavericks, form up on me, Red Section will take the lead."

Red Section took over Blue Section's usual position in the flight and I turned for home. The remaining planes in the squadron followed suit.

Judd waved goodbye standing on his wing. Soon his plane disappeared from view, as we took a bearing towards Banley.

"That was a rum do," said Jonty at length.

"Yes," I agreed.

This was one of Bentley's favourite sayings. Since he said it so often, we'd all started using it.

"And before you even start, the answer is no!" said Willie at once.

"No what?" said Jonty.

"You know what," said Willie.

The rest of the flight burst out laughing, and the tension eased as Willie and Jonty started to quarrel once more about Jonty's ballads. Things were back to normal.

As we approached the airfield, I noticed my fuel gauge was registering empty. I fervently hoped it would last until I got down but in typical fashion, considering the day we'd had, the engine cut out while I was still a little way off the ground.

"Damn and blast it! My engine's died," I said to nobody in particular.

"You're nearly there, Scottish. Keep calm," said Willie.

Fortunately, the undercarriage was already down so I didn't have to lower it manually. All I needed to do was coast it in, and from the height I was at it wasn't too difficult.

"Easy does it, Skipper," said Jonty.

The Spitfire hit the grass and bumped along for a fair bit, but the landing wasn't as bad as it might have been. I let it roll to a standstill. Redwood came running up to help me get down from the plane.

"She ran out of fuel," I told him. "We got caught up in a dogfight."

"At least it got you home," he said.

"There is that."

I left him to it, because I could see Bentley striding towards me with Audrey. He would no doubt want to discuss what had happened on the sortie.

I saluted as he came up to me and waited while he removed his pipe from his pocket. He lit it and puffed on it for a moment.

"So," said Bentley. "That was a damn rum do by all accounts."

There was a barely concealed snigger from Jonty, who was still within hearing distance. Bentley cast a look in his direction and I hastily stepped into the breach before he could say anything. Jonty had been in Bentley's bad books too many times in the past.

"Yes, it was all fine until the Focke-Wulfs suddenly appeared over Southampton."

"What the devil were they doing coming out to Southampton?" the CO demanded, as if I was personally privy to the Luftwaffe's operational decisions.

"I don't know, sir. It's rather odd."

"Yes ... yes, indeed."

He puffed on his pipe a little more, sending out clouds of smoke which caught in the gentle breeze blowing over the field.

"You don't suppose it's another blasted spy, do you?" he said, lowering his voice a tad.

I had thought about this on the flight home, but it seemed highly unlikely to me.

"I think it was probably more a case of bad luck," I replied. "Perhaps they are just testing us and their planes. They didn't seem in the mood for a fight; it was hard to get a bead on them."

"Hmm, well let's hope you're right, but this makes that little matter we discussed more important than ever," he said.

I nodded. I knew he meant the plan to steal one of Jerry's new planes.

"I'll tell those Johnnies to get a move on," he continued.

He was referring to the Marx Brothers, and no doubt they would be arriving hot foot.

"Yes, sir," I said.

"Good, good. Well, I expect Judd will be back in due course. He made it down all right, I gather."

"Yes, he did, and I managed to shoot down the Focke-Wulf that was on his tail."

"Yes, by Jove, well done! Nice to turn the tables on these blighters for once."

"It was," I agreed.

He nodded and took a few more puffs on his pipe before placing it back in his pocket.

"Right, well, jolly good. We will talk in due course," he said. "I've got phone calls to make."

I saluted and watched him go. He was immediately replaced by my fiancée, who catapulted herself into my chest in her usual fashion.

"Oof," I said, giving in at once to her determined kiss.

"I'm glad you're home," she said at length.

"Me too."

"Shall we have tea, and then later some supper?"

"Yes, yes, I'd like that. After tea, I'd better go and see Phillip."

"Yes, I suppose you should," she replied a little sadly.

In perfect harmony once more, we walked arm in arm back to the hut.

Phillip was under lock and key in the guard house, such as it was. Banley wasn't a place where a lot of prisoners were expected. In fact, detaining anyone was highly unusual. Apart from the occasional drunk, I imagined it got very little use.

He was kept in a smallish room with a bed, desk, chamber pot, and a small barred window. The bars seemed something of an afterthought. One of the guards let me in and locked the door behind me.

Phillip was lying on the single bed, staring up at the ceiling. He sat up when I entered, and swung his legs down onto the floor. He was still wearing his uniform, but the jacket was draped over the back of a chair. He would continue to be entitled to wear it until the court-martial had been completed. I noticed he had shaved, so was keeping up appearances if nothing else.

"Hello," I said.

"Hello."

He looked at me a little warily. I supposed he might be wondering what I thought of him. He should have been informed by now that I would be his defending officer. In any case, he didn't seem surprised to see me, which was encouraging. I sat in the chair opposite him.

"How are you faring?" I asked him.

He shrugged in a non-committal way. "As well as might be expected."

He didn't sound bitter, but rather resigned to his fate.

"Are they treating you well?" I asked him, hoping that they were.

"I'm fine." He brushed off my concern.

"I mean it," I told him. "Bentley wants you treated properly, fairly. If there's anything you need…"

"What could I possibly need?" he said.

"A book to read? Something to write with?" I suggested.

"A book would be nice, thank you."

He shot me a grateful smile, which disappeared almost immediately.

"I'll see to it."

We lapsed into silence while I considered how to go about things. I had never had to defend anyone before, so I wasn't sure where to start.

"Why are you doing this?" he asked me suddenly.

"Why am I doing what?"

"You know, defending me? I'm a coward. Why would anyone want to speak up for me?"

I could see he was determined to go down the road of self-castigation, which would not help his cause.

"I'm defending you because everyone has the right to a fair trial," I replied firmly.

"But you don't even know me. Why would you care?"

"I care about justice," I said. "I care that justice is properly done. In a way, not knowing you is an advantage."

"How so?"

"Because nobody can say I'm biased or swayed by friendship."

"Friendship," he said bitterly. "I will never have any friends again, not now."

"Look," I said, a little exasperated by his attitude. "I'm going to be defending you regardless, because that's the duty I've taken on and I'll see it through. I'm not here to judge you either. That's not my job."

"What is your job?" He wasn't making this easy.

"To see that you get a fair trial, and that your voice is heard in court and goes on record, regardless of what happens."

"Oh … yes … I see."

Phillip suddenly looked serious. I thought I should at least reassure him about the consequences.

"You're not going to get shot, if that's what you're thinking."

"No, I've been told that at least."

"But I can try to mitigate what does happen as much as I can."

"Can you?"

We seemed to be going around in circles, and it wasn't doing us any good. I decided instead to take another tack.

"Why did you do it?" I asked, referring to the incident where he had fled.

He sighed and looked at me for a long moment. "I don't know. I really don't know."

"Well, what was going through your mind at the time?"

"I don't know. I was just afraid. No … not afraid. I had these feelings that I could not cope. I couldn't deal with it anymore. I just didn't want to be there, so I … left."

"Why do you think you felt that way, though?"

"I don't know…"

I looked at him and I could tell that this was not true. He did know, or at least had some idea, but he evidently didn't want to tell me. I felt a little out of my depth. When I rashly volunteered to defend him, I thought I would just have a few conversations and Phillip would tell me what I needed to know. It turned out it wasn't going to be that simple. However, that being said, I knew a man who might know better than me how to approach things. I determined that I would need to go and speak to Gordon.

"I see," I said.

"Sorry," he replied, although he didn't look it.

Phillip appeared to have already given up, but I wasn't about to let him do so.

"I'll be back soon," I said. "We'll talk again."

"All right."

"I'll get you some reading material too."

"Thanks."

"Don't mention it."

I stood up and knocked on the door for the guard. Phillip lay back on the bed and started to whistle tunelessly. It sounded like 'It's a Long Way to Tipperary'. I could still hear it as I left the guardhouse.

Gordon wasn't hard to find. He was quite often hanging around in his jeep when he wasn't seeing to his various duties. True to form, he was having a quiet smoke and probably contemplating the world at large.

"Do you need to go somewhere, sir?" he asked me.

"No thanks, Fred," I said. "But I do need to talk to you."

"Oh, I see. Is it an Annie's type of talk?"

The idea was certainly appealing, and so were the tea and crumpets; however, I had to demur.

"I'd love to, but I don't think there's time to go there and back before I have to meet Angelica."

Gordon motioned to the passenger seat beside him. "Well then, how can I help?"

I sat down while he continued to finish his cigarette.

"I'm defending Pilot Officer Charlton," I said.

"I was aware, sir, yes."

"Of course…"

"And how's it going?"

"Not well." I elaborated on my conversation with Phillip and he listened carefully.

"I see," he said when I had finished.

"What do you suggest I do?"

"You have to get to the root of the problem, as it were," he said. "It's possibly somewhere back in his childhood."

"Really?"

"Yes, could be."

"Gosh," I said. "I'm not sure I'm equipped to discover such a thing. How do you know this?"

"I've read Sigmund Freud, and others. Their books are about psychoanalysis."

"Well, I'm blowed."

Gordon never failed to surprise me, although I shouldn't have been surprised to hear this at all. He seemed to be a fount of knowledge and was extremely well read. Now I had heard this, a plan was forming in my mind.

"Have you … ever done any psychoanalysing?" I asked.

"Not as such, sir, no, but I understand the theory."

"Supposing, Fred, that I asked you to come with me … to try to, erm, get to the root of things, as you said … with Phillip. Would you?"

He stubbed out his cigarette and then lit up another. He took a few drags on it before speaking.

"If you think it would help, sir, of course."

I knew I could count on him. Gordon invariably came through.

"Excellent. I don't think it would do any harm, and I'm not going to get anywhere otherwise."

"Well, in that case, I'm at your disposal," he said.

"We'll see him tomorrow then."

"In the meantime, sir, I can see your lady approaching us as we speak."

Angelica came up to the jeep. "What are you two talking about?" she enquired with a saucy smile.

"I'll tell you over dinner," I replied.

"Hop in," said Gordon.

She did so and we set off for the local village chip shop, which we visited rather often lately.

Angelica and I sat on the village green in our usual spot and ate our dinner. I told her what had transpired between myself and Phillip.

"Oh dear," she said. "It sounds as if it's going to be rather more difficult than you thought."

"Yes, which is why I've enlisted Fred's assistance. Perhaps he can help me find out something I can use in Phillip's mitigation."

"*If* Phillip will let you use it," she pointed out.

"There is that, of course."

It had crossed my mind that this might be a waste of time, if Phillip simply refused to cooperate. But I had a streak of determination that wouldn't let me give up so easily.

"Audrey says she's grateful for what you are doing for him," Angelica said after a pause to polish off the last of her meal.

"It still seems odd she fell for him so quickly," I mused.

"Does it? I told you, I fell for you almost instantly."

"Then why didn't you say?" I demanded.

"You weren't exactly in a position to listen, were you?"

She was right, as usual. I had been heavily embroiled with Barbara, a circumstance that now seemed an aeon away. Back then I never would have imagined I could fall hook, line, and sinker for a woman, but I had.

"Audrey fell in love with him; she can't help that. No more than I can help having fallen hopelessly in love with you," Angelica continued.

"Do you wish you hadn't?" I shot back at once, although I was just teasing.

"Frequently."

Her eyes danced. She could give as good as she got.

"Come closer and tell me that," I said softly.

"With pleasure."

Nothing more was said, and both of us knew we had no regrets at all about falling in love with each other. I was at least more fortunate than Audrey in that respect.

The following day, I was met by Audrey as soon as I arrived at Banley.

"The Marx Brothers…" she began as I got down from the jeep.

"I've been expecting them," I replied with a smile.

"Yes, Bentley was onto them yesterday."

"Well … lead on."

We walked together and Audrey stopped by the main building. She touched my arm briefly.

"Thank you."

I knew she was talking about Phillip.

"You're welcome, and I'm sorry … for the way things have turned out."

She gave me a tight smile. "It can't be helped. I seem to be somewhat unlucky in love."

I nodded. There wasn't a lot I could say. Perhaps this wasn't the first time for her. Her voice was a little strained.

"I really thought I'd found someone special," she said quietly.

"It's a damn shame, but I'll do my best."

"I know."

We were both well aware that the chances of them being able to continue together after Phillip's court-martial were slim. Perhaps love gives you false hope; they certainly say it springs eternal.

"Let's go," she said. "Probably shouldn't keep them waiting."

"No."

I was shown into the usual room, and I assumed this would become the mission operation room once we started.

The Marx Brothers were seated in the same spot as last time, as if they had never left it. Somehow, they always managed to give the impression of studied nonchalance. The two of them were smoking cigarettes, a habit of theirs which I noted seemed to have become more frequent over time. Perhaps their job was more stressful than they made it look. After all, constantly deceiving people must become quite wearing, as much as constantly wondering if you were being deceived.

"Ah, Flying Officer Mackennelly," said Harpo with a lazy smile.

"Forgive us if we don't get up," said Chico. "It's actually rather comfortable here."

Since I'd seen their offices, which were exceptionally well appointed, I found that rather difficult to believe. However, I declined to comment and simply pulled up a chair.

"We've spoken to your CO and he's mad keen for you to do this mission," said Harpo.

"Just as enthusiastic as we are, in fact," Chico added.

"Yes, I know," I replied, although I wasn't sure Bentley was quite as eager for the mission as they implied. I let it pass.

"You'll be pleased to hear we've got the go-ahead from the War Office, and indeed, Churchill himself," said Harpo.

"So everyone's counting on you," said Chico.

"Right."

If this was meant to fill me with confidence, it had quite the opposite effect. The new mission was fraught with difficulties.

"Have you found someone to fly the Focke-Wulf?" I asked them.

"We have indeed," said Harpo. "It certainly won't be *you*."

"Yes, I am fully aware," I said, slightly nettled. Having put that issue to bed, I didn't want to discuss it again.

"We've a test pilot who has flown all kinds of aircraft, including some German planes — before the war, but still, he's one of the best. And, more importantly, he speaks German," said Chico.

"Is he German?" I asked with interest.

"Oh no, no, no," said Harpo. "He's from Poland and hates the Nazis with a passion. He's been around a bit and escaped over here when the war broke out."

They were quick to reassure me, and I was happy to hear that he wasn't of German descent. You couldn't be sure where people's loyalties might lie, particularly if their roots lay in a country we were now at war with. We'd had enough spies already.

"We've checked him out thoroughly," said Chico. "And we're ready to vouch for him."

"That's good to know."

The issue of the pilot was seemingly resolved. We got down to business.

"What else will you need? Have you picked your chaps?" asked Harpo.

"The same team as before — I've already told Bentley."

"Good, good. You can set up your mission HQ here, as per the last time."

"We need that Mosquito, and the Lysander you promised."

"Consider it done," said Chico.

"We'll use the same planes. We've still got them all blacked-out," I said.

"Splendid!" Chico smiled.

"What are we to put about as a cover story?" I asked them, assuming they would already have thought of it. "You surely can't say it's to test our night-fighting capability again. We used that last time and in any case, nobody believed it."

"Nothing," said Harpo.

"Nothing?"

"Yes, nothing. Say it's for a mission and you can't divulge any more than that. People can think what they like."

"All right."

I shrugged. They would think that anyway, regardless of what we said, though I doubted that anyone would imagine we were going to steal a Focke-Wulf.

"If you get too hard-pressed for ideas, tell them you're going after Hitler himself," said Chico.

The two of them burst out laughing at this. I didn't entirely see the funny side, but I felt it politic to join in.

"I have to say," said Harpo, "we've had more entertainment from this squadron than most of our other missions."

"I am so glad we could oblige you," I told him coolly.

"We've got his hackles up again," said Chico.

"Alas."

These two were never abashed; everything was like water off a duck's back to them.

"I assume we should start training for our mission as soon as possible," I said.

"Yes and no," said Chico.

"Meaning?"

"We've got something else in mind," said Harpo.

"You can think of it as a practice run," Chico continued.

I eyed them suspiciously. Whatever they were planning, I was certain I wasn't going to like it.

"You're going to hit an airfield in Northern France," Harpo said with a grin.

I stared at them aghast. "Have you taken leave of your senses?" I asked.

"Not at all," said Chico. "It's the ideal opportunity."

"Ideal opportunity for what? To signal our intentions to Jerry before we've even done it?" I protested.

It seemed utterly foolhardy to carry out an attack on an airfield before we undertook a mission doing precisely the same thing. Instead of answering me, to my annoyance, they changed tack.

"Don't you want a chance to get back at these Focke-Wulfs?" said Harpo.

"Well, yes, but that's what we're doing by stealing one of their planes. Surely that's important?"

"*This* is just as important," he continued, unperturbed.

"Exactly how?"

"It'll send a message to Jerry."

Once more they were talking in riddles.

"What message?" I said with exasperation.

"That the British are not to be trifled with," said Chico.

"Are you sure it won't send a message to double the defences on every airfield in Northern France?" I asked him.

"We don't believe so, no."

"How can you be so sure?"

The Marx Brothers exchanged glances and Harpo stubbed out his cigarette. I waited while he lit up another and took a long drag from it, blowing the smoke out thankfully away from me.

"Because," he said, "there's a certain arrogance in the Nazi psyche and in the Luftwaffe, mainly from Goering. He thinks they are invincible, in spite of what happened during the Battle of Britain, and now with these new planes he really will believe it." He took another pull on his cigarette and smiled, as if he'd just played his trump card.

"We want to give him a bloody nose," said Chico, adding his halfpence worth.

Whether they were right about the German psyche, I didn't know. They probably had more knowledge than I did in that respect, since they worked for the Intelligence Services. I could still perceive flaws in their reasoning, and I said so.

"What if it's us who get the bloody nose?"

"Well, it's up to you not to get shot down," Harpo replied in the dismissive way he had of ignoring the pitfalls of their schemes.

I sighed. There wasn't any point in arguing, since it would go ahead anyway.

"When are we meant to be doing this?"

"In two weeks' time, give or take," said Chico. "We will give you a date as soon as we've finalised the target based upon intelligence."

"Two weeks ... or less?"

This didn't seem enough time to get my team back together and fully operational.

"Surely enough time to prepare, for a man like you?"

Now they were trying to flatter me.

"It's still a risk, in my opinion," I replied.

"We have to take that risk," said Harpo smoothly.

"*We?* It's *us* who are taking the risk, the pilots carrying out the mission."

They really were most blasé about other people putting their lives on the line for their madcap schemes.

"Yes, of course, we understand that."

They looked more serious than usual. Perhaps they did care after all. They sent people on missions all the time, I supposed, and many probably didn't come back. I didn't intend to be one of that number.

I refrained from asking them why they couldn't send bombers to destroy the airfield. If we were practising strafing the target, then it had to be us. It would be very similar to the actual mission, but without the plane-stealing part.

"Now, let's talk logistics," said Chico.

"You know most of it, as I said earlier," I told him. "Also, we're going to need an escort, so we can save our ammo for the mission."

"It's all taken care of. The Hurricane squadron you had last time will ride shotgun for you. They did a pretty good job as I understand it."

"Yes, they did."

I recalled that they had warded off an attack by 109s that would have scuppered the entire assassination plot as we headed for the target. We would have to fly in at low level again, and most probably at night. How the Hurricanes would fair if a squadron of Focke-Wulfs attacked us was another matter, and I didn't really want to think about it.

"When will you know about the target?" I asked them.

"We're waiting for air reconnaissance. Once they've managed to identify an airfield of Focke-Wulfs in range, it's all yours."

"And you're sure they won't expect another attack afterwards?" I repeated my concern because I wasn't convinced.

"As certain as we can be, yes," said Harpo. "We've been dealing with these people for months now, and through many intelligence reports we are beginning to understand how they think."

"I hope you're right," I said.

"Have faith," said Chico.

Faith was the last thing I had. I did have confidence that we would do the best we could, and that was about all I could hope for. All the planning in the world could go for a burton due to providence. I just hoped Lady Luck would continue to be on my side.

"I'd better get things moving then," I told them.

"Never fret, we'll be around to ensure you have everything you need," said Harpo.

"The War Office is counting on you," added Chico. "We all are."

"That is *exactly* what worries me," I replied.

CHAPTER SEVEN

I went to see Bentley after speaking to the Marx Brothers. He would be anxious to know the outcome of our discussion. His office was in the same building and so I was soon seated in front of his desk, watching him scrape out the bowl of his pipe.

I waited in silence while he performed the usual ritual. Once the room was filled with clouds of smoke, he was satisfied.

"I take it you've seen the MI6 Johnnies," he said.

"Yes, I've just come from talking to them."

"And?" He eyed me with interest.

"Did they explain their plans to you, sir?" I asked him, wanting to know exactly how much he knew already.

"Yes, you're going to steal one of those new planes. That's the idea, isn't it?" He puffed away contentedly.

"It's part of their plan, yes," I said.

"Oh, and what's the other part?"

It was obviously news to him, and I imagined when he heard the rest of the plan, he wouldn't be best pleased.

"In less than two weeks' time they want us to carry out a practice run," I said.

"Practice run? What kind of practice run?"

I certainly had his attention now, and so I delivered the punchline. "We're to go to France to strafe an airfield that has those Focke-Wulfs."

There was an ominous silence while he digested this information.

"What? What did you say?" He sounded incredulous.

"We're to strafe an airfield in Northern F—"

I got no further. Bentley was up and out of his chair, pacing the room in agitation.

"I might have bloody well known! Not content with risking my best pilots once, they want to do it bloody well twice!" he yelled, sounding most irate.

"That's about the size of it, yes."

"Bloody fools!" he bellowed furiously. "A pack of bloody fools running the show! And where has this hare-brained travesty of an idea come from?"

"The War Office, apparently…"

"The War Office, yes, I might have guessed it was the blasted War Office Johnnies. And what, pray, is their reason for doing it?"

Bentley was fairly bristling now and puffing on his pipe at an alarming rate.

"Apparently it's to give Jerry a bloody nose," I said.

"A bloody nose? Really! I'd like to damn well give them a bloody nose!" he roared. "I would certainly like to tell them what to do with their blasted clown show of a scheme, yes, I certainly would! Pack of circus clowns could do a better damn job of it and no mistake."

I waited for his anger to abate. His wrath was directed at what he saw as yet more interference in his running of the squadron and putting his pilots in danger more than anything else. He took a few more puffs of his pipe, discovered he'd used the tobacco up already, and returned to his desk. There he began the task of replenishing his pipe of doom. This had a calming effect, so that by the time he was puffing on it once more he seemed in a much more reasonable frame of mind.

"It's a good job I'm not a drinking man," he said. "I'd have drunk myself into an early grave with that lot."

"Yes, sir."

"Like a tot of single malt at bedtime, don't mind if I do, but apart from that…" He sighed. "Well, can't be helped. No use arguing with the top brass. Might as well get your chaps together and brief them. You can use the second hut as before. Apparently, I'm getting some more planes and pilots while you lot indulge in this latest farrago, but mark my words — I'm going to take my pound of flesh while I have the chance."

"Yes, sir," I said.

I knew, of course, that while he could be highly critical of his superiors at times, he would be just as invested in the success of this mission as anyone else. He knew we had to take risks, and this was just another one. The war was taking its toll on the patience and stamina of everyone. I didn't envy him the task of running the squadron.

"All right, well, naturally I never said all those things I just said," he said mildly, reminding me I had not been lightly taken into his confidence.

"My lips are sealed," I replied.

"Good, good. Now, have you been to see Charlton?" he asked, turning to other matters.

"I have and I'm planning on seeing him again."

"How's it going?"

"I … just need some time to prepare a decent defence," I said, prevaricating a little.

"Hmm, not cooperating, is he?" said Bentley, as perceptive as usual. "I'm not surprised. Never seen a fellow keener to hang himself — metaphorically speaking, of course."

"I hope I can at least get through to him," I said.

"Do your best, Angus, that's all anyone can ask."

I nodded. Phillip was the least of his worries now we had this mission to run and new pilots to integrate into the squadron.

"Very well, I'll leave you to get on with the mission."

He turned his attention back to his paperwork and I took it as a signal to leave. As I walked away from his office, Audrey caught up with me.

"Will Phillip not defend himself at all?" she asked me unhappily. She had been quietly working away during my meeting with Bentley, but had obviously overheard our exchange.

"He's reluctant to do so, I'm afraid," I replied. "But I'm enlisting the aid of Fred to try and dig a bit deeper."

"Should I talk to him?" she said.

"I'm not sure if it will help," I told her. "Not that I can stop you, if you want to see him."

Audrey nodded and turned away. I watched her go and then went outside, intending to head for the hut.

Naturally, Angelica intercepted me before I had a chance to get very far.

"Well?" she said at once.

"I'm just about to round up the chaps — and you, of course, if you want to be the comms."

"Of course, I do!"

"I'll be briefing them shortly," I said.

"Then you can brief me now."

"And what gives you special privileges?" I said playfully.

"You love me, and I'm your fiancée."

She smiled at me triumphantly, and I did not demur.

We sat down together on our bench, and I told her what had transpired with the Marx Brothers and then Bentley.

"Oh," she said when I'd finished.

"Oh? That's all you've got to say?"

She shrugged. "What is there to say? You said yourself you know what those two are like. I'm not happy you're going on two missions instead of one, but neither of us can do anything about it."

"You're rather stoic for a change," I said, having expected a less muted reaction.

She laughed and her voice took on a teasing tone. "Don't you believe it. I'm furious with them for putting you in harm's way like that! If only I was a practitioner of voodoo, I'd be sticking pins in dolls right now."

I smiled. This was the Angelica I knew. I kissed her and then we made our way to the dispersal hut to collect my team.

"You're probably wondering why you're here," I said when I had assembled the team — Jonty, Willie, Arjun, Jean, Tomas and Redwood — in the room which was to become our mission HQ once more.

"Is it something fun, Skipper?" asked Jonty.

"You might see it as fun, Jonty, yes."

I knew of Jonty's penchant for aerial combat and his perverse enjoyment of it, in spite of the danger.

"It's not to compose a ballad, if that's what you're thinking," added Willie.

"I say!" Jonty said in mock indignation.

"All right, settle down," I said, once more having to don the hat of leadership. "I've got you together because we have another mission; well, two in fact…"

They were suddenly all attention.

"Now, this might sound far-fetched, but the mission we've been given — which it goes without saying is top secret — is to steal a Focke-Wulf."

"Far-fetched?" said Willie. "It sounds like something out of a novel."

I outlined the two missions and what they would entail, while the team listened in silence. As I expected, there were questions.

"So, this isn't a joke?" said Arjun at length.

"No, it's deadly serious."

"Do you think it can work?" asked Jean.

He was a pretty straightforward individual, a stalwart in the air. I couldn't give him a positive answer.

"I don't know," I said. "If everything goes according to plan, then we've a chance, and if not then I guess it won't."

"Doesn't matter if it works or it doesn't," put in Tomas. "We have to do it anyway."

"I for one am going to take great pleasure in cutting a few of those Focke-Wulfs to pieces," said Jonty.

There were murmurs of agreement at this.

"So, what now, Scottish?" asked Willie.

"Techie and his crew will give the planes the once-over, and then we'll take them out for a spin. We need to get accurate with our strafing, so some target practice is in order."

"And the other planes?" Arjun asked, meaning the Mosquito and Lysander.

"I suppose they will arrive in due course. We'll doubtless use the same navigation method as before, with the Mosquito flying ahead and dropping flares. Until then, we're still on operational duty, so try your best not to get shot down."

It was a tall order. The Air Force expected us to fly a special mission and at the same time fly operational missions too. However, that was not my problem — it was Bentley's.

"All right," I said. "We will decamp to the mission dispersal hut and use that for the moment. As far as anyone is concerned, this is a top-secret mission and that's all you have to say."

"Let's hope there's not another spy in the squadron," said Jean.

When we arrived at the M Flight hut, we found that Bentley had obviously had some ground crew in to make it serviceable. We settled in and since we had no further orders for the day, I resolved to find Gordon and tackle Phillip once more.

Gordon and I were soon seated in Phillip's cell. He sat on the bed and looked at us warily.

"You know Fred, don't you?" I said to him.

"Yes, yes, of course," he replied.

"I've asked Fred here to help me with your defence."

"Oh? And how is he going to do that?"

Phillip was somewhat combative, it seemed. I glanced at Gordon.

"I just want to talk, sir, if you wouldn't mind," said Gordon, mindful that Phillip was still a serving officer for now.

"I suppose."

"Why don't you make yourself comfortable, perhaps?" Gordon suggested.

"I'm fine as I am," said Phillip, not moving.

Since Phillip wasn't being cooperative, Gordon elected to move things along.

"Could you perhaps tell us a little about how you came to be in the Air Force?" he asked Phillip gently.

"Is it relevant?"

I sighed inwardly. Was he going to continue to be this difficult? But Gordon was made of sterner stuff and merely batted the question back in the diplomatic way he had.

"It could be, sir, yes."

"Well…" Phillip began. "If you want to know the truth…"

"Most certainly." Gordon smiled.

"I didn't want to be a pilot, not ever. I certainly didn't want to join the Air Force."

"What did you want to do, if I might be so bold?"

Gordon was adroit at turning the conversation in the direction it needed to go.

"I wanted…"

"Yes?"

Suddenly, for the first time, Phillip came alive. He spoke with a passion I had not previously observed in him.

"I wanted to be on the stage. An actor. What a wonderful life that would have been. My whole life revolved around literature. I loved it. Shakespeare and others. They wove such magic into their words. I remember putting on plays for my mother when I was younger, and she used to love them…"

A shadow crossed his face as he mentioned her. He had relaxed a little at this memory and I felt it must be significant. Gordon did too.

"So, your mother featured quite a lot in your early life?"

"Yes … she was always there, you know… She used to come and play with me instead of leaving me to the nurse. She loved me, cared for me. She encouraged my interest in learning."

"It sounds as if she loved you very much," said Gordon softly.

"She did…" Phillip's voice cracked. "She did, but then…"

"Then?"

"She died. Horse riding accident. My father made her ride — you know, with the hunt. She hated it. Her horse bolted, and she fell, broke her neck…"

He put his head in his hands and his shoulders began to shake. Gordon's look told me that we were possibly getting somewhere. After a few moments, Phillip sniffed and sat up straighter. He dashed the wetness from his eyes.

"I understand it must have been somewhat distressing for you," said Gordon sympathetically.

"It was … in so many ways, because then … then there was nobody between me and my father…"

"Tell me about your father."

"He hated me," said Phillip bitterly. "Always has. You know what's expected from the males in the family. Stiff upper lip. Go to war and all that. I wasn't the son he wanted."

"Did he tell you that?"

"Not in so many words, but in every other way. My brother was a paragon. He always did well at school — he was in all the best teams, captain of rugby, cricket, you name it. 'Why can't you be more like Maxwell? Live up to the family name and all of our traditions.' That's what my father always used to say."

"How old were you when your mother died?" asked Gordon.

"I was eighteen, ready to go up to Oxford."

This wasn't what I had been expecting. I had thought he was far younger, but at eighteen he was still evidently attached to her.

"And then?"

"The war broke out. My brother was already in the Air Force. My father told me I had to join up too. I had no choice — I had nobody to say otherwise."

I admired the way Gordon skilfully turned the conversation. He asked intrusive questions without them seeming to be that way, and Phillip was thankfully now willing to answer.

"How was your father towards you in early life?" Gordon asked, since he had Phillip's cooperation.

"Distant."

"So he never…?"

Phillip interrupted him. "Never what? Laid a hand on me? No, my mother would not allow it. I told you, she protected me from the worst of his excesses."

"Excesses?" I said curiously.

"Oh, most people wouldn't see it as that. He schooled my brother all right, but my brother was a real boy, getting into scrapes and all that. A few painful trips to my father's study ensued. I wasn't a real boy, not to my father, I was … a sissy."

"But he didn't do that with you," said Gordon.

"No. My mother protected me, I told you. She was my rock. She understood me, she loved me, and I loved her. I loved her and she left me … to him. He hated me with a passion, don't you understand that? And he still does."

His voice blazed with a violence of feeling he had not shown up until now. Perhaps we were getting to the core of it.

"Did he ever express such sentiments to you?" Gordon asked him.

"No, he didn't have to, as I said. His whole life was all about my brother and why I couldn't be like him. I never wanted to join the damned Air Force — look what happened when I did."

There had been quite some disclosures, though I failed to see how I could use any of it. Gordon persevered.

"Why did you fly away that day … from combat?"

Phillip sighed and once more seemed distraught. "I don't know. I suppose it's what my mother would have wanted me to do. She always told me to run from a fight. If she had been alive, this never would have happened."

"Right. I see," said Gordon. He glanced at me as if to tell me he'd asked enough for the moment. I nodded. We needed to regroup.

"Thank you for being so open with us," Gordon told him. "We'll come back another day, if that's okay?"

"If you want. I don't know what good it will do. You can't help me; nobody can help me," said Phillip.

I was almost inclined to agree but I held my peace. We took our leave and I walked back with Gordon to the jeep.

"What do you think?" I asked him while he lit up a cigarette.

"Have you heard of the Oedipus complex?" he said with a smile.

"The what?"

"It's a theory by Sigmund Freud, that the child develops feelings for one parent, in this case the mother, and a sense of rivalry with the other, in this case the father. This usually happens at a young age, but for some, it never goes away…"

"And you're suggesting that Phillip…?"

"Was somehow in love with his mother, yes … and perhaps his father sensed it."

"Good God!" I was flabbergasted.

"It is just a theory, naturally. I'm no Freud."

"Yes, but we can hardly use that in his defence," I protested. I couldn't imagine whoever was acting as judge in the court-martial buying it.

"No."

"Think of how it would sound."

"I am aware of that," he said sympathetically.

I felt stymied and no further forward. I had taken on an impossible task with no way of mitigating Phillip's actions.

"Then what on earth am I to do?"

"Appeal to their better nature?"

"The better nature of the Air Force?"

"Far-fetched, I know…"

We both laughed at this. The Air Force would look after you, if you conformed. Those who did not ended up in the Mavericks. To those who couldn't even do that, the Air Force wouldn't be kind.

"Thanks for trying, Fred," I said, feeling a little hopeless.

"You're welcome, sir," he said. "If I can think of anything further, I will let you know."

I left him and returned to the hut. It was obvious that Phillip's mother had been a big influence in his life and somehow shaped his thinking. There would, however, be no sympathy for that at all, I was sure of it. He had signed up and would be expected to do his duty, just as his father had compelled him to do. There was also the issue of his father being an Air Vice-Marshal. I could hardly bring his name into disrepute. While I had damaged my own career quite extensively with my previous peccadilloes, I had to some extent regained some kudos during recent service. I could not imagine my reputation would survive disparaging one of the top brass, however. Perhaps appealing to their better nature was all I had.

We spent three days strafing dummy planes. The Marx Brothers had at least come through on that score, and the planes had been placed at a nearby artillery range we'd used before.

"Do you think we're getting any better, Skipper?" Jonty asked me, as we sat drinking tea outside the hut, having completed our training for the third day.

"At least some of us can hit the bloody target," Willie observed caustically.

"Are you saying I'm a poor shot?" Jonty said, bristling at once. "I'll have you know my father made me shoot targets for hours on end until I was a damn fine crack shot."

"All very well for pheasants," Willie shot back.

"All right, all right," I chided my friend. "Jonty's doing perfectly well, Willie, and you know it."

"He's probably better than all of us," said Willie. "I was just winding him up; it's the Kiwi way."

"Philistine," said Jonty with a smile.

The two of them seemed to enjoy baiting each other, or rather Willie liked to bait Jonty.

"In answer to your question, Jonty," I said, "I think we can always use more practice, but I'd say the accuracy is pretty good, and it needs to be."

We had deliberately had one of the dummy planes painted red so that it stood out, and we had to avoid shooting it if possible. Some ground crew had been assigned to check the planes after each pass and tell us whether we'd succeeded. They then patched up all the holes so that by the time we had flown back to Banley, rearmed and refuelled, the targets were ready to go again. God knows how much ammo we had used up, but I wasn't satisfied until the six of us firing in unison could strafe all the other planes without hitting the red one at all.

Then when we managed that, we did it again and several times more. At the end of the third day, I felt we were at least ready for the first mission, if not the second.

As we sat talking, I noticed a speck on the horizon getting larger by the second. Since there was no siren, I assumed it was one of ours. It was, and within a short space of time, the Mosquito we were expecting thundered in. It was a big twin-engine beast constructed entirely out of wood. However, for all of that, it was fast and had been a godsend on our previous mission. It taxied to a standstill, and shortly afterwards the familiar figures of Flight Lieutenant Michael Cranford and Flying Officer Gervais Montpellier were seen striding towards us. Michael was a tall man in his late twenties, with grey eyes, black hair and a moustache. Gervais was shorter, with fair hair and striking blue eyes. He was French and by all accounts a supreme navigator, while Michael was the pilot. Gervais had escaped from France in the nick of time, before the Germans took over.

"Hello, Angus," said Michael as they came up to greet us.

We were all on first-name terms after the last mission.

"Good to see you," I said, shaking hands with them both.

"*Ah bon, c'est très bien aussi*," said Gervais with a smile. Although he spoke perfect English, he would often drop a few French phrases in too.

"I gather you need a little help," said Michael.

"Yes, indeed," I replied. "Let's go in. You can renew your acquaintance with the chaps, and I'll brief you properly later."

"I could use a cup of tea," said Gervais. "Isn't that the English way?"

We all laughed.

"It certainly is, and that, at least, we can provide."

After giving Michael and Gervais some time to catch up, I went over what I knew of the mission with them. Gervais let out a low whistle.

"This is brave, hmm? Or perhaps foolish? I am not sure which."

"I think it's both," I replied. "But orders are orders."

"And who is this pilot, the one who is to steal the plane?"

"We've not met him yet. I suspect he won't arrive until after the first mission."

I assumed he wasn't needed until we were actually ready to steal the plane. He'd just be kicking his heels otherwise, and if he was as good as they said, he'd be needed for test flying in the meantime.

"We've seen a bit of action ourselves," said Michael. "Pathfinding for bombers and so forth. We got to fly a couple of sorties in a fully armed Mosquito too."

"That was fun," said Gervais.

"Gervais likes shooting — he's somewhat trigger-happy," Michael told me with a wink.

"Ah, I just like to shoot Nazis. They've stolen my country!" Gervais protested.

Michael laughed.

"I don't think they are anyone's favourite, to be honest, and now they've got this new plane," I said seriously.

"Yes, well, let's hope we can pull this off then."

"We shall, never fear, now that Gervais is here," said Gervais.

"He hasn't lost any of his Gallic pride," said Michael, smiling.

"We need all the help we can get, frankly," I replied.

The other two nodded, their expressions becoming serious too. For all we might joke, this mission wasn't going to be a walk in the park, not by a long chalk.

"What do you need us to do first?" asked Michael.

"We'll refresh our navigation skills and do some night-time practice runs, if that's all right with you?"

"You're the mission leader — whatever you say," Micheal said.

"I am, for what it's worth."

I wasn't enamoured of the job, but now I'd been asked to do it by Bentley, I would do the very best I could.

"It's worth a lot," said Michael. "You did a great job last time."

I inclined my head in thanks, yet still the mantle of leadership didn't sit easily on my shoulders. Perhaps that was what made one a good leader, like Bentley. I didn't know.

CHAPTER EIGHT

Seven days later, the Marx Brothers returned. A meeting was called in the mission room by Bentley. They had said we'd be attacking the first target within two weeks, and I was pretty sure that time had arrived.

The six of us, plus Angelica, the Mosquito team, and those ground crew who needed to be privy to the mission orders were assembled. Angelica sat next to me and tucked her arm in mine. She smiled up at me a little tremulously. I knew what would be going through her head at this point. She would be worried about the impending mission and my safety in particular.

"Do you think this is it, Skipper?" said Jonty speaking quietly.

"I rather think so, yes," I replied.

"Good show!"

"That's you all over, eager to go and get killed," said Willie.

"Pfft, not if I have anything to do with it," said Jonty scornfully.

I was about to hush them when Bentley walked in, and we all stood to attention. Audrey was beside him, and they were followed by the Marx Brothers.

The four of them made their way up to the front. There was a map on the wall which had not been there before, and papers on the table behind them. As per usual, in no hurry to begin, Bentley produced his pipe. He had apparently loaded it up before the meeting, so instead of his normal ritual, he put it straight into his mouth and lit it. He puffed on it with satisfaction, and I noticed the Marx Brothers light up their now ever-present cigarettes. Poor Audrey was sandwiched between clouds of smoke. She wrinkled her nose, though I imagined she must be used to Bentley's pipe smoke. After a suitable interval in which we all waited quietly, Bentley spoke.

"I'm sure it won't come as a surprise to you," he said, "that we've now got our mission target for Mission One. Our colleagues from MI6 will shortly brief you on the details. Before they do, I just want to say that I have the utmost confidence that you will do what's needed to bring this off successfully. Everything we can put in place has been done to try and ensure that. We've got the Mosquito team here, and a fighter escort to the target just like last time, in order to save your ammo in the event of an attack."

He paused and took a few more puffs before continuing.

"It goes without saying that I'm immensely proud of you and of this squadron. I'm sure you will live up to all expectations. It's time we gave Jerry a taste of his own medicine, and we intend to do so through your sterling efforts. I will hand you over to our MI6 chaps now for the briefing proper."

Bentley was pretty good at rousing speeches when needed. I didn't disagree with his sentiments: we did our best, every one of us, against all the odds.

Harpo and Chico moved centre stage, and they really did remind me for a moment of a music hall double act. I expected them to break into song at any moment.

"Thank you, Squadron Leader Bentley," said Harpo. "As you are aware, this mission is critical as a practice run for the real event. However, it's also a chance for us to show Jerry that he's not dealing with an enemy who is simply going to lie down because he's got a new toy. Oh no! We're going to show him that we can strike when and where he least expects it."

There was a shuffling of feet but everyone was intent on what he was saying.

"This first mission, or Mission One, as your CO has said, is to hit an airfield in Northern France where there is at least one squadron of Focke-Wulfs stationed," said Chico, taking up the refrain. "We have codenamed the entire mission Operation Sunrise, of which this is the first part. What I am about to share with you is, needless to say, highly classified and must not leave this room. A flight plan has been carefully worked out by your RAF backroom people, and you need to try and stick to it in order to give the mission every chance of success."

Harpo spoke again, which was typical of the way they ran things, taking it in turns.

"Fortunately, Jerry has set up an airfield in an easy location. However, we know that it is likely to be moved at any time, so we've set the date for your airstrike for two days hence. You will leave in the early hours of the morning, timed to arrive at sunrise over the airfield. We figure this time of day is best to catch Jerry half asleep."

There was some laughter at this. It was true that dawn attacks were often more devastating in their effectiveness.

"This also means," Harpo continued, "that you will have some light to see what the hell you are shooting at. So apart from anything else, this is a chance to put all the practice you've done to good use. Your main mission is to take out as many planes as you can, then get the hell out of there as fast as you can."

"Preferably in one piece," quipped Chico.

"Yes, indeed — we need you for Mission Two."

There was some polite laughter at this, although it wasn't really that amusing to put your life on the line. Being lighthearted in the face of adversity was the British way, but deep down we knew the risks of a mission like this.

"Any questions?" asked Chico.

"Is there any ground support?" I asked him. "Or are we on our own?"

"It's possible the resistance may join the attack, but don't count on it. You need to assume you're on your own."

"And try not to get shot down over enemy territory," said Harpo. "Jerry will want to question you about the mission and future plans. Although they abide by the Geneva Convention, they aren't above a little coercion if they feel it might be profitable. In any case, they won't take kindly to our strafing their airfield…"

He left the rest unsaid, but it was enough. I glanced at Angelica and read the concern on her face. I had already been shot down once and it would be playing on her mind now it had been mentioned.

"If there are no more questions, then I'll hand out the mission orders, target coordinates and so forth," said Harpo.

We spent some time covering the details, and then Bentley wrapped things up.

"We will convene for a final mission briefing in two days' time," he said. "In the meantime, get some more practice in. God knows you'll need it. Make sure you are fully *au fait* with everything — I shouldn't need to tell you. That's all for now."

Before leaving, the CO came up to me.

"Angus, a word, if I may?" he said.

"Yes, sir."

He drew me aside, then took a few puffs on his pipe. On discovering the tobacco was spent, he gave a dissatisfied grunt and replaced it in his pocket with the bowl, as usual, sticking out the top.

"I've postponed the court-martial for the time being," he said. "This mission is more important. We'll try to get it done afterwards, assuming you are ready with your defence?"

"I've not had a lot of time to prepare yet, sir."

"Well, don't fret about it for the moment. Charlton can keep a bit longer as far as I'm concerned, and the Johnnies up at Fighter Command can stew on it. Yes, indeed."

"Yes, sir, I'll do my best to get onto it after this mission."

"That's the ticket," he said with a smile. "Anyway, I'll leave you to it. I'm sure you've plenty to do."

With that, he left, and I returned to my seat to study the papers with the call signs, codewords and so forth. It was a process of preparation that was becoming all too familiar.

After the briefing, I went to see Phillip. I had promised him some books and the means to write if he wished. It would be better for him to be doing something rather than nothing. Also, Gordon had recently suggested during one of our morning chats on the way to the airfield that Phillip writing down his thoughts might be cathartic. With this in mind, I had procured some books, including a volume of Shakespeare's plays, as well as a notebook and some writing implements.

When I was let into Phillip's cell, he was lying on his bed, staring at the ceiling. There was little else for him to do.

"Hello," he said, sitting up.

"Phillip, I've brought you some books, a notebook, a pen and some pencils," I said.

I put them on the table. He reached over to take them while I sat down in the chair.

"Thank you for the books," he said, looking through them. "Some of my favourites. I appreciate it."

"I gathered you like Shakespeare."

"Very much," he replied with a smile. He hesitated. "As for the notebook — what am I to do with that?"

"Maybe write down your thoughts? Your feelings? I thought it might help pass the time."

I was tentative rather than trying to force it on him, but he nodded.

"Perhaps, yes."

"Are they treating you well?" I asked him.

"As well as can be expected," he replied. "I don't see anyone much…"

"No, I suppose not."

He was quiet for a moment, considering something.

"Is Audrey…?" he asked tentatively.

"She's somewhat distraught," I replied. There was no point in dissembling. It was the best I could say, and she evidently had not been to see him.

"Well, give her my … regards … and tell her I'm sorry about the way things turned out."

He had meant to say "love", I was sure of it. I wondered if perhaps I should talk to Audrey. What harm could it do, for them to see each other?

"Your court-martial won't be for a while," I said.

"Oh?"

"There are … other priorities."

It was the most diplomatic way I could put it, since I obviously could not tell him about the secret mission.

"I see. Well, I suppose that means I can call myself an officer of the RAF for a little longer," he said with a sigh.

"Yes," I said. "Yes indeed."

He said nothing further, and I didn't have anything more to ask him at this juncture.

"Let me know if I can get you anything else," I said. "We'll talk again soon, about your defence."

"If you like."

He had the demeanour of a man who had simply accepted his fate. I got up to go.

"Thanks again, for the books," he said.

"Don't mention it."

I left feeling rather sad that it had come to this. He would be a footnote in history very soon, a line in a journal somewhere, and there didn't seem to be a damn thing I could do to prevent it. I could make a speech about how he really was a decent fellow, but his reasons for his act of cowardice could hardly be made public.

As luck would have it, I bumped into Audrey on my way back from the guardhouse.

"Have you seen Phillip?" she asked me.

"I've just come from there," I said.

"Is he…?"

"As well as you could expect. I took him some books and a notebook. Bentley says the court-martial will not be until after the mission at least."

"I know." She bit her lip.

"Why don't you go and see him … unless it would be too painful?"

She shot me a chagrined look and I noticed a shine in her eyes, as if they held unshed tears.

"You probably think me a coward for not seeing him," she said softly.

"I don't think anything of the sort," I replied.

She was determined to castigate herself regardless. "And a fool. A fool for falling in love with someone not only younger than me, but who I hardly even know."

"Of course not. You can't help your feelings," I told her.

I was surprised at myself, but now I was in love I knew how it went.

"I feel like a damn fool," she whispered.

A tear ran down her cheek, followed by several more. As much as I wanted to comfort her, I felt that would be crossing a line.

"Don't feel that way," I said, trying to use words instead. "You're not a fool — or if you are, then all of us who fall in love are fools."

She nodded and dashed the tears away. "You're right." She sniffed. "I should go and see him. I've stayed away because I don't want to be hurt, but that's selfish."

"Nobody could blame you," I replied gently.

"No, I will go and see him, for his sake, and for mine too."

"I'm sure he will appreciate it," I said.

"Yes, yes." She touched my arm lightly. "Thank you, Angus."

I watched her walk away towards the guardhouse. Sometimes the things we want the most can never be, and not because of anything we've done ourselves. It made me glad for what I had with Angelica, regardless of the tricky subject of marriage that was still to be settled.

Two days went by very quickly, as they always did when preparing for a mission. The night before the final day, Angelica arranged for the two of us to stay at our favourite hotel. We could have viewed the mission as just another sortie, but it felt different. It seemed far more likely that some of the team would not come back, no matter how well-organised and careful we were. Things could always go wrong.

Angelica and I shared a nice supper together and then went up to bed. Angelica liked to keep something special for occasions like this, and make an entrance from the bathroom. She was wearing a sheer black nightdress which left little to the imagination. The sight of her in a state of déshabillé like that was guaranteed to raise the temperature and it did. Angelica was a passionate woman and she saved it all for me. I felt exceptionally lucky.

We lay in the half-light in each other's arms.

"I wish you didn't have to go, darling," she whispered.

"I know," I said, forbearing to give her some trite phrase about duty. She knew all of that already, and it didn't make it any easier. A small voice in my mind wondered once again why she wouldn't let me marry her, but I stilled it for fear of spoiling the moment. It wouldn't do to leave on a sour note for the mission.

"I know you'll come back, because you have to," she said, still whispering.

"Then I will," I replied because I couldn't say anything else.

"Now, show me how much you're going to miss me while you're out there…"

The mission was only a few hours, but to her it would probably seem like an eternity — a yawning chasm from which I might never return. I kissed her and surrendered to the moment, letting it take us wherever she wanted.

Gordon picked us up from the hotel in the morning, and noted we were both a little subdued.

"Today the day, is it, sir?" he asked.

He didn't know about the mission *per se*, but he also didn't miss a trick. There had been a bustle of preparation with the planes that were being made ready for the final sortie. He also knew that Angelica and I often spent a night away together before something important.

"You're in the wrong profession, Fred," I joked. "You should have been a detective."

"Oh no, sir," he replied. "That would be far too fatiguing."

I wondered what he'd do once the war was over, and if he'd remain in service. The life seemed to suit him, and he did pretty much as he pleased in the position of batman.

Nothing more was said, and he dropped us off as usual.

"Good luck," he told me. "I take it you won't be needing a pickup this evening?"

"No, that's all right," I replied. I'd be eating supper on the base with the rest of the team, then catching some sleep before the early morning start.

"Jolly good. See you tomorrow then."

With a smile and a wave, he let out the clutch and was gone.

"I suppose this is it," I said to Angelica.

"Yes."

"Better get to it."

The day was spent going over the flight plan several times, the code words, and everything else we needed to know. We studied the aerial reconnaissance photos, and the maps too. Intelligence had confirmed that nothing had changed at the target as far as anyone knew, and we had the green light.

The blacked-out Spitfire Mark V planes we were using had four Browning .303 machine guns and two 20mm canons. This combination delivered quite a punch, particularly for the strafing mission we were about to undertake. The fuselage had been fitted with glare shields, since this had proved to be a problem for night flying on the previous mission. We also had extra fuel tanks to give us more than enough to cover the trip. We would be getting in as close as we could to the targets, as we had practised, in order to do the maximum damage. The only unpredictable thing was the positioning of the enemy planes, although from the photographs they looked to be lined up all in a row. We'd come in from the side, strafe them, and then turn back for another run. In theory, it should be easy.

Theory and practice, however, are two different things, as we'd discovered already. After dinner, eaten with the rest of the mission crew, we went for a final briefing. There was little to be said other than final words.

As we sat together in the mission room, Angelica put her hand in mine and squeezed it gently. I glanced at her and noticed her lip tremble just a little.

Bentley, Audrey and the Marx Brothers walked in at that moment. All eyes turned to the front. Bentley took out his pipe and lit it up, in time-honoured fashion. After only a couple of puffs, he spoke briefly.

"I don't have a lot to say, except that I know you'll do the best you can. I realise that these missions are a lot to ask from anyone, but nobody is prouder than me of the way you've stepped up to take them on. Regardless of what happens tonight, you are all a credit to this squadron. I'm not going to wish you luck, but I am going to tell you to make sure you bloody well come home, and that's an order!"

He smiled as he said the last part, and there was a ripple of laughter. This was Bentley's style.

He motioned to the Marx Brothers and Harpo stepped forward.

"I know we're probably not the most welcome sight at the airfield," he said. "But you, all of you, are a most welcome sight to us. Without you and people like you, we can't win this war. So, we thank you, and the War Office thanks you too for what you're about to do."

"Good luck and Godspeed," said Chico, adding his mite.

"Right then," said Bentley. "Enough said. I'm sure you all need to get in some kip before the off, so we'll leave you in peace and see you when you return."

They filed out of the room, and we repaired to the hut. We would sleep wherever we could, and Angelica refused to leave my side. The others let us snuggle up together in one of two beds put there for the pilots, and very shortly a hush fell over the room.

In the early hours, I awoke to the ringing of the phone. The night duty staff had been tasked with waking us at the appointed hour. We had to leave early in order to hit daybreak once we reached the airfield. After last-minute preparations, it was time to go.

Angelica held me tight and kissed me with all the passion she could muster.

"Get home safely," she whispered.

"I will."

"I love you."

"I love you too."

On those final words, I turned, letting go of her fingers and walking to my plane. The others were already getting into theirs and the roar of the Merlin engines cut through the early morning silence. I strapped in and fired up the kite.

"Goose Leader, you're clear to go," said the control tower as we taxied into position. Goose Flight was our codename. The Mosquito was designated Magpie.

"Magpie airborne," said Michael as the Mosquito thundered into the air ahead of us.

"Roger, Control," I said, as we followed them up into the darkness.

It swallowed us up quickly. I thought of Angelica, but she would already be running back to her post on comms. We were relying on bearings alone, and the Mosquito to guide us. As we'd quickly learned from the previous mission, everything looked different at night and navigating just from our Spitfires was well-nigh impossible. The Mosquito was essential to our success. It would give us a bearing and drop a flare codenamed a "firework" at each waypoint on the trip there and then back again.

The Hurricane escort — codenamed "Falcons" — would fly above us and join us over the Channel.

I felt the adrenaline starting to course through me in anticipation of what was to come. It was extremely dark, all told. The other Spitfires were visible only as black shapes and from the flare of the exhausts.

Radio silence was essential in order to give the Germans as little chance as possible of picking up our comms. They would be listening for transmissions, naturally, so no clue of where we were going could be given. The less chatter the better.

The monochrome landscape slipped by underneath us as we maintained a decent height. Once we crossed to enemy territory, we would drop down as close as we could to the ground. This would help avoid detection but conversely, it meant remaining alert at all times to the terrain.

The airfield we were to hit was just a little to the south of Calais and not far from the coast. I considered that we were lucky in this respect. Naturally, we had no idea of the position of the airfield for the second mission. We crossed the coast at Eastbourne and would fly just south of Boulogne then up through enemy territory, attacking the airfield from the south. It was a dangerous manoeuvre, but a considered one which would give us the least chance of detection. Coastal flying was hazardous because the Germans had many coastal defences from Calais to Boulogne, but just past there we could clear the coastline and go inland — hopefully without too much trouble.

We reached Birling Gap and the radio crackled to life.

"Goose Leader, this is Falcon Leader joining you for the ride."

It was the Hurricane squadron, our designated escort. I was relieved to hear the familiar voice of the flight leader who had been part of our last mission.

"Glad to have you aboard, Falcon Leader," I replied.

"Roger. We've got your back. Take it easy on the way to the Carnival."

The Carnival was our mission codename for the target airfield. It would probably be apt once we had lit it up with exploding aircraft.

"Wilco. Thanks."

Of course, none of us would be taking it easy, although the Falcons would fly above us and keep a lookout.

"Goose Flight, we'll descend to approach level on my mark," I told my team.

When we hit the correct spot on the edge of the French coast, we had to turn inland. Then we'd go as low as we could all the way to the target. Below us, the sea was inky black. It felt as if we were in a void. The white shapes of the sand dunes appeared just north of Hardelot-Plage. We had determined that this was an easy landmark to spot, even in the darkness. We had to turn on the correct bearing and head into enemy territory.

"Magpie, we're over bandit country now," I said. I gave them our bearing and hoped for the best. They couldn't drop a flare so close to the beach, someone might see it.

"Roger, Goose Leader, dropping the firework in five."

"Roger," I said. "Goose Flight, we're going down."

I went as low as I could along with the rest of the flight. The Falcons would maintain position about one thousand feet above us. The dunes ended and then we were almost skimming the treetops of a forest as we started to cross it. This part wasn't particularly comfortable albeit necessary.

"Goose Flight, look out for the firework," I said. It was essential we spotted it for the next bearing. This process had all worked beautifully before, but there was always a first time for things to go wrong.

Tense minutes passed by. All the while my attention was on the ground, shooting by below us. The plan was to head for a forest west of Boulogne and then go north. We had to miss the main town of Boulogne for obvious reasons.

We left the forest behind and flew over open fields and land. This was a relief but it also made us more of a target. Would the roar of our engines get picked up? What was more, the grey light of dawn would be emerging very shortly. We would no longer be under the cloak of darkness.

I began to wonder if we'd missed the flare, as I couldn't see it. It should have been dropped by now.

"Firework at two o'clock," said Falcon Leader suddenly. Relief flooded through me.

"Roger, got it," I said as I clocked it too.

From his height, he was able to see further than we could.

"Firework spotted, Magpie," I told the Mosquito team.

"Roger, here is your new bearing."

It was Gervais. He gave us the heading and we turned as one. I could vaguely see the shadow of the dark forest on our right, as we finally headed north. We would be over the target in several minutes. Tense seconds passed as the miles ticked by.

"Searchlight, at six o'clock," said Tomas urgently.

This was all we needed. A Jerry ack-ack battery nearby must have heard our engines. I could see the beam of light piercing the sky and then another. We had to put some distance between us and those lights as fast as we could.

"Left, bank sharp left," I said frantically, turning away from the light. We were still continuing north but we would now be off our bearing. I was more concerned about the searchlights for the moment. The bearing would be the next issue.

A few more nail-biting minutes went by as we moved further away from the searchlights still piercing the sky. Then, thankfully, they went off.

"Falcons, keep them peeled in case they send up a search party," said Falcon Leader.

He was right. If we'd spooked Jerry, they would probably scramble a squadron to fly a patrol. I just hoped we would be gone before that happened. I continued to head on our bearing, knowing we were now off course.

"Mosquito, we had to deviate," I said.

"What's your heading?" asked Gervais.

I told him and there was silence, no doubt while he figured out what to do. I hoped it would be soon. The light of dawn was beginning to show and the sun would crack its smile at us very rapidly after that.

"We're dropping a firework now," said Gervais.

I looked out for it, though it would be less visible because it wasn't so dark. I anticipated the Falcons would spot it if we couldn't.

There was always a point where we might have to call off the mission, but I hoped this wasn't it. If we lost our ability to find the target, we'd have to return home. All these eventualities had been discussed. Another minute went by and there was still no sign. Then, thankfully, the radio crackled to life.

"Got it, there's the firework," said Falcon Leader. "Twelve o'clock dead ahead."

"Saved our bacon, Falcon Leader," I said gratefully.

"That's our job."

There was a smile in his words. We headed for the flare and got a new bearing from Gervais. The landscape was rapidly resolving into greens and browns as daylight began its journey out of the night. I felt we must surely be nearing the target. There was a mist rising from the landscape. I didn't like that — what if there was too much mist to see the enemy planes? Had the Marx Brothers thought about that? I became more anxious as the mist began to thicken below us.

"Goose Leader, the Carnival is dead ahead, three minutes," said Gervais.

This was it — we were on. We were about to hit the airfield. The mist blanket was swirling around. There was hardly any time to think in those moments. It was in the hands of the Mosquito crew as to whether we would be on the right approach. There was no second guessing or time for an observational pass. We had to go straight in, do the damage and get out.

"Goose Flight, attack formation," I said tersely, putting my faith in providence.

We dropped lower, as low as we possibly could. There was a belt of trees ahead now and over it would be the airfield. We fanned out in a line, and I slipped the safety off my guns. The others would be doing the same. My heart began to race, pumping nineteen to the dozen. You never know what you're going to see until you get there, no matter how many air reconnaissance photos you might have looked at.

The tree line rushed up towards us and then we were up and over. Right on cue the sun came up and spread its golden light across the landscape. Miraculously, the airfield was clear of mist. It opened up onto a vista of green fields, huts, a hangar, and various vehicles. There was no time to take it in. Only one thing mattered and there they were, spread out before us: two full squadrons of Focke-Wulfs on the ground, like sitting ducks. We closed in and then I gave the order to fire.

"Let them have it."

Six Spitfires opened fire in unison. It must have been an earth-shattering sound. Just as we'd practised with the dummy planes, the bullets ripped across the field and into the fuselages of the Focke-Wulfs. Then came one explosion after another, but we had already passed right over them.

"Let's go again," I said, wanting to capitalise on our good fortune. Several planes were still intact. This was a good thing; it showed we had learned some precision. Still, we needed to take them all out this time, if we could. We had each picked our targets carefully, just as we had trained to do. It had actually worked.

We pulled a tight turn, circled back and dropped down again. Figures on the ground were running now for the remaining planes, frantically trying to get them. They were too late. We opened fire once more, cutting them down and scything into the remaining planes. There were more explosions, fires breaking out everywhere.

Suddenly, tracers started flying past my canopy. The ack-ack had managed to get themselves into action and had opened up. There wasn't time for another go.

"Goose Flight, break off. Let's get the hell out of here," I said.

We turned and ran, just as we were supposed to. We weren't there to be heroes; we were there to do a job and get out.

"Now, isn't that a glorious sight?" said Jonty with satisfaction, as we banked past the airfield awash with burning planes.

"Yes, but let's focus on getting home in one piece," I told him, wanting to get as far out of range as possible.

"Aye, aye, Skipper," he replied, unable to keep the jubilation out of his voice.

"Goose Flight, we've got your back, never fear," said Falcon Leader, wanting to reassure us they were covering our retreat.

"Roger," I replied.

I felt that if we were attacked now by Focke-Wulfs, then that confidence might be misplaced. Our best bet was to make it back to Blighty as fast as we could.

Gervais gave us a bearing and we headed rapidly for the coast. The mission had been a remarkable success, but we had not been able to stay around and really see the results of our handiwork. Now we had lost the cover of night, I was concerned Jerry wouldn't be far behind us. No doubt they would have scrambled at least one squadron in defence of their colleagues.

We left the coastline and streaked at low level out across the water. I was glad we'd made it thus far, but we certainly were not home and dry. I took us up higher once the English coast was within striking distance. Were we really going to get away scot-free? The question was answered almost immediately.

"Bandits, coming in fast nine o'clock," said one of the Falcons in alarm.

"Leave it to us, Goose Leader. We've got this," said Falcon Leader.

I looked at my fuel gauge — it was all right, but I doubted I had much ammo left, if any. We'd certainly unloaded at the airfield. I would have been surprised if any of us had anything left. It would be futile to take on the Jerries. Besides, that was what the Falcons were there for.

"Goose Flight, head for home. Leave the Jerries for the Falcons," I told them.

We could hear Falcon Leader giving the order to engage.

"Break, Falcons, break."

Over to my left, I could see the Hurricane escort splitting up their formation and turning on the attack. Nobody said anything, except Jonty, who seemed to take exception to my orders.

"Damn it, Skipper," said Jonty. "I've never run from a fight."

"Jonty, stay on course," I told him firmly. This was no time for one of his starts. However, he wasn't willing to let it go so easily.

"Skipper, I've still got ammo. I can't let them all get shot down."

"Jonty, leave it — that's an order!" I said again. When Jonty's blood was up, it really was hard to manage him. Agreements were there to be followed and the mission planes were a priority, as were the pilots.

Behind us, the dogfight was receding, but it seemed as if the Falcons were getting the worst of it.

"Well, if you say so, Skipper," said Jonty, sounding aggrieved.

"Listen to the man and do what he says for once," Willie put in.

No sooner had he spoken than a Focke-Wulf broke off from the dogfight with the Hurricanes and decided we'd be a better target.

"Damn it!" I swore.

"There's a bandit following us," said Arjun. "What shall we do?"

"I know," I said. "I've seen it."

I was considering our options when the decision was taken out of my hands.

"That's it," said Jonty, turning his plane. "Sorry, Skipper, but I can't let him catch us."

"Damn!" I said again, annoyed. "Break, Goose Flight, break. We'll stop this bandit but do not engage the main pack; I repeat, do not engage the main pack."

Jonty was heading straight back for the Focke-Wulf that was in pursuit. I swore under my breath. Why couldn't he ever obey orders?

Within moments he was twisting and turning with the Focke-Wulf. It was quicker than him and soon got on his tail. Fortunately, the other Jerries were too busy with the Falcons, but that could change, as I'd seen at least two Hurricanes go down.

Jonty was a skilled pilot, but the Jerry was getting the better of him. It seemed par for the course with these new planes. I managed to catch up to them and got the German in my sights while he was preoccupied with Jonty. I pressed the fire button but nothing happened. I'd used up all my ammo.

"I'm out — ammo's gone."

"I'm not," said Willie, who had followed me in on my wing. He fired off a couple of bursts, hitting the Focke-Wulf in the tail. It lurched sideways and started to spin downwards.

"I say! Good show, Kiwi!" said Jonty with glee.

The Jerry got his damaged plane under control and started to head for the French coast. A Hurricane spotted him and broke off from the main dogfight. He swooped down on the Jerry plane with his guns blazing. The Focke-Wulf started to smoke and dived rapidly towards the Channel. The next moment it hit the water with a tremendous splash.

At the same time, the Jerry planes decided it was time to break off their attack and head for home. Perhaps they were also out of ammo.

"Still here, Goose Leader?" said Falcon Leader, turning the remainder of his squadron back to Blighty. "I thought you were going home?"

"We thought we'd give you a hand," I said sardonically.

He laughed and said, "Thanks all the same, but best you get off now."

"Thanks again," I said.

"Don't mention it. We lost a couple."

"Sorry."

"Take care, until next time. We'll follow you, but I don't think they'll be back."

I turned my attention back to my team. "Goose Flight, let's go home ... including Jonty," I said, allowing my irritation to show.

"Sorry, Skipper," said Jonty as they formed up.

"All very well, but it's not me who is likely to be unhappy about this latest escapade," I told him.

He didn't answer. He knew Bentley was bound to be mightily displeased. Jonty had a history of disobeying orders, but at least this time he had an excuse — the Focke-Wulf had pursued us. That, however, would not deter Bentley from remonstrating with him.

"The mission was a success, though, Scottish," Arjun reminded us as we crossed over the English coastline.

"Yes, well done, Goose Flight," I said.

We had certainly done what we set out to do, and no doubt everyone would be pleased. It had given us some much-needed practice for the real mission. I now felt far more confident we could pull it off. Perhaps there was a method in the madness of the Marx Brothers after all.

CHAPTER NINE

Banley soon hove into view, and we landed without incident. The Falcons had left after escorting us some of the way home. As I taxied my plane to the standing, I could see we had a reception committee. Bentley was there with Audrey, the Marx Brothers, and our ground crew.

I jumped down from the wing. A figure detached itself from the waiting group and hurtled towards me at top speed. I braced myself as Angelica flung herself onto my chest.

"Thank God. Thank God, you're here," she said, her lips finding mine. "I was so worried."

I kissed her, oblivious to the spectators. No doubt this had become a familiar sight to them in any case. Angelica stopped kissing me a few moments later, and then moved to my side, holding my hand. We walked together with the rest of the M Flight to where Bentley was waiting.

"That was a good show," the CO said, beaming from ear to ear. "A damn good show, well done!"

He shook my hand and then the hand of every man in the flight. The Marx Brothers did likewise, making suitable appreciative comments.

"We'll debrief shortly," said Bentley. "But I'm sure you're all famished."

It was true, we were hungry, and I was surprised but grateful to find that just like the last time a bit of a spread had been laid on in our mission room.

"We should go on more missions," Jonty quipped with a mouthful of sausage roll, "if this is what happens after them."

"Ah, yes, Butterworth," said Bentley, who overheard this remark and fixed him with a beady eye.

Jonty quailed a little under his gaze. I was certain Bentley would not let the incident pass. He'd no doubt heard the comms, or it had been relayed to him.

"Got a little lively, did you, after the mission?"

"A Jerry plane attacked us, sir. I had to take action to defend the flight," said Jonty.

"Indeed, so I gather. But why is it always you in the thick of it, Butterworth? Tell me that! And I gather it was Cooper here who saved your bacon."

Jonty looked quite hot under the collar all of a sudden as Bentley buttonholed him.

"Yes, well, these Fockes are hard to deal with sometimes."

"Just like orders, eh, Butterworth? Hard to deal with?"

Bentley took out his pipe and lit it up. He puffed on it while Jonty squirmed uncomfortably under his gaze.

"I have no problem with orders, sir," said Jonty.

"Really? That a fact, is it?" said Bentley, looking exceptionally sceptical.

"Yes, sir."

Bentley decided not to tease him any further. "See that it stays that way."

"I certainly will, sir," said Jonty, relieved when Bentley left off baiting him and went to converse with the Marx Brothers.

"Phew! That reminded me of our housemaster, old Bagshaw, when he'd called us to his study," said Jonty once Bentley had moved away.

"You're like Peter Pan," said Willie sardonically. "The boy who never grew up."

"I say!" said Jonty, looking most put out at this rather perspicacious observation.

Fortunately, just then Bentley called the room to order. We sat down and waited for him to speak. He was busy tamping in some new tobacco and then he lit it up.

"Well done, all of you," he said. "That seems as if it went like clockwork, almost…"

Once again Jonty came under his gaze, and he kept his eyes firmly to the front.

"Yes, well," Bentley continued. "As good as it was, you all know that was only the first part of the mission and you've got to go again. The MI6 chaps want to say a few words on that score."

Harpo took a drag on his cigarette. "An absolutely first-class mission," he said. "Those are the kind we like. We've also had some intelligence from the ground, and it confirms you destroyed all the Focke-Wulfs stationed there."

A cheer went up at this. All of us felt very keenly about these new planes, and to have achieved that result was certainly welcome.

"It's a bloody nose for Jerry," said Chico. "Just as we wanted."

"With that in mind, we are going to let things simmer down before the second strike," said Harpo.

"Yes, Jerry will be on the alert now, expecting another attack," Chico added.

This was exactly what I had said to them when they had mooted the first mission, so I wasn't best pleased. At the same time, it would be sensible to wait.

"We'll give it a couple of weeks," said Harpo. "By then, Jerry will very likely think it's a one-off, and there will be other matters to claim their attention."

I took that to mean other operations, or possibly there would be clandestine action from the resistance.

"We will be back in touch once we've identified your target for Mission Two, and in the meantime keep yourselves prepared."

Bentley chipped in. "What he means is don't go and get yourselves bloody well shot down. M Flight will not run any patrols for the moment as Fighter Command has very kindly acceded to my request to give us more planes and pilots, so the main squadron is up to strength. Obviously, there are more reprobates out there than I thought."

He smiled at his joke and there was a ripple of laughter through the room.

"You need to keep yourselves in readiness and on form. That means continued practice, so that you keep needle-sharp. Now, any questions?"

"When is the pilot who is flying the Focke-Wulf going to be joining us?" asked Arjun.

"He will be here in good time," said Harpo. "He's busy flying a captured Messerschmitt at the moment. We need him to be absolutely confident he can fly the Focke-Wulf without a problem."

"How will he know? Surely the controls will be different?" asked Jean.

"Not that different, we suspect," said Chico. "He will be far quicker at identifying what to do than someone who has never flown a German plane and who can't speak the language."

I noticed Bentley looking pointedly at me, and I put on my very best innocent expression. Angelica nudged me in the ribs and shot me a mischievous smile.

"All right," said Bentley, when no other questions were forthcoming. "Make yourselves scarce for the rest of the day, then get back to it tomorrow."

He left shortly afterwards with the Marx Brothers. Having been stood down for the day, the flight dispersed.

"I'm off to get myself some shut-eye," said Jonty. "Do you want a lift back to Amberly, Kiwi?"

"Don't mind if I do," said Willie.

I was left alone with Angelica.

"Well?" she said.

"Well, what?"

"Are you wanting some shut-eye too?"

Her expression suggested her thoughts were far from any idea of sleeping.

"Why don't we take a drive somewhere?" I suggested mildly.

"To our hotel?"

I laughed. She was exceptionally forward, but I had grown to like it.

"You have a one-track mind," I said.

"Where you are concerned, yes. Especially when I can get you all to myself."

I was not one to demur. I was equally enamoured of her. Would it last a lifetime? Would we even *have* a lifetime? I put these thoughts to the back of my mind.

"Then let's find Fred."

Once at the hotel, we repaired to our room, where we indulged in each other's passion until late afternoon. Hungry once more, we went out in search of sustenance. A small pub in a nearby village afforded us a rather pleasant late repast. The landlord kindly rustled us up some bread, cheese and pickles. It was a typical ploughman's meal with a smattering of salad to go with it — I suspected from the pub garden.

"This is delightful," said Angelica.

"The pub, or the lunch?"

"No, silly, being here with you."

Since we were so much in harmony, I was of a mind to broach the subject of marriage once more. I had left it for a suitable interval; perhaps now she'd be more willing to talk about it.

"Can I ask you something?" I said, after consuming another mouthful of the delicious bread and cheese.

"As long as it's not about marriage," she replied with a smile.

My face must have fallen at once because she put out her hand.

"*Was* it about marriage?" she said quietly.

"It was actually, but if you'd prefer not to discuss it…"

I was a little hurt by what I perceived as an immediate rebuff.

"Don't spoil it," she said. "Please don't spoil it."

She meant, of course, our accord with each other. I fought an impulse to say something cutting, because I knew that truly would ruin things and probably the rest of the day. Instead, I opted for a milder tone.

"I wish you would tell me why you don't want to talk about it."

She was silent for a long while, and we ate the rest of our meal.

"I have spoiled it, haven't I?" I said at length, unwilling to endure it any longer.

"No, no … no, you haven't…" She immediately took my hand and looked imploringly into my eyes.

"Then why?"

"I … I can't tell you," she said.

"Can't … or won't?"

"I … both. It's complicated … and it's not the time."

I shook my head. "You always say that," I protested.

"Because it's true."

"Then when will it be time?" I said, defeated.

"It's not because I don't love you or because I don't want to be with you," she said passionately. "Because I do, more than anything in the world, and I love you more than you can ever know, I really do."

I sighed. She got under my defences every time I was nettled. She had a knack for it. I had long since realised we were together, to some degree, on her terms. Given my wayward behaviour with her from the beginning, I most probably deserved it too.

"You know you're..."

"Frustrating, incorrigible..." she supplied helpfully.

"Certainly both of those, yes." I couldn't help smiling.

"I will tell you, soon," she said. "I just can't say when soon will be..."

With that, I had to be content.

"Then let's walk back to the hotel, and let me show you just how frustrating you are," I said.

"I'll look forward to it."

Hand in hand, we left the pub and turned the topic of conversation to less contentious things.

"Do you feel better?" she said, kissing me softly in the half-light of the evening. We had gone down for dinner and repaired directly to our room.

"Better for what?" I enquired.

"Well, have you got rid of your frustrations?"

I chuckled. "I'm not sure..."

"Then we need to make sure you do."

"Indeed."

She snuggled in close to me and sighed contentedly. These were good times, just her and me together. What if we could be that way every night? I wondered if familiarity might cause the passion to fade. But I was beginning to realise it wasn't just about passion — there was so much more. I genuinely enjoyed her company. She was my boon companion, my best friend. She was the person I shared nearly everything with, and if that was love, then I was in it for the duration. What would marriage bring that I didn't know about? Was it the unknown that made her reluctant? How could I know if she simply wouldn't say?

"Don't fret, darling," she said softly, turning to kiss me.

"I wasn't."

"Yes, you were. I saw you frowning. I'll always be here for you. I promise you that."

We kissed and I was once again lost in her.

Fred picked us up in the morning after breakfast and took us back to Banley. Audrey came and found me almost immediately upon my arrival at the dispersal hut.

"Bentley wants to see you," she said as we walked.

"Is something amiss?"

"No, not that I know of. I think it's to do with…"

"Phillip?"

"Yes."

No doubt Bentley wanted to wrap up things with Phillip and get the court-martial over with.

"Did you see him?" I asked her before we entered the main building.

"Yes, yes, I did, and I'm glad."

"Then I'm glad too."

She smiled and let me into Bentley's office, then took her usual seat at her own desk. She put her head down and appeared to be focusing on her work. However, I was certain she would be taking in every word.

Bentley was sitting at his ease, behind his desk. He glanced up as I entered, and I saluted. He motioned me to sit. From his demeanour, I could tell he was not in a sunny mood. He fiddled with his pipe for a moment, before deciding to empty it. Then he scraped it out with even more care than usual, filled it, lit it and sat back, puffing for what seemed a long while. He definitely had something on his mind.

"I had a visit," he said, finally breaking the silence. "From Air Vice-Marshal Charlton."

I didn't need telling who Air Vice-Marshal Charlton was — he was obviously Phillip's father. This might account for Bentley's annoyance.

"Yes," repeated Bentley. "Air Vice-Bloody-Marshal Charlton. You probably want to know what he wanted, don't you?"

I did, of course, but it was a rhetorical question and I felt sure he was going to inform me.

"Well…"

He did not let me finish. "I'll tell you what he wanted. He wanted to know why I had not finished prosecuting his blasted son for cowardice, that's what he wanted."

He was deceptively quiet as he said it, and I wasn't fooled. Anyone who knew Bentley well would know this was the calm before the storm.

"And do you know what I said?" he erupted, suddenly getting out of his seat and pacing the room. "Do you? Hmm?"

He pointed his pipe at me in an accusatory fashion. I didn't like to interrupt him in full flow, so I didn't answer.

"I said, yes sir, no sir, three bloody bags full, sir, that's what I said! And why? Because that's what it takes to make sure I bloody well stay in charge of this squadron!"

Bentley puffed frantically on his pipe and looked almost apoplectic. Then he continued to vent his wrath about the Air Vice-Marshal.

"I didn't say what I wanted to say, oh no! I didn't say, actually we've got better bloody things to do than prosecute your damned offspring. Funnily enough, there's a war on, and there are special missions underway as we speak, but no, your blasted court-martial takes precedence over all of it!"

Having vented his spleen to his satisfaction, he put the pipe back in his mouth. Clouds of smoke issued forth but having got his ire out in the open, he seemed calmer. After a moment he resumed his seat.

"I may have mentioned a little more than I meant to just then," he said in a milder tone.

"Yes, sir."

"So, you won't repeat it, or I'll have your guts for garters!"

I wasn't planning to, but Bentley was a man who liked to spell things out.

"My lips are sealed," I assured him.

"Good, good. The long and short of this … meeting … with the Air Vice-Marshal is that I will convene the court-martial in three days' time regardless. So, you had better get yourself prepared."

"Is there a point?" I asked him, rather rashly in the wake of his tirade.

"Is there a point to what?" His voice immediately took on a dangerous edge.

"I meant, sir," I said, quickly before he went off again, "I meant, is my defence going to make any difference?"

"Hmm." He smoked his pipe and ruminated on this question for a moment. "I won't let it be said that Charlton did not have a fair trial. So, in short, yes, there is a point to you defending him. I'm not about to let you back out of it, if that's what you're thinking."

"I wasn't, sir," I said, not wishing to become another target for his frustrations with the Air Vice-Marshal. "It's just that I don't have much of a defence, all told."

"Ah."

I felt it incumbent upon myself to explain. "The thing is, if I *were* to defend him properly, then things would come out about his upbringing and, well, I don't think it would be politic … if you see what I mean."

"I take it you mean his father…"

"Yes, and his mother…"

"His mother?"

Since we were exchanging confidences, I decided to take him into mine. After all, he might think better of Phillip if he knew what I knew. He heard me out in silence. When I had finished, he repeated his entire pipe of doom routine again before commenting further.

"I see, well, all of that makes a lot of sense. A lot of sense indeed, though not much use to Charlton now," he said when he was once more puffing contentedly on his pipe. "Even if you could say it, it would be unlikely to go down well. More than likely he'd be sent for psychiatric evaluation and so forth, but it would not change the outcome. Also, he might not want you to say it. Have you asked him?"

"You are right, I'm sure," I agreed. "And I don't think he would want me to, no, sir."

"In which case," he said, "you'll just have to try to say something about him being a decent chap and all that, anything you can, just for the record."

"Yes, sir."

"I know it's unsatisfactory —" he pointed the stem of his pipe at me — "but we are living in unsatisfactory times. Those who refuse to do their duty are regarded as pariahs, and that's all there is to it. I cannot change that and nor can you. The Air Force has to take a hard line, or everyone would be doing it. Don't you see that?"

I did see it, but I also couldn't understand that mindset. I was brought up with a sense of duty and nothing could stand in the way of it. We were all different, though, as I had discovered during my time in the Mavericks. Perhaps I had mellowed a little myself. I had some sympathy for Phillip, but the Air Force was a well-oiled machine and if you were a faulty cog, you would get discarded without mercy.

"I do, sir, yes."

"Very well, then your duty is to do the best you can in this regard, without bringing the Air Vice-Marshal's name or reputation into it, understood?"

I had already decided upon this course of action and Bentley had the right of it, unfortunately.

"Completely, sir."

He nodded, satisfied. "Very well. Audrey will give you the handbook on the court-martial procedure. Get yourself *au fait* with it while you're at it."

"All right," I said.

"Good, and well done again for what you did on the mission. Let's hope the second part goes as well as the first."

"Yes, sir."

I waited, as I hadn't been completely dismissed. It seemed he had something more to impart.

"Do I perceive you and Sergeant Kensley have made up after your quarrel?" he said bluntly.

"I wouldn't exactly call it a quarrel," I protested.

"Call it what you like," he said acidly. "But I don't doubt you had made a cake of yourself, thus causing it in the first place."

The fact he immediately attributed the disagreement we'd had to something I'd done spoke volumes about his opinion of my ability to hold down a relationship. But he wasn't wrong.

"We've made up, sir, yes."

"Good, good."

He smiled to himself. Why he had such a vested interest in seeing me settled, I didn't know.

He turned to the papers on his desk, and I took that to mean the interview was over. I left his office and decided it might be best if I went to see Phillip. At least I could prepare him for his fate.

I was let into Phillip's cell and found him sitting on the bed, reading a book. As I entered, he put it aside.

"Well?" he said, somewhat belligerent in tone.

"Well, what?" I was taken aback.

"Well, what do you want?" he demanded.

Since I wasn't expecting him to address his defending officer in this fashion, I was somewhat bemused by his attitude.

"I came to tell you about your court-martial," I said.

"Really? And why should I give a monkey's about it?" he shot back.

"Is something amiss?" I asked him.

"Oh, what could possibly be amiss," he said bitterly, "when your own father comes to see you, and calls you a damn coward to your face!"

I got the picture. The Air Vice-Marshal had not only been to see Bentley.

"What happened?" I asked, taking a seat.

"What happened? I'll tell you what happened!"

"Yes, please do."

It would probably be good for him to get it off his chest. His shoulders sank a little.

"I hadn't seen my father for a long time, until today," he began, a little more quietly.

I waited to see what would transpire.

"He asked me how I was, and so forth. I didn't really know how to answer him, because I wasn't expecting to see him. After all, why should he come to see me? I'm not exactly his favourite son…"

He shot me an anguished look, but I could see the anger behind his eyes.

"I told him I was as well as could be expected. I thought perhaps he had come out of the goodness of his heart, but no…"

I stayed silent, waiting for him to continue.

"He could have said anything. He could have said he was sorry things had to come to this. Perhaps that he was sad I had ended up this way — anything, anything to show that he damn well cared, but do you know what he said?"

I shook my head.

"He said he'd come so that he could look into my face and see what a coward looks like."

I must admit I was shocked. For a father to say such a thing to their child, no matter what they thought, seemed unnecessarily cruel.

"So, I said to him…" His voice was now pitched low, almost a growl. "I said, well go on then, look at the coward, because that's what you made me. Yes, *you* bloody well made me like this. You bullied me, you made me afraid of you, but guess what, I'm not afraid of you anymore."

I nodded slowly, but he hadn't finished.

"He said it wasn't his fault, it was my mother's fault. That's when I lost my temper. I finally told him exactly what I thought of him, all the things I had never said all these years. Then I told him to get out. I said I'd spare him the trouble of disowning me, because I was disowning him. I told him to rot in hell — that was my parting shot."

He let out a hollow laugh. I stared at him in admiration, because somehow, I was looking at a different Phillip. His back was straighter, and he suddenly seemed more confident. It was almost as if he'd faced his inner demons and won.

"You know the thing I regret most?" he asked me suddenly.

"No, I don't. Tell me," I said.

"I regret that I did what I did up there on the sortie. I regret that I played into his hands by running away. But I'm damned if he'll call me a coward again!"

He got up and paced the room in an agitated fashion.

"If only I could have that time again, if only. But now I'm marked, branded for life as a coward."

He sat back down on the bed with a thump, his anger spent.

"I've messed it all up, and now I've no chance for redemption."

Unfortunately, he was right. There would be no second chances, not with the Air Force, and probably not with many people outside of it once it was known what he had done.

Now he had let out his wrath, he turned his attention to me.

"So, what was it you came here for?" he asked in a far more reasonable tone than before.

"Your court-martial is in three days' time, and I came to tell you. I also need to come up with something to say in your defence..."

I trailed off. It was better to be honest. He thought about it for a little while.

"You can say I regret my actions, that I wish I had that time again to undo the harm I've done, not only to myself but to the squadron. You can say that I'm sorry," he said softly.

I nodded. It seemed reasonable, if unlikely to change much.

"I will say that if you wish it, but I'm not sure it will help."

"It doesn't matter. It's the truth. I'm glad my father came here today. I finally saw things for what they are. It's just a shame I saw them too late."

"I'm sorry too," I said. "I'm sorry I can't do more to help you."

"No," Phillip replied. "It's time I learned to fight and stopped running away. My mother was wrong. It's running from a fight that has been my mistake all of my life. I have to pay the price for that."

I was much moved by this speech, and what had just transpired. I really wanted to help him, if I could.

"I'll do my best for you," I said. "I'll make the best damn speech I can muster."

"Thank you," said Phillip. "I'm grateful."

We shook hands; somehow it seemed fitting. He'd had an epiphany, that much was clear. It was just a shame it hadn't come sooner. I left the guardhouse in a pensive mood.

"Where have you been?" said Angelica, arriving by my side as I returned to the hut.

"I've been to see Phillip, if you must know, after seeing Bentley."

"Oh, do tell?"

Her arm was tucked into mine in customary fashion, and we went together to our bench. Once seated, I told her what had transpired.

"I'm impressed," she said when I'd finished. "Impressed with Phillip for standing up to his father."

"Yes, but it's a shame he hadn't the guts to do it sooner," I said.

"Sometimes you need to have your back to the wall before you feel able to act," she replied softly.

"Oh?" I had a feeling this was suddenly no longer about Phillip.

"Yes, because ... I know. Sometimes, if there's something you want — someone — and you can't have them... Well, sometimes you have to take action."

She was referring to herself. It took me back to the first night I'd kissed her. She had pretty much goaded me into it. I had still been dithering over Barbara, but Angelica had stuck it out. Her back was certainly to the wall then.

"Yes, yes, I see," I said with a smile.

"Do you?"

"Yes."

I was slow at times where women were concerned, but I certainly got the subtext. It was amazing how we could have two completely different conversations at once.

"That's why I love you," she said.

"I was wondering," I said, returning to the main subject, "if you might help me write my speech, for the defence?"

"Of course I will."

"Thank you," I replied.

"Can I tell Audrey what you told me, about Phillip?"

I shrugged. "Why not? It might help her."

"Yes, perhaps it might."

Her arms wound around my neck, and her lips found mine. We kissed gently and then more passionately.

"I was always going to get you, no matter what. You know that, don't you?" she whispered.

"Yes, yes, I do."

"Only one more mission to go," she said.

"Until…?"

"Until it's over."

As I kissed her again, I thought it was a vain hope. With the Marx Brothers, it might never be over. They kept turning up like a pair of bad pennies. Who was to say there wouldn't be another mission, and then another? I said nothing further. If it helped Angelica to think that way, then I would hold my peace.

CHAPTER TEN

Three days passed in a whirlwind. It was surprising how time could fly when you were preparing for something unpleasant. In this case, it was two things, the first being the court-martial and the second Mission Two.

The second mission was very much on my mind, and we recommenced strafing practice at the nearby gunnery range. I knew that we had to be incredibly precise in order to leave one plane standing. Logic dictated this had to be the one at the front of the pack, so the pilot could take it and get away. That was a tall order and one which I wasn't entirely sure was going to work, even though the first mission had been a success. However, we had to give ourselves the best chance, which came down to more practice.

Writing the speech for the court-martial was also quite a task. It had never been my forte to pen any amount of prose, and I'd struggled at school when required to write essays of any length. However, this is where Angelica came to my rescue. I discovered her to be something of a wordsmith, and then she informed me she had won the English prize at school more than once for her compositions.

"I never knew this about you," I said when she told me.

"You see, you don't know everything, and that's as it should be."

"Is it?"

"Of course, I need to have something in reserve to keep you guessing."

She laughed and I caught her round the waist to kiss her.

"I know," she said. "I'm incorrigible."

"I was thinking irredeemable," I countered.

"That too…"

Angelica had turned my thoughts about Phillip into something that sounded rather acceptable. I refused to allow myself to think of the futility of what I was doing. Phillip had a raw deal, and he was going to pay a price for it. The least I could do was try to make him sound like a decent person. Angelica would arrange for Audrey to type up the speech.

We talked about the proceedings together, as I now had the orders for it in my possession.

"Do you know this person, Flight Lieutenant Alfred Morgan?" she said.

He was the prosecuting officer. He wasn't from our squadron, as Bentley felt the prosecution had to be impartial.

"No, I don't know him, and I suppose that was the intention," I said. "It couldn't be someone from here. A lot of the chaps feel Phillip deserves everything that's coming to him. I know some don't, like Jonty. I think Jonty sympathises with his plight. At least Morgan will be impartial, I hope."

"Oh, yes, I see."

"Morgan is already here," I said.

"Have you met him?"

"No, I don't think it's a good idea. I feel that I should keep him at a distance, since we are on opposite sides. He's interviewing various witnesses. I suppose he might be asking you…"

I trailed off and she pursed her lips. Angelica might be called as a witness, since she was on comms at the time of the incident. She knew that if she was ordered to be a witness, she'd have to do it.

"I've only got one witness," I said, not wanting to dwell on this eventuality. "He's a friend of Phillip's who did his flight training at the same time. I managed to get hold of him, and he has agreed to at least try to bear witness to Phillip's good character."

"I suppose that's something," Angelica agreed.

"Well, it's not much but it's better than nothing."

"Do you think Charlton *will* be drummed out of the Air Force?" Angelica wondered.

"I'm afraid I don't know, and I wouldn't like to guess. All I can do is try my best."

I had visions of what the drumming out would be. I had heard tales. The commanding officer would assemble the entire squadron, and then ceremoniously rip the badges of rank and the pilot's wings from the clothing of the guilty officer. He would then be escorted away, never to return, for all I knew with drums actually being played during the proceedings. It seemed harsh, and daunting. I couldn't imagine Bentley taking any pleasure from such an event. I could also imagine that Air Vice-Marshal Charlton would want his son humiliated in such a fashion, since it seemed he was that kind of man.

"Whatever happens, I love you for standing up for what you believe in," Angelica whispered.

The appointed hour of the court-martial arrived at last. It was set for early in the morning, and the officers who made up the panel had arrived on the airbase from other squadrons.

"Are you ready?" Angelica asked me before I entered the room designated for the court-martial.

"As I'll ever be."

"Good luck."

She kissed me and left me to it. There would be no spectators allowed other than those officers called to be witnesses, and Squadron Leader Bentley. Morgan had decided not to call Angelica as a witness since she was my fiancée.

Even under oath he probably felt she might be biased. I was glad she didn't have to testify.

I knew Bentley had done all he could to ensure there was a fair trial. The handbook was explicit about everything, including the layout of the room. I entered and took in the surroundings.

At one end of the room, facing the court, was a long table, behind which would be Phillip's judges once the court-martial was in session.

The President of the court was to be Wing Commander Edward Smithson, a senior ranking officer. He would oversee the proceedings. To his right would sit Squadron Leader Howard Brinkman, who was the Judge-Advocate and a Barrister-at-Law appointed by the Department of the Judge-Advocate-General. Next to him would be Flight Lieutenant Alan Fisher, Senior Member of the panel, and on the left of Smithson would be Flight Lieutenant Norman Barraclough, Junior Member of the panel.

Four people to judge one man on a matter of cowardice. It didn't seem like very good odds as far as Phillip was concerned.

To the left of the panel's table was the prosecutor's table, and to the right was mine, the defending officer. Next to the prosecutor's table was a stenographer to record the court proceedings. I was a little shocked to discover it was Audrey. This would surely be hard for her to take, but perhaps she had volunteered. She flicked a glance at me and gave me a tight smile. I returned it briefly, wishing I could say some words of comfort or reassurance.

There was a chair for the witness in front of the prosecutor's table, and two chairs for the accused and his escort in front of mine. My witness was sitting behind my table, and the prosecution witnesses were behind the prosecutor's table. Bentley was sitting to my left as I entered the court. There was also a court orderly, a sergeant, who was charged with telling us when to stand, sit and so forth.

I walked over to my table and put down my papers. Almost immediately Morgan came across to me and held out his hand. I supposed this must be how things went.

"Sorry to meet you like this, as an adversary, old chap," he said at once. "These occasions are always fraught, I'm afraid."

I shook his hand and he seemed quite affable all told. I had stuck to my resolution not to speak to him prior to meeting him at the court-martial; it seemed more politic.

"You've done this before?" I asked him.

"I'm afraid so. Have you?"

"No," I said. "And I rather hope not to have to do it again."

"Good luck," he said with a smile.

"Thanks."

I wondered if he really meant it, or if that was just something people say before a battle. I sat at the table and mentally prepared myself for what was to come. The witnesses called by the prosecution were Judd, Tomas, Colin, and Gerald. Four people to corroborate that Phillip had left the field of combat was probably enough, although the entire flight had witnessed it. I turned to Pilot Officer Clarence Donaldson behind me, my witness. He was a young, fair-haired fellow Scot. I had met him briefly beforehand.

"Are you ready?" I asked him.

"Yes, yes, of course," he said.

"Thanks for doing this."

"I'm happy to. It's a damn shame…"

Just then, the sergeant called the court to order.

"Attention in the court, senior officers in the room."

We stood to attention as the panel entered. Of the four of them, Wing Commander Smithson was the oldest at around forty years of age and quite distinguished in appearance. The other three were probably in their thirties, each smartly turned out in dress uniforms. They took up their designated positions behind the table for the panel.

We sat when they sat, and then Smithson addressed us.

"For the record, this is a legally convened court-martial," he said. "It's my job to ensure that the proceedings are fair and right for all concerned. We will hear the charges laid, followed by a plea from the accused. After which we shall hear evidence from the prosecution and then the defence. Finally, you both will have a chance to address the court before we retire to consider judgement. Is that all clear?"

"Yes, sir." Both myself and Morgan affirmed our understanding.

"Good, and if you have any questions during the proceedings, you may address them to me."

He paused for a moment, and I looked over at Bentley. He was sucking on his empty pipe and no doubt felt the lack of opportunity to smoke it. If Smithson noticed this, he deigned to ignore it. Bentley and his pipe were inseparable.

"Very well, bring in the accused," said Smithson.

Phillip was escorted into the room by a corporal. He was in uniform but not allowed to wear his cap; this was apparently in case he attempted to fling it at his judges. The corporal carried it for him, instead. The person who had written the court-martial procedure had thought of everything. Phillip glanced at me, and I smiled encouragingly. Then he sat down, and his escort sat next to him.

"Proceed with the charge," said Smithson. "The accused will stand."

Morgan stood up also to read the charge as the prosecuting officer.

"You are Pilot Officer Phillip Charlton?" he said.

"I am," said Phillip in a clear voice.

"You are accused of cowardice in the face of the enemy. It is alleged that you left the field of combat during an aerial engagement, and that you disobeyed a direct order to return," said Morgan. He then went on to specify the date and time of the offence, and various other details.

When he had finished, Smithson spoke again.

"Pilot Officer Charlton, how do you plead?"

I had already discussed this with Phillip, and there was no option but to plead guilty. It would be impossible to prove otherwise, and to try to get out of it might go harder against him.

"Guilty, sir," said Phillip loudly and clearly.

Audrey was typing and I could see she was stony-faced.

"Very well, be seated," Smithson told him. "We shall hear the evidence from the prosecution, and then from the defence. After closing statements, we shall determine our course of action."

There was very little for me to do, as the four prosecution witnesses were called one after the other. Each of them told the same story, describing how Phillip had fled the field of combat. Tomas shot me a look of apology. He had no choice as to whether he was a witness or not. Whatever he might feel about Phillip, Tomas and I were friends.

As the evidence was given, the expressions of the panel became more and more forbidding. Once the last witness was called, I wondered if there was anything I could do to mitigate the situation at all.

"Flying Officer Mackennelly, you may call your witness," said Smithson to me, giving me no further time to muse on it.

"Sir, I call Pilot Officer Donaldson," I said.

I waited while Donaldson took the stand across from me and swore an oath on the Bible. I took a deep breath and began.

"Pilot Officer Donaldson," I said, "you've known the accused for how long?"

"We were at school together," he replied. "Then we went to flight school — Phillip was posted to a different squadron to me."

"So can I take it you've known Pilot Officer Charlton for a number of years?" I asked him.

"Yes, quite some time, yes."

"And in that time, could you describe what you know of his character?"

Donaldson considered the question for a moment, amid silence in the room.

"He was always a good sort," he said. "A loyal and true friend. He would even take the blame for things I did, and the punishment too." He smiled as he said it, reminiscing.

"So might it be fair to say, he had your back?"

Donaldson nodded eagerly. "Yes, he did. I mean, he wasn't one to get into a fight on his own account, but if someone threatened me, he'd be in the thick of it. He'd protect me."

This was quite a promising answer, I felt. I had mentioned the questions I intended to ask when I had talked to him. We hadn't gone into details, though, as there wasn't time. So it really was down to what he said on the witness stand.

"So, Pilot Officer Charlton, in effect, was a person who wouldn't run from a fight?"

This was a difficult question because I knew Phillip's mother had told him to run and not get into fights.

"No, certainly not if it involved his best friend. I could rely on him."

I smiled and flicked a glance at the panel. They remained impassive, but I persevered.

"You said you could rely on Pilot Officer Charlton. Would you say the same about your time at flight school?"

"Yes," Donaldson said at once. "On the exercises, Phillip was always in the thick of it, and in our dogfight practices too. He was a pretty good pilot all told, shaping up well."

It didn't seem like much, but it was something. I went on to ask him the key question.

"Given he was all you say, what was your reaction on discovering that Pilot Officer Charlton had left the field of combat?"

Donaldson hesitated before answering. "Well … I have to say I was surprised. I never expected it, not the way he had always been."

This was a good answer which gave me the opening I wanted. Whether it would weigh with the judges, I didn't know.

"So would you say it was out of character for him to have done that?"

"Yes," Donaldson replied, this time without hesitation. "Yes, I would. He's always been a plucky sort."

"Thank you."

I had made my point, and there wasn't much mileage in trying to labour it.

"No more questions," I said to Smithson.

"Very well," said Smithson. "Flight Lieutenant Morgan, do you have any questions for this witness?"

Morgan stood up. I had not asked his witnesses anything. There was no point — I couldn't refute what they said since I had been there myself.

"Yes, sir, I do," he said.

"Proceed."

He turned to Donaldson with a deceptively mild expression on his face.

"Pilot Officer Donaldson, have you been in combat?" Morgan asked him.

"Yes, sir, yes, I have."

"And what was it like?"

I saw at once where this was leading. Morgan was out to destroy my witness's testimony.

"It was pretty much hell, sir, if I'm honest."

"Hell," said Morgan with a smile. "Slightly different from a fight with some lads at school, wouldn't you say?"

Donaldson grimaced. He had also twigged what Morgan was up to, but since he was under oath he had to answer truthfully.

"If you put it that way, I suppose you're right."

"You *suppose* I'm right?" pursued Morgan. "In a schoolyard bout of fisticuffs, nobody is likely to die, are they?"

"Well … no."

"So, it's not the same, is it?"

Morgan was good, I'd give him that, and a little ruthless with it. I supposed it was his job to pursue the result he felt Phillip deserved. It didn't make me like Morgan any better for it at the time, though.

"No," said Donaldson, looking a little defeated.

I was chagrined to discover Morgan hadn't finished.

"When you were at flight school, is it not true that Pilot Officer Charlton liked to kick up a lark?" he said.

My heart sank; he was thorough. He must have somehow obtained access to Phillip's records, and that would be damning.

"I'm not sure what you mean by a lark," said Donaldson evasively.

"Is it or is it not true that he buzzed the office of the CO with his aircraft?"

Donaldson nodded reluctantly. "Yes, it's true."

Morgan continued. "And is it or is it not true that he was found *in flagrante delicto* with one of the WAAFs?"

"I believe so, yes."

Donaldson looked very uncomfortable now and didn't want to look at his friend. Phillip remained impassive; perhaps he was simply accepting the fact that this wasn't going to go his way.

"You believe so? Do you know so or do you not?" Morgan was starting to sound just like a barrister in a real courtroom.

"Yes, yes, he was."

"Which is why he didn't go to the same squadron as you, correct?"

"Yes."

Morgan had made his point — Phillip did not have an unblemished record. Everyone in the room knew the Mavericks was where the unwanted pilots were sent.

"So, whilst you might impute that Pilot Officer Charlton had a good character or, as you said, his act of cowardice was out of character, that's perhaps not quite so, wouldn't you say?"

"No, I suppose not," said Donaldson, defeated. "But those were not serious things. When the chips were down, he always had my back."

Morgan ignored this last attempt by Donaldson to recover some ground, because he knew he had done it: he had discredited the testimony of my witness as he had set out to do.

"No further questions," said Morgan. He shot me a look of satisfaction which made me dislike him. The affability at the beginning was simply a front. I was annoyed but, nevertheless, I would press on with what I was going to say, because it needed to be said.

"Do you have any more questions, Flying Officer Mackennelly?" asked Smithson.

"No, sir," I said.

"All right, then if we've heard all of the evidence, we can proceed to the summing-up. Flight Lieutenant Morgan?"

Morgan stood up again. "The evidence in this case is cut and dried. There can be no doubt that the accused, Pilot Officer Phillip Charlton, fled the field of combat. This has been corroborated by four witnesses who were there at the time, including his flight leader, Flight Lieutenant Judd. Charlton disobeyed an order to return to the field and left, committing an act of cowardice — an act to which he has already pleaded guilty. The single witness brought by the defence to testify Charlton's good character has unfortunately illustrated the difference between camaraderie at school and courage in a time of war. He also could not deny that the accused already has a blemished record with the Air Force; therefore, we don't accept the assertion that he acted out of character. We do not believe there are any circumstances to mitigate his actions, and that is the entire case for the prosecution."

Morgan nodded to me as he finished, as if to say, "Beat that." It seemed the whole thing was a competition to him and not someone's future on the line.

"Thank you, Flight Lieutenant Morgan," said Smithson. "Flying Officer Mackennelly, do you have anything you wish to say on behalf of the accused?"

I stood up. This was it.

"Yes, sir, I do," I said.

"Proceed," said Smithson.

Four pairs of eyes swivelled towards me as I prepared to address the panel. My hand shook a little with the paper containing my speech. I cleared my throat and tried to imagine Angelica looking at me encouragingly.

"Pilot Officer Phillip Charlton," I began, "is…"

I stopped. There was the distinct distant thrum of aircraft engines. As pilots, we had become fine-tuned to it.

"Go on," said Smithson, when I didn't say anything further. I was straining to hear what sounded like a large number of planes coming closer.

"Ahem … yes … sorry… Charlton is a man and an officer who…"

I got no further. I noticed that Bentley was also suddenly very alert. Then, without warning, the air-raid siren sounded. Smithson looked annoyed but before he could say anything, one of the ground crew burst into the room.

"It's a raid! We're being raided!" he yelled. "You need to take cover!"

Bentley was up at once and very much in charge. This was his squadron, regardless of the court-martial.

"Angus, get out there and get those bloody planes in the air, now! That's an order!"

I didn't hesitate on hearing this — my only thought was our precious Spitfires. The court-martial and protocol forgotten, I left the room at high speed.

Behind me, I could hear Smithson shouting, "The proceedings are adjourned. Take the accused away — everyone take cover!"

Then I was running for the airfield. I could see other pilots heading for their planes, and in the distance, what looked like a squadron of Focke-Wulfs was closing in fast.

Suddenly, behind me, I heard Phillip's voice.

"Sir, sir, wait."

I turned around and was surprised to see him running towards me. His escort had disappeared, or perhaps he'd given them the slip.

"What are you doing here? You need to get to safety!" I shouted as he ran with me.

"Let me take one up. I want to help — I swear, I'm not going to run. I'm not a coward."

"Don't be a damn fool," I said.

"Please…"

I had no time to argue and besides, what difference did it make now? He was damned if he did and damned if he didn't.

"Fine. If you can find a plane, take it, get up in the air and get stuck in — I've no time to debate it with you. But don't you dare bloody well disappear."

"I won't, I swear — I have to do this. I have to show them."

"Just go on, then — there's no time!"

I ran for my M Flight Spitfire and jumped into the cockpit. I hadn't time to see if Phillip had found a plane or not, or to consider the consequences of his actions or mine. My sole focus was to get us airborne. Spits were firing up their engines and taxiing out. I did the same and then throttled up. The Focke-Wulfs were almost upon us as I got airborne. The rest of M Flight was with me as I took off.

"M Flight, break, break, let's take them," I said over the radio.

"Mavericks engage, quick as you can." It was Judd. He would be leading the rest of the squadron.

The Jerries saw they had lost the element of surprise and broke formation. Nevertheless, they came at us on the attack. There was no doubt that they had intended to strafe our airfield, but there wasn't time to consider how or why. We had fortunately prevented them from destroying our planes wholesale, but we could still lose a few regardless.

I picked out one of the approaching planes and flew at it. He flipped away in predictable fashion, although I squeezed off a burst just the same. It went wide of the mark. I took up the chase. The air was suddenly filled with gunfire and chatter.

"I'm on him, I'm on him."

"Watch out!"

"There's one on your tail."

"Damn it, I'm hit! I'm bloody well hit!"

One of our Spitfires went down and burst into flames.

I stayed on the Focke-Wulf I was chasing. He was expertly avoiding me, and his evasive manoeuvres were much faster than mine. Out of nowhere another Spitfire from the main flight appeared, and tracers fired across the bows of the Jerry. He turned away, but the Spitfire fired again. Bullets ripped into the canopy and the Focke-Wulf went into a spin.

"Thanks," I said.

"You're welcome, sir." It was Phillip; he had shot down the Focke-Wulf.

He had managed to get into a plane after all. He sheared away and went back into the fray. I hadn't the leisure to contemplate where he'd summoned his newfound courage from, because I found myself now on the receiving end of gunfire.

A line of tracers slid across my bows in front of me. I banked sharply and went into a dive. Another Focke-Wulf who had opened fire followed me doggedly, so next I tried weaving left and right. He was still quicker than I was. I pulled some tight turns, hoping to evade him. But it wasn't working.

My next trick was to go up into a steep climb. The Spitfire responded nicely and for a moment he was just far enough away for me to loop over. I did so, and then I was behind him. He flicked his craft wide of my gunfire and turned away. I gave chase.

The chatter continued in the background. I heard a familiar war cry.

"Tally-ho!"

Jonty was hallooing in typical fashion, and no doubt enjoying every moment of it. Over on my left another Spitfire went down, fortunately not one from M Flight. The Mark Vs seemed to be faring better than the older models, though we had had some of the Vs delivered to the rest of the squadron recently too.

The Focke-Wulf I was chasing decided to try the same trick I'd pulled on him. He went up and looped over. I had anticipated this move and followed him. Although the G-forces kicked in, I still managed to stick on his tail.

He turned again and accelerated away, disengaging. I turned away too and headed for the main pack. The fight was still very much on. I could see another Spitfire which looked like it was Willie's being run down by a Jerry fighter. I dived towards it and fired. I managed to hit the tail, causing the Jerry's plane to jerk sideways. The Jerry left off chasing Willie and started to fly away.

"Thanks, Scottish," said Willie.

"You're welcome, Kiwi."

I decided not to let the Jerry go and gave chase. I was gaining on him when I clocked a shadow on my right.

"Damn!" I swore softly.

I had not been paying attention — it was another German plane. I turned just in time to face him, but he was close. I realised he had me in his sights.

"Blast," I said, wondering if my time had finally come. I waited for him to fire while simultaneously trying to bank away, knowing it was probably too late. Everything that followed happened in a few seconds, though it seemed like minutes at the time.

I heard Phillip once again as the radio crackled to life.

"I've got you — I've got your back."

His plane came in from out of nowhere, catching the Jerry unawares. I saw that he had a chance to make a kill.

"Shoot!" I shouted. "Shoot him!"

"I can't, sir, no ammo, but don't worry. I've got him."

Divining his intention, I cried out, "Don't be a fool!"

"I have to do this — I've got no choice. I'm not a coward — tell them that!" he said.

Phillip's plane kept coming and the Jerry saw him too late. The Spitfire collided and took the Focke-Wulf amidships in a tremendous explosion.

Everything sped up once more; reflex action kicked in and I banked away sharply to avoid the flying shards of metal coming at me.

Once out of range, I watched the two planes spiralling to earth. Phillip was dead and so was the German pilot. Phillip had given his life to save mine.

The main dogfight was starting to break up, and as I flew back into it, the remaining Focke-Wulfs turned and ran.

"M Flight, let them go," I said. There was no point in trying to chase them down, and I had no idea how much ammo we had left. One thing was clear: we'd foiled what must have been a plan to decimate our squadron.

"Mavericks, break off, stay in the air until we're sure they are gone," said Judd.

M Flight settled behind me in formation. We all stayed airborne a while longer, but the Germans became smaller and smaller specks in the distance. Once it was perceived there was no longer a threat, we decided to land.

As might be expected, Bentley was waiting for me when I jumped down from my plane, but before I could attend to him Angelica was running towards me at top speed. She flung herself into my arms.

"You're home, thank God, you're home," she whispered.

I kissed her fervently, realising I was lucky. If it hadn't been for Phillip, I would probably be dead. After a few moments, I gently detached her arms from around my neck.

"I have to speak to Bentley," I said.

"All right."

She clutched my hand tightly while I walked up to where Bentley was patiently observing us. He was busy filling his pipe, so I waited until he had lit it. He regarded me steadfastly for a few moments before speaking.

"What happened up there, Angus?"

"With regard to the Jerry planes?" I played slightly dumb until I knew where the conversation was leading.

"I'm not talking about the Jerry planes." He took a puff of his pipe. "I'm talking about how one of our pilots smashed their Spitfire into an enemy fighter."

"Well, yes, he saved my life," I said.

Beside me, Angelica pursed her lips and squeezed my hand. Bentley was joined by Audrey, who came hurrying up to us. He had probably told her to get into one of the bunkers.

"Who exactly saved your life?" Bentley continued with interest, although I was sure he knew full well.

"Phillip, sir," I said at length.

Audrey's face was a tight mask as she tried to control her feelings.

"Charlton," said Bentley with a wry smile. "And how precisely did he manage to get into one of the Spitfires?"

"I don't know, sir, it just … happened…" I shrugged. I wasn't about to divulge the conversation I'd had with him beforehand, since it was probably quite damning for me.

"Just happened? Hmm … indeed…"

The CO continued to puff on his pipe without showing any sign of wanting to end the uncomfortable conversation.

"Sir … I believe he … wanted to show the world that he wasn't a coward," I said, trying to mitigate things just a little.

"I see. And you know this how?"

"I heard the conversation, sir. Phillip … I mean Pilot Officer Charlton … said it before he crashed into the German plane," Angelica suddenly piped up. She would have been on the comms.

Bentley smiled at this. He had a soft spot for Angelica; no doubt that was why he allowed the two of us so much latitude with our public displays of affection.

"Really? And what exactly did he say, Sergeant?" asked Bentley with interest.

"He said something like… 'I have to do this. I've got no choice. I'm not a coward — tell them that…' just before he smashed into the Jerry, sir."

I flicked a glance at Audrey, whose expression was unreadable. However, her eyes were shining with unshed tears.

"I see, and that's what you heard too?" he asked me pointedly.

"Yes, sir," I nodded.

"And you know nothing about how exactly he escaped his escort and got into a Spitfire?" Bentley asked me once again.

"No, sir, nothing at all. It was pandemonium out there..."

"Well, see that you stick to that story when you're asked about it at the court-martial," he said, cutting me short.

"Yes, sir."

"Right, I've got to speak to Judd..."

I saluted and Bentley turned away. Audrey didn't follow him, and Angelica went up to her. She took her in her arms. Audrey burst into tears.

I left them to it and went to see to my flight; hopefully, none of them had been shot down. I was pretty sure Bentley knew I hadn't told him everything about Phillip, but he was prepared to let it lie. There would be repercussions from the raid, and that was a far more important consideration. Phillip had saved my life. I could never forget that either.

CHAPTER ELEVEN

I stood in front of the panel after the court-martial reconvened. Smithson eyed me askance as I related what had happened to Phillip. When I had finished, he folded his arms and said nothing for quite a long while.

"You've no idea how Pilot Officer Charlton evaded his escort?" he said at length.

"No, sir."

That part at least was true.

"And you've no idea at all how he managed to get into a Spitfire and take it up into the air?"

"No, sir, I don't."

Smithson didn't really look as if believed me any more than Bentley did. However, he seemed to be willing to let it pass.

"What were you going to say about Charlton, before the air raid happened?" he said, changing the subject.

"I had a speech prepared, sir, just to say that I felt what he did was out of character. Now this has happened, I feel it to be even more true."

"All right, let's hear it then. You can read it out now," he said.

"Don't you think that under the circumstances…" I began, wondering why he would want me to do such a thing.

He cut me off while regarding me with a fulminating eye. "No, Flying Officer Mackennelly, I don't think! These proceedings have been unceremoniously interrupted by events which are arguably unwarranted but necessary. However, I'm damned if I will allow the protocols of this court-martial to go for a burton. We will finish this properly, and a proper judgement will be given, regardless of whether the accused is demised or not!"

"Yes, sir."

"Good, in which case you can get on with it."

Not wishing to make him any more irate, I went over to my table, picked up my speech and began to read.

"Pilot Officer Phillip Charlton is … or rather was … a man and an officer who perhaps joined the Air Force somewhat reluctantly. At least I know he might have wanted to do something else with his life, but then the war came along. His father and family set great store by the tradition of the RAF, and he perhaps felt that he had to follow in those footsteps. Whatever his personal ambitions may have been, the fact remains that he *did* join the Air Force…"

I paused. The panel was listening to me with interest.

"I am sure he did so with every intention of succeeding as a pilot. I don't think any of us join up with any other desire than to acquit ourselves well. I submit that Charlton was no different. As you've heard from the witness and his lifelong friend, Charlton always had his back when younger. He also acquitted himself well as a pilot at flight school. I did not know Charlton very well, but he was a personable man who seemed ready for the fray. Overall, I do believe that to be true."

I checked myself slightly, but the panel were still attentive.

"All of us as pilots know that combat is a very different thing. It probably affects us all in different ways. I personally have flown many combat missions and been shot down twice, and so I know the gamut of emotions one can run through on these occasions. Charlton was new to combat, and we are facing a far deadlier foe now that the Luftwaffe has the Focke-Wulf — a plane to which we have no real answer. This is testing for an experienced pilot, let alone a new pilot unused to combat.

"It's my view from what I know of him and conversations I've had with him, that Pilot Officer Charlton's actions on the day in question were out of character. I believe him to be a man of good intentions, and none of us can know what personal demons another is fighting. I know he feels … felt … a deep remorse because of it. He told me, just before this court-martial, that he wished he was able to have had a second chance to show that he wasn't a coward."

This was quite poignant now in the context of his death.

"What he did was, in the eyes of the Royal Air Force, unconscionable. I am sure he understood that too and was ready to face the consequences of his deeds. However, I would like to ask the court to perhaps consider the man, as well as his actions, and perhaps show some leniency if it possibly can. I'm no bard, but I'm sure we all know the quote from Shakespeare which begins: 'The quality of mercy is not strained' and that's what I'm asking today from this court for Pilot Officer Charlton."

I paused and gathered my thoughts. That was the end of the speech; however, in light of the events of the day, I had something I wanted to add.

"I should also add that what happened today demonstrates that Charlton meant what he said to me. He said he wasn't a coward, and he wanted a second chance. Somehow, he got that chance, and surely that endorses how out of character his previous actions were. I hope and indeed ask that this will be taken into account when you consider what judgement you intend to pass on him, albeit posthumously."

I put my papers down and waited to be dismissed.

"Thank you, Flying Officer Mackennelly. The panel will retire for a short while to consider what ruling we will make in this case," said Smithson in a far more reasonable tone than before.

"Attention in the court," said the sergeant of the court.

The panel left the room, and I sat down to wait. Morgan glanced over to me and nodded in approval. Bentley left the courtroom too, no doubt to smoke his pipe. Phillip's cap had been placed on his chair to represent his presence.

After half an hour the panel returned.

"Attention in the court," said the sergeant once again.

The panel were seated and then Smithson stood up. He looked rather serious, but I presumed that was his customary expression for delivering a verdict.

"This has been an unusual case," he said. "One for which there is also no precedent. In fact, I don't recall ever having an air raid during a court-martial before where the accused took off in an aeroplane and went into combat."

He smiled ever so slightly at this.

"The fact remains that Pilot Officer Charlton did commit an act of cowardice in front of the enemy."

My heart sank. They were going to discredit him after all.

"However, to mitigate this he then — perhaps foolishly — took a Spitfire and flew into combat against an incoming enemy raid. Which brings us back to the unprecedented events."

Smithson paused once more, and I wondered now what the outcome would be.

"During this raid, he apparently not only managed to shoot down one German plane, but he also deliberately crashed his Spitfire into another, saving the life of a fellow officer." He sighed. "Thus, committing an act as brave as it was foolhardy."

The punchline was coming, and it could go either way. Smithson's demeanour told us nothing.

"So, we are faced on the one hand with a proven act of cowardice to which the accused pleaded guilty, and on the other an act of extreme bravery by the same man. There is really nothing to cover such a situation in law or within the scope of court-martial proceedings."

He looked around the court as if daring us to contradict him. A faint spark of hope lit in my breast.

"It is, however, within my power as President of this court to rule on decisions which perhaps might be out of the ordinary. We have, in fact, deliberated quite carefully on this case. It's my view and the view of this panel that redemption is sometimes possible."

My heart soared on hearing this; they were going to do the right thing after all.

"While Pilot Officer Charlton's act of cowardice shall remain as a matter of record, so shall his act of bravery also be recorded to counter it. However, as regards these proceedings, I rule that they be dismissed on the basis that a sound and proper verdict cannot be reached. That is the opinion of us all, and that is the end of this hearing. The court-martial is now dismissed."

"Attention!" said the sergeant, as the panel swept from the room.

Morgan came over to me. "That was a turn-up for the books."

"Yes," I replied. "I'm glad of it. It was the right thing to do."

He did not comment. I wondered if he disagreed. It didn't matter anyway, considering the result.

"Good speech, by the way," he said with a smile.

"Thanks."

He held out his hand and I shook it. As he left, Bentley arrived.

"You can come and see me in my office, Angus," he said shortly.

"Now, sir?"

"As soon as you like ... yes."

"Sir."

He turned on his heel and left. I wondered what it would be about, and decided I should not keep him waiting.

As I was about to depart the courtroom, I felt a hand on my arm. It was Audrey.

"Thank you, for what you did for Phillip. It means a lot."

"That's okay," I said.

"When nobody would speak for him, you did. I won't forget that." She smiled.

"Bentley wants to see me," I said.

"Oh, then I suppose you ... we ... had better go."

"Yes."

Angelica waylaid us as soon as we left the courtroom.

"Where are you two going?" she demanded. "And what happened in there?"

She claimed my hand at once in a slightly possessive manner. Although she didn't see Audrey as a threat *per se*, where I was concerned all women were potential rivals in her eyes. Given my past behaviour, I could hardly blame her for that.

"I've got to see Bentley," I said.

"You two go and have a few moments," said Audrey, taking in Angelica's pursed lips and mulish expression. "I'll distract Bentley for a little while... I'm sure he can wait."

Angelica smiled immediately.

"Shall we go to our bench?" I asked her.

"Why not?"

"I'm proud of you," said Angelica once she had heard the whole of it.

She slipped her arms around me and kissed me.

"And to cap it off, I got to give your speech after all," I said.

"It was your speech. I just embellished it," she replied, unwilling to let me give her the credit. She was quite modest, all told.

"It seemed to go down well."

"What do you think Bentley wants?" she said, turning the subject.

"I don't know."

"Well, perhaps you had better go and find out. You've probably kept him waiting long enough," she laughed.

"And whose fault is that?" I shot back.

"Who is more important?" she countered.

"Touché. Come on then, walk me to his door."

As it turned out, Bentley had a visitor and I had to kick my heels in any case. A circumstance which Angelica was more than happy with.

An hour later, I was finally seated in front of Bentley's desk while he replenished his pipe of doom. Audrey had shown me in and then left again, saying she had to attend to something. Bentley didn't seem to mind, and his attention was wholly taken up with his pipe ritual. Once this was complete and he was smoking it cheerfully, he seemed ready to broach the matter on his mind.

"Angus, now this blasted farrago is done with, you can tell me the truth about what happened with Charlton, and no more of your blasted flummery…"

I wasn't sure I wanted to tell him. "Sir, I…"

"Don't flannel me, Angus. Let's just pretend, for a moment, that I'm not your commanding officer, shall we? Now, I know you had something to do with him getting up in that plane. So, tell me the truth and it shall go no further."

I sighed. He had me there, and in fact, he sounded rather like my father for a moment, who set great store by telling the truth. He really gave me no option.

"Well, sir, I don't know how he escaped his escort, but as I was running to the planes, he caught up with me…"

Bentley smiled with satisfaction, as if he had known this all along.

"I thought so," he said. "Go on."

I told him what had transpired between myself and Phillip, and he listened without interrupting, puffing contentedly on his pipe until the end.

"I see," he said when I'd finished. Then he pointed the stem of his pipe at me. "You know you took a damn big risk that he didn't scarper, don't you?"

"I know, sir," I said. "But something told me he wouldn't."

"And you consider yourself a great judge of character, do you?" he said with some acerbity.

"Sometimes, sir, yes."

"Good job it didn't all go wrong then, isn't it?" he said.

"Yes, sir, indeed it is."

"All right, well, I just wanted to know what actually went on, and I'm glad you told me. It's no more than I expected, but there we are. Anyway, I've made up my mind about something else, and this just confirms that decision."

"Oh?"

"Yes, I had a visitor, as you probably know."

"I —"

"None other than Air Vice-Marshal Charlton, as it goes. He hot-footed it over here, although I believe he was staying nearby in any case."

He waved his pipe around as he said this and puffed out a few more clouds of smoke.

"Naturally, he was upset about his son's demise. I was sympathetic… Anyway, he asked me what I was going to do about his son's burial or service or whatever … and do you know what I said to him this time?"

"No, sir."

Bentley smiled with what could only be immense satisfaction. "I said, 'Your son will be buried with full honours like the hero he is, in keeping with the honour of this squadron. He gave his life in the service of his fellow pilots, and I for one should think that's enough for any father, sir.'"

I smiled too. Given what had transpired between Bentley and the Air Vice-Marshal before, I could imagine Bentley took great delight in saying what he said.

"How did he take it?" I asked.

"What could he say? His son *is* a blasted hero, after all. He had to put that in his pipe and smoke it, hmm!" Bentley chuckled at the recollection. "Got to take your victories where you find them, eh, Angus?" he went on, meaning just for once he'd bested the top brass. "Yes, so we shall make some arrangements once Charlton's … remains … have been recovered."

I wondered what would be left of Phillip after the explosion. In any case, they could perhaps just bury an empty coffin if needed. Bentley wasn't going to pass up the opportunity to celebrate his small triumph.

"All that being said, I'm concerned about this raid," said Bentley, frowning.

"Yes, it came out of the blue," I replied.

"Rather seems like a tit for tat, would you not agree?"

"It had crossed my mind."

"So, I'm wondering how they knew it was us, and where did they get that information from?" said Bentley.

"I was thinking the same thing, but I'm pretty sure there will be two people who know if anyone does."

"Those blasted MI6 Johnnies — yes, exactly!" said Bentley, looking annoyed. They were certainly not his favourite people.

"Shall I…"

"I've already put a call in to them," he said. "I expect we will see them tomorrow. In the meantime, we lost a couple of planes in that damned nonsense, and we're lucky it wasn't more."

"Do you think this will jeopardise Mission Two?" I asked him.

"It's certainly a question for those two reprobates," he said. "Anyway, enough said. No doubt we will find out more when we see them."

"Yes."

Audrey slipped into the room and hovered as if she wanted to say something.

"Yes, Audrey?" said Bentley, noticing.

"Sir, the Air Vice-Marshal…" She trailed off.

"What the bloody hell does he want now?" Bentley demanded.

"He wants to see Ang— I mean Flying Officer Mackennelly, sir."

"Oh?"

"Most particularly, sir, yes."

Bentley looked at me as if it was all my fault and I shrugged. I had no idea what an Air Vice-Marshal would want with me, let alone one who was Phillip's father.

"I suppose you'd better get off and see him," said Bentley, sounding most aggrieved. "And if he asks you about it, stick to the story you told to the court-martial!"

"Of course, sir, the other thing was between you and me."

"And so it shall remain," said Bentley, pointing his pipe stem at me once more. "Off you go. You can tell me what he wanted some other time. I've got plenty to do after that bloody raid."

"Yes, sir."

I saluted and left the room. Audrey accompanied me.

"What does the Air Vice-Marshal want?" I asked her.

"I've no idea."

"I'm sorry about all this," I said. "It must be hard."

"At least Phillip died a hero," she said.

"Yes."

She opened a door and let me into another office. I guessed that she must have been attending to the Air Vice-Marshal's needs while I was seeing Bentley. I soon saw what those needs were. He was sitting at ease with an open bottle of whisky and a half-empty glass on the table. I supposed if my son had just died, I would have done the same.

He looked like an older version of Phillip and a little more careworn. He had grey hair and blue eyes, unlike his son whose eyes had been brown. Other than that, the family resemblance was clear enough. His hat, the peak covered in gold braid, sat on the table.

I stepped smartly up to where he sat and saluted. He returned a perfunctory salute in acknowledgement.

"Sit down, Flying Officer Mackennelly, is it?" He motioned to a chair.

I did so and waited to see what he had to say.

"Drink?" he offered, indicating the bottle of single malt. Although I was partial, I decided against it. Besides, there wasn't another glass.

"No thank you, sir," I said.

He nodded in acquiescence, as if it was of no consequence to him either way. In truth, he had the look of a slightly broken man.

"Do you know why I asked to see you?" he enquired, picking up the glass and taking a sip of the whisky.

"Not really, sir, no."

"You were to defend my son, were you not?"

It was delivered as a statement of fact, rather than in a combative tone.

"Yes, yes, I was — at least, I was to try my best to do so."

That was the truth, and he no doubt had heard that the court-martial had been dismissed without a verdict. I wondered if this rankled, or if he wanted to remonstrate with me for defending his son. However, it turned out to be none of these things.

"He probably thought I hated him, Phillip … I didn't. I just wished for something I couldn't have."

I stayed silent. This didn't seem to warrant an answer. He took another drink and poured out another half measure from the bottle.

"Have you ever done something you bitterly regret?" he asked me suddenly.

"Yes, frequently," I replied, feeling that he wanted some honesty.

He nodded. "Well, it's a new thing for me … regret … and now I'm past being able to change it."

"I'm sorry," I said, for want of anything better to say.

"I'm sorry too. Sorry that the last time I saw Phillip, I called him a coward. Sorry that he told me I was no longer his father. That he disowned me. My last memory of my son ... is him telling me to rot in hell."

I did not know what to say to this self-castigation, and I felt it wasn't my place to comment.

"Perhaps if your son could be remembered, sir, as a hero ... rather than as a coward..."

"Yes, yes, good point. Not much consolation, but good point."

He took another sip of his whisky.

"Did he say anything to you? After I went to see him?" he asked.

"He said..." I hesitated. I couldn't tell him how Phillip had really felt in that moment. "He said he wished he had that time again, so he could show you he wasn't a coward after all..."

That at least was the truth.

"Did he? Hmm ... well, he certainly proved *that*, and now he's dead..."

His tone was acidic but full of pain. He was obviously a proud man, and like they often say, pride comes before a fall.

He let out a heavy sigh. "If you ever have children, do right by them ... not what you think is right *for* them," he said.

"I'll try and remember that," I said.

"Thank you, for being willing to defend Phillip when his own family had abandoned him. When I had abandoned him. You might not think it, but it means a lot. I just wanted you to know that."

He fell silent, staring morosely past me, as if I wasn't there. After a few minutes, I decided to break into his reverie.

"Will that be all, sir?"

He started slightly, as if he'd forgotten that I was there.

"Yes, yes … that will be all, thank you."

I got up and saluted. Before I left the room, I glanced back. He was staring at nothing, as before. There was certainly a part of me that felt sorry for him. There was another part that said that you reap what you sow. The Air Vice-Marshal had certainly illustrated the second point very clearly.

The following day, Audrey came to collect me from the hut. There had been much discussion among M Flight about the raid and what it meant for our mission. I couldn't give them any answers.

As I stood outside drinking a brew, Tomas came up to me.

"Ah, Scottish, this a rum do, no? Like Bentley says."

He put an arm around my shoulder for a moment.

"I'm afraid so, yes," I agreed.

"Do you think…?" He eyed me speculatively.

"Do I think what?"

I knew full well what he was going to say.

"Do you think there is a spy in the squadron … another one?" Tomas had a flair for the dramatic.

I sighed and shook my head. The problem was he might possibly be right. I hoped not.

"I don't know, and I need to speak to the Marx Brothers first."

It was my diplomatic answer before he tried to rope me into another escapade.

"Well, if there is, you and me, we will find him … yes!"

"Let's not go there, shall we?" I said. The last thing I needed was another Tomas-style adventure.

"If you say so," he shrugged. "But if there is … then…"

He was nothing if not persistent, but to my immense relief, Audrey appeared and cut the conversation short.

"The Marx Brothers are here," she said.

"Oh, good, good," I replied.

"Ah, yes ... now we will see," said Tomas in ominous tones before he returned to the hut. "We will see."

At the entrance to the main building, we encountered the Marx Brothers, who were lounging against the wall smoking cigarettes.

"Ah, Flying Officer Mackennelly, good to see you," said Harpo, flicking his cigarette end to the ground and stamping it out.

"That remains to be seen," I replied.

"Still got his hackles up," remarked his colleague, following suit and extinguishing his own cigarette.

"Let's not keep Bentley waiting," I said, ignoring this.

In short order, we were seated in Bentley's office. The CO busied himself with his pipe and was soon puffing out clouds of smoke. Beside me, the Marx Brothers lit up also, and their fumes joined Bentley's in making the place smell like a pub on a Saturday night. Audrey was at her desk and couldn't quite disguise her distaste. I was probably the only one who noticed, however.

"Had a spot of bother, we hear," said Harpo as his opening gambit.

"Spot of bother!" said Bentley, becoming irascible at once. "Is that what you call it? We were raided by a squadron of Jerries and two of our planes were shot down! It's a miracle it wasn't more."

"Indeed, very regrettable," said Chico, unperturbed, taking a drag on his cigarette.

"Regrettable? What do you mean, regrettable?" said Bentley, firing up even more. "You sound as if you already knew something about it!"

"Not quite, no," said Harpo.

"Meaning what?" demanded Bentley. "I need to know if I'm looking for a spy in my blasted squadron, yet again! That raid certainly did not target us by accident."

"It won't be necessary," said Chico.

Bentley started to puff on his pipe at an alarming rate — a sure sign that he was about to explode.

"What do you mean, not necessary?" he said, keeping his temper with an effort. "Explain yourselves, please, without talking in damn riddles."

"What my colleague means is that we already know who the spy is," explained Harpo.

"What!"

Before he could say any more Bentley was up and out of his chair.

"You mean to say you know who they are? I demand to know at once! Which member of my squadron is it? Answer me, damn you!"

He brandished his pipe like a sword of Damocles, pointing the stem at Harpo, who did not appear the least bit perturbed.

"It's nobody in your squadron, I assure you," said Harpo smoothly.

"What? Right ... hmm ... oh, I see."

Now he'd been disarmed, Bentley took a few more puffs on his pipe to calm himself down then resumed his seat. His reaction to Harpo and Chico was the result of long-standing frustration on his part with the pair of them. He had not entirely forgiven them for their charade over Lawrence Calver's 'demise', aside from the fact that their presence at Banley always seemed to spell trouble.

"Sadly, it wasn't one of yours," said Chico. "It was one of ours."

"One of your spies?"

"Regrettably, yes."

"Care to elaborate further?" said Bentley, giving him a look that very much conveyed the impression that they better had do so.

"Spying is a tricky business," said Harpo.

"Even when you're sure someone is on your side, you can't always be sure," said Chico.

I was pretty certain that if they continued in this fashion Bentley would have another fit, but I held my peace.

"We have discovered a double agent," said Harpo.

"In the ministry," added Chico.

Bentley looked from one agent to the other and back again, astonished.

"How did this happen?" he said.

"How does anything happen?" Harpo replied.

"It's a mystery," said Chico.

"When I asked you for some answers, I didn't expect twenty questions!" said Bentley in a voice of icy calm.

Harpo and Chico exchanged glances and seemingly decided not to goad Bentley any further.

"The truth is we don't know. We just became aware that someone was feeding information to the Germans directly from our department," said Harpo.

"How long has this been going on?" Bentley asked him.

"We don't know," said Chico.

"There seems to be a lot that you don't know," said Bentley, looking pardonably annoyed.

"That's the business of spying, I'm afraid," said Harpo dismissively.

Bentley seemed to resign himself to their evasive behaviour, and moved the subject on to more practical considerations.

"All right, so you found out and what did you do about it?"

"We eliminated the problem," said Chico coolly.

My blood ran slightly cold at this. I had a notion that their idea of elimination was very likely a bullet to the head or something worse.

"After we got the information we wanted..." Harpo added.

That confirmed it. It was definitely something worse.

"All right, so you had a spy in your midst, and they fed information to Jerry. That's how they knew it was our squadron that carried out the raid. Am I right so far?" said Bentley.

"That's it," said Chico.

"Perfectly stated," said Harpo.

I could almost hear Bentley grinding his teeth at their continued insouciance.

"And do they know about the second mission, the Germans?" said Bentley, somehow keeping a check on his temper.

"We don't believe so," said Chico.

Bentley looked extremely unhappy at this disclosure. "You don't believe so? You don't know for sure? The fate of a team of people rests on whether you know or not!"

"Yes, we are aware of that, and that's why we're looking into it."

Bentley rolled his eyes. He'd heard enough and came to a decision.

"Well, if you aren't sure, then I'm standing down the mission until you bloody well are sure," he said.

"Perhaps that might be the best course of action," Harpo agreed.

"Perhaps? Perhaps?" Bentley was once more infuriated. "I'm not risking my pilots on perhaps. Unless you can tell me for certain that Jerry has no idea we're going to try and steal one of their planes, I will not sanction this mission any further! And you can tell that to Winston Churchill himself for all I care."

Perceiving that they had pushed Bentley to the end of his rope, Harpo assumed a more diplomatic tone.

"I'm sure there is no need for that," he said. "I will inform the War Office that the mission is on … erm … standby, pending further intelligence. In any case, we will have to review the airfield that we propose to attack, and there is a lot of coordination to be done first."

"Right," said Bentley. "You can keep me informed then."

"Indeed, we will," said Chico, getting up to go.

"You can stay, Angus," said Bentley, before I had a chance to move.

"We will be in touch," said Harpo.

"Soon," said Chico.

They left the room with alacrity, clearly not wishing to court Bentley's wrath any further. When they had gone, Bentley sighed wearily. He emptied his pipe, scraped the bowl and refilled it with studious attention. Then he lit it and sat back in his chair.

"Those two will be the death of me," he said. "Absolute bloody scoundrels, the pair of them. Beating around the bush, never giving a straight answer to anything. God knows I'm glad I never decided to work in Intelligence. How we ever get anything sensible out of them I have no idea. A couple of blasted comedians, that's what they are."

Having vented his spleen about the Marx Brothers, he seemed satisfied.

"All right, well, as we don't know how long these chaps will take, your flight can get back to active duty. You can start tomorrow. We've got enough spare planes. You can make up a second smaller flight and start running patrols separately to Judd. If, and only if, those goons come back with something more positive, we will restart the mission," he said in a more reasonable tone.

"Sir," I replied.

"Good, then be off with you. I've got work to do."

He was smiling when he said it, and I was glad not to be thought guilty by association with the Marx Brothers. I had to privately agree with Bentley that they were a most frustrating pair.

Angelica came and found me after I left Bentley's office.

"You look tired," she said, taking in my demeanour.

"The Marx Brothers are enough to tire anyone out," I replied with a laugh.

"Could you use a night away?"

"With you?"

"Who else?" Her eyes were dancing.

"Yes, why not?"

CHAPTER TWELVE

As it was still the afternoon, we decided to get Fred to drive us to our hotel. Angelica went to obtain dispensation to take the afternoon off, and I headed for the dispersal hut to stand the flight down for the evening before we left. There would be questions, and I had to answer them.

"I've got some news," I said to the assembled flight.

"Aye, aye, Skipper, what's the crack?" said Jonty.

"Let the man speak," Willie admonished him.

"Am I stopping him?"

"All right," I interrupted them before they could start arguing. "None of this can go any further, but we now have some information from MI6 about the raid yesterday."

They all listened patiently while I gave them a brief rundown of the situation.

"Well, I'm blowed," said Arjun.

"Ha, I knew this would be the case," said Tomas triumphantly.

I forbore to remind him he'd said it was a spy in our squadron rather than MI6. I was rather glad it wasn't our squadron.

"Does that mean we're back on active duty?" asked Jean.

"We will run routine patrols when asked to do so. We will continue to stay in our flight, and I'll be leading it," I said.

"And if one of us is killed?" asked Arjun.

"I don't know," I said. "I suppose we will have to replace them…"

There was silence. Losing a pilot would mean that a replacement wouldn't have gone through the mission training. It was a risk we had to take.

"You know what Bentley would say," said Tomas.

"What would he say?" Arjun asked him.

"He would say, 'Don't you bloody well get killed, or I will have your guts for garters.'"

There was laughter at this, and also at his remarkably accurate impression of Bentley. He was quite a good mimic.

"Be that as it may," I said, "try not to take any risks. If we have to engage the enemy, keep it tight. If they run, let them go."

"Do you really think the mission will go ahead?" asked Willie.

"I'm not entirely sure," I said. "But knowing the MI6 chaps, it is very likely."

"I'm up for it," Jonty put in.

"You always are," Willie said.

"What's the point of being a pilot if you can't shoot some Jerries?" Jonty shrugged.

Willie rolled his eyes.

"I'm standing the flight down until tomorrow," I said.

There were no more questions, so I left them to it. Fred dropped Angelica and me off at the hotel, and we decided to take a stroll before tea. There was a river nearby, and after a walk along the banks, we sat down on a convenient public bench.

"This is such bliss," said Angelica, putting her head on my shoulder.

"Yes, yes, it is," I agreed, feeling suddenly at ease with the world. "I'll be glad when the war is over; then things like this won't have to be an interlude."

"Will you?" She sat up and looked at me strangely. "I'm not sure I want it to be over, after all."

This was the last thing I expected her to say, and it broke the spell.

"What? What do you mean?"

"Well, when this war is over, and if we are married, then I suppose we'll go and live in a little house somewhere and I'll become the little woman at home while you go out to work…"

She put her hand up to her mouth as if she'd said too much.

"Damn it," she said. "I didn't mean to tell you…"

"Is that what you think?" I interrupted her.

"Yes … it is. I'm sorry…"

"Well, go on. Now you've started, tell me the rest."

She regarded me for a moment before coming to a decision. "Well, then I suppose, you know… I'll have dinner ready, get your slippers while you read the paper, and sit there meekly like a good wife should."

I laughed at the picture she had painted. "Sounds rather nice," I said, smiling. "Though I can't imagine you sitting meekly."

She didn't take the joke. "Oh, stop being horrid. I don't want *that*. I don't want to become … a … a Miss Nobody," she said vehemently.

"You wouldn't be a Miss Nobody. You'd be a Mrs Mackennelly," I said, still with a slightly teasing tone.

"Oh, you always laugh at me, make fun of me. You don't understand at all how I feel. That's why I didn't want to tell you!"

I was contrite at once. "I don't always do that, do I?"

"No, all right, but you are doing it now. I'm being serious, and you're not listening."

"Did I say I wasn't listening?" I demanded, somewhat nettled, although she was right — I had been teasing her when I should have been paying attention.

"Stop it, stop answering everything with another question as if I'm stupid. I'm not stupid, and I'm not your *little* woman!" she said furiously.

Things had escalated once more.

"I never said you were."

I moved to put my arms around her, hoping to mend things, but I had severely underestimated the strength of her feelings.

"Don't touch me! I told you before, I don't want you to touch me when I'm angry," she shot at me, her eyes flashing.

"Okay..." I said and backed off.

"I don't want to get married," she said, pursing her lips.

"You don't?"

"No."

I was taken aback. I didn't know how to answer her or allay her fears, but I tried.

"How about if I tell you, it won't be like that for us?"

She shook her head. "But it will. The war will be over. Men will come back from the war and take back their jobs. Women like me will be relegated to being second-class citizens like we always were. We'll end up just like my mother and father."

"It doesn't have to be that way," I said.

"But it will be, no matter what you say..." Her voice broke slightly.

"So, you don't believe me, even if I promise you?"

"No, I don't."

She was adamant, and I knew better than to argue with her. At least she had finally been honest with me, not that it really helped.

"All right." I sighed and capitulated. "We won't get married, then. We'll remain as we are. Is that better?"

She nodded.

"Can I hug you now?"

She nodded again and I took her in my arms. Then without warning, she burst into tears. I held her while she cried against my shoulder. She had probably been holding all this in for a very long time. I had to admit I had not thought much beyond marriage or what would happen after the war. It seemed as if I would need to, if she was ever to be reassured. What would I do after the war? Remain in the Air Force? Get demobbed? I didn't know.

After a while, she stopped crying and sat up.

"I'm sorry, darling. It doesn't mean I don't love you," she said in a small voice. "Just because I can't marry you."

"It's all right, but can we … stay engaged?"

"Yes, of course."

It looked like it was going to be a long engagement after all. We walked back to the hotel in silence. Angelica kept looking up at me as if she was afraid of what I might think of her now. She obviously felt very deeply on the subject. I had to be willing to listen to her fears and respond to them somehow. I put the issue to the back of my mind, hoping to talk to Gordon.

That night she was more loving and passionate than ever. It was as if she was trying to make up for what she'd said.

"I'm sorry," she whispered, as we lay together in the dark and she nestled in the crook of my arm.

"Don't be sorry. I needed to know how you feel."

"Even though it might hurt you?"

"You haven't hurt me," I said. "Or changed my feelings."

"I was beastly to you…"

"Look," I said. "I love you and I will always love you, no matter what."

"I love you too."

We were due to return to Banley the next morning. At breakfast, Anglica was unusually quiet.

"What's up?" I asked as I ate a plate of eggs on toast.

"I just hope you're not angry," she said, putting down her knife and fork.

"About what?"

"About what I said last night, and why I can't marry you."

"No, of course not. I'd be quite a damnable cad if I was," I said.

"Well, you're certainly not a cad," she said with a mischievous smile.

"Meaning?"

"I'll tell you later…" She leaned over and kissed me.

Gordon picked us up in the jeep. Angelica resumed her usual sunny mood, laughing and joking with him. When we got to Banley, I kissed her before she went to the comms room.

"You're everything to me, everything," she whispered. "Don't ever forget it."

"Was that what you wanted to tell me?"

"Yes."

Then she was gone. I watched her go, while Gordon lit up a cigarette and studiously looked the other way. I lingered for a moment longer, pondering the events of the previous night.

"Is everything all right, sir?" he enquired in his perceptive way.

"Sort of," I said. "At least I have an answer about … you know … though not exactly the one I was expecting…"

"Ah, indeed."

A trail of smoke made its way skyward in the still air.

"Yes, we'll make a date for Annie's soon and I will enlighten you."

"I'll look forward to it."

I wanted to discuss things with him. He could usually shed some light onto the things I felt unable to fathom.

I nodded and went to the hut, leaving him to finish his cigarette and muse on the world at large.

Not long afterwards, we received orders to run a patrol, just M Flight. Bentley was as good as his word, and we were not going to be off the hook. Angelica brought the sheet of paper with the orders and handed it to me wordlessly.

"What's the crack, Skipper?" said Jonty as I read them.

"We're to go up the Channel, north of Southend…"

"Again? How many more times?"

"More times than you'll have hot dinners, I should imagine," said Willie unsympathetically.

"There's a fair bit of shipping going up that way," said Arjun. "At least that's what I've heard, anyway."

"Oh well, nothing to be done about it," added Jean.

"No," I said.

"Well, I don't like it. That's our unlucky run," said Jonty. "I've said it before, and I'll say it again…"

Angelica's hand stole into mine, and she shot me an anxious glance.

"I'm pretty sure you haven't," said Willie at once.

"I am damn sure I have."

"Well, I haven't heard you."

"Well, I have…"

"All right, all right," I intervened. "Airborne in fifteen minutes, chaps, so let's get ourselves sorted."

Willie and Jonty broke off arguing and started laughing instead. They elected to have a final brew and I spent a few moments with Angelica. Shortly afterwards we headed for our kites.

Angelica said farewell in her customary fashion.

"Come back safe," she whispered with a parting kiss.

"I will."

The black Spitfires had been put in the hangar for the time being, and we'd been given some camouflage Mark Vs to use instead. I was glad they were Vs, since this model could just about hold its own against a Focke-Wulf.

"M Flight, form up," I said as we left the ground behind us. Angelica watched us go, before returning to her post.

We flew the familiar route to Southend, dipped our wings at the Navy and headed out to the middle of the Channel. Then we turned north.

It was a sunny day, and quite warm. Had we not been on the lookout for enemy fighters at every second, it might even have been quite pleasant. As it was, we had to be constantly on the alert and scanning the skies. Once we got parallel with Cromer, we'd turn back for home. It seemed routine, but nothing was routine anymore. Death could come from any direction once you were airborne.

Below us, the sea was pretty calm with the odd fleck of white disturbing the blue. A convoy of Navy ships was heading north, and we passed over them. It was much the same for them, I mused. They would be expecting an attack from below and we were watching out for attacks from above. German U-boats had been having a field day with our convoys by all accounts. I couldn't think which was worse, being shot down or drowning in the ocean. I decided I'd rather die in a blaze of glory if I had to than sink into the icy depths.

I snapped myself back to the task at hand as a flicker in the distance caught my eye. The sun was flashing off the canopy of an approaching aircraft. I made out several more. It was Jerry, right on cue.

"Bandits, three o'clock," I said. "Break, M Flight, break. Let's look lively."

We peeled off and headed for the fray. It was better to engage than wait for them to come to us. They didn't show any sign of backing off in any case.

We were soon within range of each other. They were Focke-Wulfs, but at least there were only six, so we were evenly matched. Except with these planes, the odds were always in their favour.

I picked one out and went on the attack, throttling up as I did so. There was nothing for it but to take them head-on. The Focke-Wulf turned towards me and fired off a burst before flipping away. I gave chase, and he led me a merry dance. These planes were nimble, and very difficult to draw a bead on. However, despite that, I was sticking doggedly to him.

The radio chatter was punctuated by Jonty's 'hallooing' and general warnings to each other to 'watch out'.

I fired at the Focke-Wulf a couple of times, but he was too quick. Each time he moved tantalisingly into my sights, and then as soon as I squeezed the trigger he wasn't there anymore.

"Damn you, stay still!" I heard Jonty say in exasperation as he tried to chase one of the planes down. He was having no more luck than me.

"Look out, Jean," said Tomas suddenly. "There is one behind you."

"I've got him," said Arjun, trying to intercept.

A quick glance showed me Jean's plane being actively pursued. The Jerry fired at him several times, and he just about evaded it each time. There was one burst of tracers which looked as though it had hit home, but Jean's plane didn't go down. I assumed he had got lucky. Arjun's persistence paid off.

"Got you!" he said at last. A burst from his guns hit the pursuing Jerry across his wing. The German flicked his plane away, and the Focke-Wulfs broke off the attack. It didn't seem as if they were that serious about it anyway.

"Let's go home," I said, watching the specks dwindle into the distance. "Form up."

The Focke-Wulfs had left intact, and fortunately so had we.

"That was a bit of a damp squib," said Jonty as we headed for Banley.

"So sorry none of us got shot down," said Willie. "We'll try harder next time."

"Don't you two ever stop?" Arjun cut in.

"I'll stop if he does," said Jonty.

"Chance would be a fine thing," Willie shot back.

The banter continued until, thankfully, we landed. I jumped down from my kite just in time to hear a shout from Jonty.

"Jean, I say, your leg — you're bleeding!"

I looked at Jean and his trouser leg was indeed soaked with blood. I ran over to him as he started to keel over.

"Quick, let's get him to the medical facility," I said.

Four of us picked him up and carried him as fast as we could to the medical unit. Doctor Vivek Ramachandran came outside, tutting at the sight. We put Jean on the bed in the treatment room and one of the nurses shooed us all out.

"Come back later. I'll let you know how he is," said the doctor.

With that, we had to be content. The others dispersed, but I hung around outside the hut. Angelica appeared shortly afterwards with a mug of tea.

"You're a lifesaver," I told her.

"What happened?" she asked, handing me the mug.

"I don't know. He must have been hit, unbeknownst to us," I said.

"I'm glad it wasn't you," she whispered. "Is that wrong of me?"

"No, I'm glad it wasn't me too."

She laughed. It seemed callous, but whenever someone died or got injured, it was natural to feel glad that this time you were spared. We all wondered if somewhere out there was a bullet, or a bomb, with our name on it, and we had just not met it yet.

Bentley arrived along with Audrey while I was sipping my tea.

"What's occurred, Angus?" he demanded.

"We encountered six Focke-Wulfs, sir, and somehow Jean got shot in the leg. I'm not sure how bad it is."

"I see."

He frowned and took out his pipe. He lit it and started to puff on it methodically.

"Well, let's hope it doesn't keep him from flying," he said philosophically.

I said nothing. If Jean couldn't fly, we'd be a man down. How would that affect our mission, let alone anything else?

It wasn't long at all before Doctor Vivek came out of the medical facility.

"Ah, a delegation, how nice," he said affably.

"What's the situation?" Bentley asked.

"I'm afraid your man has sustained quite a serious bullet wound in his leg; he's lucky it wasn't worse."

Bentley's face fell. "Oh, oh dear."

"He'll be off active duty for some time," said Dr Vivek. "I might need to transfer him to the local hospital so they can take a look at it."

"All right, I see," said Bentley, not looking happy at all.

"He lost some blood but said he hadn't felt anything. Probably due to the adrenaline during combat."

"Can we see him?" I asked the doctor.

"Yes, but not for long, mind."

"You go, Angus. Give him my regards," said Bentley. "Best he doesn't have too many people at once."

In the treatment room, Jean was lying on the bed with his leg heavily bandaged.

"Sorry, Scottish," he said, looking contrite. "I caught one, I'm afraid."

"Can't be helped," I said. "And it could have been worse."

We both knew he could be dead instead of injured.

"The doc says I'll fly again, but not for a while."

"Yes, you need to do what he says," I told him.

"What about the mission?"

"I don't know," I said with a shrug. It was the least of my worries compared to the life of one of my pilots.

"I let you down…" He trailed off.

"Enough of that talk. Do what the doctor says. If there's anything you need, I'll arrange it."

"I'm fine. I just feel a bit weak."

"Take it easy," I told him. "Bentley sends his regards."

I stayed a while longer and then went outside again. Angelica was still there, but Bentley was gone.

"I'd better go and tell the chaps," I said.

"I'll come with you."

She slipped her hand into mine, and we headed for the hut.

The following morning, predictably I found myself in Bentley's office. Audrey had collected me as soon as I arrived at Banley. He was in the middle of his pipe ritual, so I waited, watching him tamp the tobacco into the bowl, and then light it up. He puffed away for a few moments, savouring the tobacco. I listened to Audrey typing and she kept her head down as usual.

"Lifesaver, this pipe," Bentley remarked. "Keeps me sane."

I nodded and he smiled. I supposed most of us had some kind of talisman, and this was his.

"Jean's been transferred to the hospital," he said. "So he's off duty for a while. I spoke to Vivek about it earlier, and he seems confident he'll return to active duty."

"All right," I said. "What about the mission?"

He grimaced. "Yes, the mission. Well, ordinarily I would say I'll give you another pilot and you can train him up, but I've had a phone call from those blasted spies, and they will be down here in a couple of days."

He puffed out more smoke, looking agitated at the thought of the Marx Brothers arriving in our midst once more.

"And you know what *that* means," he continued.

"The mission is on?"

He nodded. "That's what I think, yes."

"But we've only five planes," I protested.

"I know…" He trailed off.

"You told them?"

"Oh, I told them." He sighed heavily, and puffed even more vigorously on his pipe.

"I suppose they are not inclined to call it off or postpone it."

"No, I am afraid not."

"I see."

I relapsed into silence. The mission was difficult enough with six planes, but one less? Two days wasn't enough to get any pilot up to speed on the strafing. We'd done many practice runs to become that accurate.

"If you want me to take it further," he said, "I'm ready to do so."

He meant escalate it up the chain of command, for all the good it would do.

"Let me talk to the chaps and see if we think we can still do it," I said.

"All right. Let me know in short order."

He sat thoughtful for a few moments longer.

"In the meantime, we'll have that funeral service for Charlton, and you can stop flying sorties. I can't afford to lose any more pilots, and I shouldn't have put you up there yesterday in the first place."

"It's not your fault, sir…" I began.

"Yes, it is, Angus. It's very much my fault," he said, pointing the stem of his pipe at me. "But it can't be helped."

I was sure he was under many competing pressures, and I had no idea what duties the squadron was being asked to fulfil. How could he refuse, anyway? Bentley was a man of integrity, however, and felt every setback very keenly.

"I'll go and talk to M Flight," I said.

"Yes."

I got up to go and he turned his attention to the papers on his desk.

As it turned out, the rest of the team were not averse to going with five planes, in spite of my misgivings.

"We can still do this, Skipper," said Jonty optimistically.

"What do you reckon, Kiwi?" I asked Willie.

"In for a penny," he shrugged.

Jonty looked triumphant.

"All right, I'm agreeing with you this time," said Willie. "But it doesn't mean you can start up with the ballads."

"I never mentioned ballads," Jonty protested.

"Arjun, what are your thoughts?" I said, intervening before they started an argument. I also wanted to make sure everyone had their say.

"Well," said Arjun, after considering things for a moment. "It obviously shortens the odds, but even with five planes, we should be able to destroy the Focke-Wulfs. Maybe we can get in some practice, though?"

"Good idea," I said.

"There is a saying in my country," said Tomas. "Luck favours the brave ones. So, I say, let us just do it and be brave."

"By Jove, yes," agreed Jonty at once.

"Luck favours the foolish in your case," remarked Willie wryly.

"I say…" said Jonty, then stopped as he probably recalled some of his more foolhardy actions.

"All right," I said. "It seems that we're game for it, so I'll inform Bentley. In the meantime, Arjun has the right of it: we need to get in some practice. I'll talk to Techie and get things in motion."

Bentley greeted the information that M Flight was ready to fly the mission with equanimity. I set up the strafing practice for the next day, and then sought out Gordon while Angelica wasn't around.

He was in his jeep having a smoke and smiled as I approached.

"Is it Annie's time?" he said, divining my intention.

"Yes, I rather think it is."

Within a short while, we were sitting in Annie's tearoom with the customary tea and crumpets. I ladled butter and jam onto one while it was hot, and Gordon did likewise.

"You implied you had some news, sir," said Gordon after we'd both consumed one crumpet each. He busied himself with the next.

"Yes, Angelica finally told me why she doesn't want to marry me," I said.

"I'm all ears," said Gordon, taking a sip of tea.

I furnished him with an account of what had passed between me and Angelica, and he listened attentively. When I had finished, he took a bite of his second crumpet and chewed on it meditatively.

"She has a point," he said at length.

"A point?"

"Yes, after all, what she says may well be true. While the war is on women are being drafted into all kinds of jobs, but when the men return after the war, the forces won't be able to afford to keep them all on, so they'll want their jobs back."

"Yes, I see," I said.

I had not thought about it much. Since I was the son of a laird, it probably wouldn't have occurred to me.

"Your fiancée is a remarkably perceptive young woman," he continued. "She has seen her horizons, which were hitherto blocked to a large extent, opening up with new opportunities. Imagine being let out of a cage… You wouldn't want to go back, sir, would you?"

I was struck by his reasoning. "Yes, yes, I see."

Gordon continued to expand on his theme. "Think of it this way, sir. Women have had to fight for all they've got — the vote, the right to work and more. So, for someone of the calibre of your fiancée, the prospect of languishing at home isn't one she relishes."

He returned his attention to his crumpet and finished it off. I did likewise.

"Now you put it that way, it makes a lot of sense."

He inclined his head. Gordon had a knack for seeing both sides of an argument.

"The war has changed many things; I'm not sure they'll ever go back to the way they were."

I poured out two more cups of tea. I mused on the fact that a mind like his seemed wasted in the role he had allotted himself.

"So, what do I do about it?" I asked him.

"Wait for her to resolve her misgivings," he said. "In her own time."

This wasn't the solution I'd hoped to hear.

"But what if that takes a lifetime?"

He laughed. "I very much doubt it will, sir. Given what she's gone through to get you, I doubt she's going to let you go so easily. She just needs time to make her own decision about the future."

I sighed. "I suppose I might have guessed you would say something like that."

"Marriage is made of compromises," he said. "That's why I've not married, at least not yet. I'm not very good at compromising."

I lapsed into silence and drank my tea. Gordon lit up a cigarette and smoked it contentedly.

"But I can't predict the future," I said. "I can't say what will happen to us when the war is over. I can't give her the promises she seems to want because I simply don't know."

"You don't have to." He smiled. "She'll come around in her own time. She'll make her own plan, have no fear."

"Will that plan include me?" I asked with interest.

"Undoubtedly, sir."

I shook my head. Angelica was more strong-willed than me, and she probably always would be. Gordon's words were reassuring, nevertheless. I paid the bill and we returned to Banley.

Angelica found me shortly afterwards.

"Were you out with Fred?" she asked.

"Yes."

"At the tearoom?"

I nodded.

"And do you feel better now?" she said.

"I do."

I didn't ask her how she had worked out I needed to talk to Gordon; she seemed to just know.

"Then kiss me."

"That seems to be your answer for everything," I teased.

"It's like tea, a cure for all ills."

CHAPTER THIRTEEN

The strafing practice sessions proved fruitful, and I began to feel hopeful that the mission might be successful after all. Even with five planes, it seemed as if we should be able to pull it off.

A day later, Bentley assembled the squadron for the funeral service for Phillip. It was unusual to hold such an event, but I supposed that Bentley wanted to expunge the stain of cowardice from the squadron. Honouring Phillip's courage was a way of ensuring he would be remembered as a hero through his selfless act.

It was arranged for his remains to be buried at the local church. The coffin was processed into the church for a brief service. This was attended by Air Vice-Marshal Charlton and Phillip's brother, Flying Officer Maxwell Charlton, as well as the pilots, and others, from the Mavericks. A guard of honour preceded the coffin. It was borne up the aisle and set in front of the altar.

The local priest said a few words, as did the squadron chaplain, and then Bentley got up to speak.

"We are here to particularly honour Pilot Officer Charlton," he said.

Angelica sat beside me in the pews up at the front, as did Audrey. I wondered if Bentley was missing his pipe, since he couldn't smoke it in the church.

"Pilot Officer Phillip Charlton came fresh to our squadron, and as we all know he experienced some difficulties regarding combat. However, I'm not going to dwell on those."

This was his way of glossing over the cowardice and moving on to the more fruitful topic of Phillip's heroics.

"Whatever he may or may not have done," said Bentley, "there can be no doubt that Charlton died a hero. No doubt at all."

He glanced sternly around the congregation as if daring any of us to deny it.

"It was Napoleon Bonaparte who once said, 'True heroism consists in being superior to the ills of life, in whatever shape they may challenge us to combat.' That is perhaps what is demanded of a pilot in the RAF: being superior to the ills of life. And we are certainly faced with an ill. The ill of the scourge of Hitler's Third Reich across the Channel. The ill of war and all that it entails. All of us here are faced with the daily challenges of combat in the air, and this squadron has always risen to that challenge.

"And so it was, when this squadron was subjected to a potentially deadly attack by the Luftwaffe, we rose to the challenge. In the thick of it was Pilot Officer Charlton. He shot down one of the attacking Focke-Wulfs, a feat in itself as all of us know. However, not content with that, and out of ammo, he deliberately flew his plane into another enemy fighter in order to save the life of a fellow pilot. He sacrificed his own life without hesitation, and in that moment showed true courage. The courage we have come to expect from pilots in the Mavericks."

Bentley paused. The church was silent, absorbing the weight of his words. I looked over at Audrey, who was crying silent tears. Angelica had slipped her hand into her friend's hand and squeezed it gently to comfort her.

"So, we shall remember Pilot Officer Charlton as having exhibited courage in the face of the enemy at the expense of his life. He will be remembered as a hero. May he rest in peace."

It was a short speech but to the point and nicely put. Bentley stood down from the podium, and the priest led us in prayer. Phillip's father did not speak, and neither did his brother.

The coffin was processed out of the church to the grave. The squadron flag was taken from the coffin, ceremoniously folded up and handed to Air Vice-Marshal Charlton. The coffin was then lowered into the grave, and three volleys were fired over the grave by the accompanying escort. The last post was sounded by a bugler, and then the priest said the last rites. After this, the funeral party broke up.

While I was standing with Angelica, waiting for the others to depart, Bentley came up to us. He was smoking his pipe with some satisfaction at finally being able to do so.

"That all went rather well," he said, puffing away.

"Yes, sir, good speech by the way."

"Hmm, yes, well, you know, sometimes we need to show publicly what this squadron's made of..." He trailed off with a smile on his face.

He had achieved the result he wanted. There would be no medal for Phillip, but his memory would not bear the mark of cowardice. I felt that alone would have been important to Phillip.

I spotted Maxwell walking towards us, and Bentley excused himself. Phillip's brother looked very much like an older version of Phillip.

"Flying Officer Mackennelly?" he said with a smile.

"Yes."

"I'm Maxwell. I just wanted to say thanks. Thanks for defending Phillip."

"I did what I felt was right and I'm sorry for your loss," I replied diplomatically.

He seemed to hesitate for a moment, as if he wanted to say something more.

"I always loved my brother," he said. "Even though he probably thought I didn't. I wish I'd done more for him. He had a raw deal."

I suspected he meant from his father, but didn't want to articulate that thought.

"He never said a bad word about you," I told him truthfully.

"Well, that's good to know. Anyway, what's done is done. I will miss him, you know."

I reached into my pocket and pulled out Phillip's notebook. I had brought it with me, thinking I would give it to his father, but his brother seemed a more worthy recipient. I held it out to him.

"You might like this," I said. "Phillip wrote some things in it while he was under arrest."

Maxwell took it and shot me a keen glance.

"Did you read it?" he asked.

"No," I told him. I genuinely had not. I was tempted, but I felt that Phillip's private thoughts should be left to his family.

"I wouldn't have blamed you if you had," he said, with a smile. "But thank you."

I nodded. There wasn't much else to say. He had been notable by his absence when Phillip was in trouble. Hindsight was a wonderful thing.

"Thanks again, for all you did," he said when I offered nothing further.

He shook my hand and walked away. I watched him go, wondering how he really felt, and how much their father was responsible for their seeming estrangement.

I took a stroll with Angelica. Some of the chaps had repaired to the pub, but I wasn't in the mood.

"I hope I never have to come here on your account," she said as we walked.

"I hope not too," I replied.

"The mission will be soon, won't it?"

"Yes, I believe so."

"I wish it wasn't," she said quietly.

I held her hand tighter, since there was nothing I could say.

The following day the Mosquito returned. They had left after the first mission, and now that the second was imminent they were ordered back. Shortly afterwards a Lysander landed at the airfield too. This was carrying the pilot for the Focke-Wulf and would take him to the target for the drop-off.

I went out to greet them and was joined by the others, who were curious to see the newcomers. Angelica appeared at my side and slipped her hand into mine. She would know they had landed from the comms traffic.

Two pilots ambled up to us, leaving the squat Westland Lysander behind them. It was a rugged aircraft, and these had been used for reconnaissance and supply drops, as well as artillery spotting. However, the versatile aircraft was increasingly deployed to drop and recover agents from France. The Lysander pilot introduced himself. He was tall, fair-haired, in his late twenties and sporting a moustache.

"I'm supposed to report to Flying Officer Mackennelly," he said, surveying our little group.

"That's me," I told him, stepping forward.

"Flying Officer Frank Jameson," he said, holding out his hand.

I shook it. He indicated his fellow pilot, a slightly shorter man around thirty, also fair-haired and with piercing blue eyes.

"This is Flying Officer Jarek Gorski," he informed us. "He's to fly the Wulf."

"Welcome," I said, shaking his hand also.

"Thank you, I am glad to be here."

Gorski spoke excellent English, though his accent was quite pronounced.

I introduced them to the rest of the team. Tomas immediately fell in with Jarek, both being from a similar part of the world. There followed an animated conversation between them while they were ushered by the others back to our hut.

I hung back with Angelica and watched them go.

"Do you think he can really fly the Focke-Wulf?" she asked me.

"So the Marx Brothers tell me," I replied.

"I suppose we'll have to take their word for it," she said acidly. Nothing those two told us could be taken as gospel and we both knew it.

"Yes ... because we don't have any choice."

"Come on, I suppose you should join the others. I can't monopolise you all the time," she said, smiling.

I stifled a quip; we engaged in quite a bit of banter, but sometimes it backfired.

"Yes," I said instead, wanting to be diplomatic.

"Yes, meaning you think I *am* monopolising you?" she teased as we walked to the hut.

"I didn't say that."

"Oh, so you *want* me to monopolise you?"

"I didn't say that either!" I said, exasperated.

She laughed and broke off baiting me. After about half an hour during which I chatted to the newcomers, Audrey arrived.

"Bentley's called a briefing," she said. "With the Marx Brothers."

"Oh, they're here, are they?" I sighed, although it was inevitable. Their presence brought the reality of the mission ever closer.

"Yes, I'm afraid so."

"All right. I'll gather the crew."

Shortly afterwards, we were all sitting expectantly in the mission room. Bentley bowled in with Audrey and the Marx Brothers. He immediately took out his pipe and lit it. While we waited for him to speak, the Marx Brothers took out a couple of cigarettes and did likewise. The three of them were like a smoker's convention.

"I'm sure you've been expecting this," said Bentley after puffing away for a few moments. "The second mission is officially on, and the MI6 chaps here are going to brief you. I know you're missing one of your pilots, but Angus here assures me you're ready to go with five planes, and so that's what we'll do."

He moved back to allow the Marx Brothers to continue. Harpo took one more drag on his cigarette before stepping forward with his colleague.

"Mission Two of Operation Sunrise," he said, "will take place in three days' time."

"We will hand out precise timings on the day," said Chico, taking up the refrain. "But suffice to say it will run in a similar fashion to Mission One but to a different airfield, for obvious reasons."

He put his cigarette to his lips and the end glowed as he took a pull on it, waiting for Harpo to continue.

"The Lysander will drop Flying Officer Gorski near the airfield in question, and the local resistance will get him to the target. M Flight will hit the target at dawn and obliterate all the planes bar one. That will be the one that Gorski will take," said Harpo.

"All things being equal," said Chico, continuing, "Gorski will take off and bring the plane back to England, under your escort. You will, of course, have the Hurricane squadron escorting you there and back. In addition, due to the importance of this mission, a second squadron will scramble to rendezvous on your return trip, providing extra cover. This should reassure you as to the priority attached to this mission by the War Office and the chain of command."

I was rather pleased to hear this, and Angelica flashed me a smile too.

"Yes," said Harpo. "You need to get that Focke-Wulf back to our shores intact at all costs. A lot of people are counting on your success."

Harpo extinguished his cigarette and lit up another.

"Now, my colleague here will go over the location of the airfield," he said.

Chico revealed the map on the wall which had hitherto been covered up, and indicated the airfield we were to attack. It was located near Étaples just behind Le Touquet, which though on the coast was further down into French territory, thus increasing the hazardous nature of the journey. The black Spitfires carried extra fuel so that would not be a problem. I assumed that the reason for picking the field was that Jerry would think it unlikely to be prone to an attack. Getting out of there would be even tougher given the likelihood of squadrons being scrambled against us.

There were recent reconnaissance photographs for us to study too. The approach to the airfield was easy enough — straight in from the coast and it was right there. It had been a former French civilian airport by all accounts. The downside was it was very close to the town, and troops would no doubt be garrisoned nearby. We would have to be in and out as fast as we could. The Lysander had to get near enough for the pilot to be within striking distance. There were plenty of open fields at the southern end of the airfield. The Lysanders had a very short take-off and could land in small spaces. It would leave before us and drop the pilot under cover of darkness.

There was still so much that could go wrong. It was one thing to strafe some planes, but quite another to have a pilot attempt to steal one in the middle of that pandemonium. As the meeting broke up, Harpo and Chico wandered over to me.

"All ready for the fray, Flying Officer?" said Harpo amiably.

"Apart from the hundreds of things which could go awry, yes," I replied.

"Ah, optimistic as usual," said Chico with a smile.

"I'm realistic rather than optimistic," I told him.

"Have faith, old chap, have faith," said Harpo, taking a drag on his cigarette.

So far, faith with these two had got us into a lot of hot water, so I wasn't reassured.

"We'll get some more practice in," I said. "I just hope that Jarek can get that plane out of there."

"Oh, he will, never fear," said Chico. "We've absolute faith in that."

"That's what worries me," I shot back.

The two of them laughed.

"We love your sense of humour, Flying Officer," said Harpo.

"See you in a couple of days — if you need anything let us know," said Chico.

Angelica had remained silent during this exchange but once they'd gone, she shook her head.

"I'll be glad when this mission is over," she said.

I nodded. "You and me both."

Three days went by very quickly. I took M Flight out for more strafing practice, and we did a couple of navigation runs with the Mosquito to ensure that our navigation skills were fresh. I noticed that Jonty had befriended Jarek, and the two of them spent a lot of time in animated discussion.

"What's with those two?" I asked Willie as we stood drinking tea.

"I don't know, but I'm happy to enjoy the peace."

I smiled. He and Jonty spent almost all their time together, so I didn't quite believe him, but I let it pass.

"Well, what are they talking about?" I asked him.

"Oh ... planes. Particularly German planes."

"Planes?" I said, surprised. "Since when has Jonty been interested in planes?"

"Since that fellow got here, apparently," Willie said sardonically.

I couldn't imagine what Jonty and Jarek had to say to each other. Jonty had never seemed interested in planes other than flying them. However, I let them be.

The night before the mission Angelica and I stayed at our hotel. If this was our last night together, then we wanted to remember it. Passion flowed freely, as always, and we lay quietly together afterwards in the darkness.

"If you don't come back," she said softly, "I will always remember us like this."

"I've every intention of coming back," I replied.

"Yes, but if you don't..."

"Then remember that I love you more than anything in the world," I said, kissing her.

"I love you more..."

I could make out her smile in the half-light. Even at times like this, she was irrepressible. I kissed her and we were lost in each other once more.

The following morning, a briefing was called and final coordinates were issued, along with flight plans and call signs. We spent the day going over everything and then just before it was time to turn in before our early start, we assembled once again.

Bentley was in the mission room with Audrey, but the Marx Brothers were absent. I assumed they probably had nothing further to add. Bentley lit up his pipe.

"Just a few words I want to say, really," he said. "I'm not here to tell you how vital this mission is and all that flannel — you already know it. Instead, I want you to know that the most essential thing to me is that you come back. Do what you have to do and get out of there pronto. I don't need any more damn heroes. I need intact pilots able to carry on the war effort."

He puffed on his pipe for a few moments, allowing his words to sink in.

"Each of us has lived with the ups and downs of this squadron since the war started. A bloody fine squadron it is too. I'm damned if I'm going to be arranging five funerals, so make bloody sure you make it back here, and that is an order!"

To emphasise his point he brandished the stem of his pipe at us. This was a classic Bentley pep talk. I knew how deeply he cared about the people under his command.

"All right," he said. "To coin a phrase from Cole Porter in *Fifty Million Frenchmen*, I think it was, 'Do that voodoo that you do so well.' Get some sleep, good luck, Godspeed, and dismissed."

We rose as one and applauded spontaneously. In his own way, Bentley could be most inspiring. He probably hadn't wanted the Marx Brothers there so that he didn't have to toe the party line. I also didn't know he was a Cole Porter fan — it seemed you learned something new every day.

Bentley came up to me as the others were leaving the room.

"Take care, Angus," he said. "I'm sure this young lady is counting on you returning to her."

He smiled at Angelica, who nodded in affirmation.

"Yes, sir, I'll do my best."

"You'll do better than that!" he said irascibly. "And make sure that fool Butterworth doesn't do anything stupid while you're at it."

Jonty's ongoing history of escapades had not been forgotten, and Bentley never failed to bring it up at the slightest opportunity. Jonty would never live it down.

"Yes, sir."

"That's the ticket."

I returned to the hut with Angelica, and the chaps once more let us use one of the beds so we could lie together and sleep. But sleep didn't come easily, as the mission played on my mind.

"Try to sleep," she whispered. "Or you'll be no use to anyone."

"I'm trying," I whispered back.

"It will be okay. I feel it will be okay."

I kissed her and closed my eyes at last.

The hut phone sounded our wake-up call, and I was broken out of my slumber. It was time to go. We did our final preparations, and in the darkness, we went out towards our waiting planes. Angelica held me tightly to say farewell.

"Come back," she said softly.

"I will, I promise."

She kissed me then, deeply, as if it might be the last time.

"I love you," she said.

"I love you too."

She watched me go. I climbed up onto the wing of my plane. Redwood was there to ensure I was strapped in and then I fired up the prop. The roar of five Spitfires and the Mosquito split the night air. The Lysander had left earlier, needing the cover of darkness to drop Jarek at the rendezvous. I could just make out Angelica still standing in the dim glow of the runway lights as I started to taxi my kite out onto the runway.

"Viper airborne," said Gervais, as the Mosquito took off.

We had new codenames for each mission.

"Blackbirds, this is Blackbird Leader," I said. "Let's go."

I throttled up and M Flight took off in formation. We followed the set bearing and maintained the required speed. We would be joined, as usual, by the Hurricane squadron as we crossed the south coast. Their codename for the mission was Otters.

We flew directly south towards Hastings, where we'd cross the Channel on a bearing to take us to Étaples. It was a dark night with little moon, but that wouldn't last too long since dawn would soon be breaking.

Flying across the landscape at night was a different experience, and I was glad the Mosquito was ahead of us, marking the way. There were no lights to be seen at all, with all the towns in blackout. We relied on Gervais and Michael completely. Hence it was imperative to find each flare they dropped to get the right bearing for the next.

We flew over the Thames, then Rochester and Maidstone. I wondered whether people in their houses below heard us, and perhaps wondered if we were friend or foe. There was plenty of time to think on the journey, which seemed interminable at times, even though in reality it was relatively short.

"Firework dropped," said Gervais as the radio crackled briefly to life.

"Roger," I said.

Now we had to keep our eyes peeled for the flare. We were at a reasonable height, so I thought it should not be too difficult.

"Firework at two o'clock," said Jonty, who saw it first.

"Roger. Viper, we've got the firework."

"Roger, Blackbird Leader." Gervais gave us a new bearing which we would take once directly over the flare. The next flare would be dropped between Hastings and Fairlight Cove. Then there would only be one more just before the target.

A few minutes later the Mosquito dropped the last flare before we left the coast. Bang on time we left the safety of English shores and then we were over the Channel.

"Blackbird Leader, Otters are on station," said the Hurricane squadron flight leader as they joined us.

I had been watching out for them, but their planes were also black and hard to see. They seemed to be far better suited to night flying than we were.

"Roger, Otter Leader," I said.

"We're with you all the way," he replied cheerfully.

"Thanks, much appreciated."

We lapsed once more into silence. The dark water flashed by below us. Over to the east, the sky was starting to go grey — sunrise wasn't far away. By that time, we'd be over the target. I wondered if Jarek was in position by now, and hoped he was. There was no way for him to tell us and just like the Marx Brothers had said, we had to take it on faith.

I began to make out the French coastline up ahead. It was time to drop down lower.

"Blackbirds, descend to approach height," I said, pushing the stick forward. I took the Spitfire as low as I dared, and the others followed suit. I could see them flanking me on either side in an uneven arrowhead.

My pulse began to quicken as we got closer. All of the practice would come down to just a few minutes of intense action.

"Blackbirds, dropping the last firework, then it's all yours to Trafalgar Square," said Gervais.

That was the codename for the target. Jarek was Weasel One. I didn't know how they picked these names, and wondered if they simply drew them out of a hat. They had to be different each time to confuse any enemy monitoring our transmissions.

"Roger," I said.

"Firework to your two o'clock," said Otter Leader.

"Roger, got it."

This was it. The flare was dropped just south of a coastal town called Saint-Cécile Plage and then we would turn due south and follow the beach to an estuary inlet. Directly to the right of that would be the airfield.

I could feel the adrenaline kicking in as we sped over the extensive tract of beach. As we went lower it made everything seem that much faster.

"Blackbirds, attack position," I said, taking the Spitfire down as close to the ground as I dared. The sand was now really flashing underneath us, and I just hoped to God that Jarek was ready because it was now or never.

"Otters breaking off — we'll be waiting," said Otter Leader.

They would circle a little way off while we strafed the airfield. We had prepared as best we could, but there was no substitute for the sight of the actual target. Then instinct and training would take over.

We barrelled up the estuary, and I could see the airfield and runway ahead on our right. If I had been religious, I would have said a prayer, but instead, I thought of Angelica. I had one aim: to get the job done and get back home to her.

"This is it, Blackbirds. It's Trafalgar Square. Stand by," I said, slipping off the safety on my trigger.

Dead ahead now were the Focke-Wulfs all lined up on the ground and with unsuspecting German pilots hopefully asleep in their beds. I turned a little to the left and then back towards the planes to approach them at an angle.

"Leave the front one," I said. "Take the rest."

The sun was rising, and suddenly the silent waiting planes were bathed in its light. This was the start of the golden hour. Some might say God was smiling on us. If there was a God, I hoped he was. On any other day, this would have been an amazing sight, but not today. There was no more time to admire the view.

"Fire," I said, giving the order and simultaneously pressing the trigger.

Instantly the guns and cannons roared from all five Spitfires, kicking up the runway and cutting a swathe of destruction across the Focke-Wulfs. Several planes caught fire as we passed over them. I could see that the one in front was fortunately still intact, but there were also more at the back of the line untouched. We needed to destroy those too.

"Let's go again. Take the rest," I said, banking sharply.

As one we flew in on the attack once more and thundered out our deadly message. The remaining planes exploded. So far, we'd taken Jerry by surprise. There was no answering ack-ack, but I doubted this would pertain for long. No doubt the airfield had anti-aircraft guns, but even a normal rifle could hit us at the height we were. We crossed over the line of burning planes and circled again. There was no sign of Jarek.

"Where's Weasel One?" I said, concerned.

We still had ammo, which was good, but if Jarek wasn't able to take the remaining Focke-Wulf, we were sunk. I wondered if he'd made it after all when Arjun shouted, unable to keep the excitement out of his voice.

"There he is! I see him!"

I was relieved to see a figure running full pelt towards the Focke-Wulf. We circled again, watching him with bated breath. Was he going to make it? For a moment, I was sure of it. Then suddenly I wasn't.

"There's a bandit, on the ground!" shouted Willie.

A jeep was hurtling towards him and a German soldier standing and firing at him.

"Take it down!" I yelled, but Tomas was already on it.

He swooped down, guns blazing. The jeep exploded in flames, but it was too late. Jarek had been hit. His body lay unmoving on the runway.

"The Weasel is down," said Willie.

I reacted immediately. This was exactly what I had dreaded, and now it had happened.

"Damn and blast it!" I swore in frustration. "Abort the mission, abort," I said at once. "Let's destroy that last plane."

All of this effort, and it was all for nothing. We took another circuit around but now I was concerned we got out quickly. If one lot of Jerries had turned up, more would surely follow.

"Skipper, wait. Don't shoot the plane," said Jonty, breaking out of our formation. "I have an idea."

"Blackbird Two, what the hell are you doing?" I shouted.

Without warning, Jonty's plane was on an approach to land on the runway. I could hardly believe it.

"Pull up, Blackbird Two, pull up now!"

But Jonty wasn't in a listening mood.

"I've got this, Skipper," he said. "Weasel told me how to fly the plane. I can do it!"

"You are insane! Will you pull up!" I said despairingly.

"Sorry, Skipper, it has to be done. We're not leaving empty-handed," said Jonty with determination.

There was nothing for it but to go to his aid.

"Cover him, for God's sake," I said to the others as we broke formation too.

"I'm taking the ack-ack," said Tomas, flying towards a gun emplacement and opening fire.

In the meantime, Willie flew at the airfield tower and raked it with gunfire. All of this would help provide a distraction. Jonty was committed to his folly, and we had to back him up.

Fortunately, he had landed his Spitfire unscathed and taxied it into position beside the Focke-Wulf. Then he jumped down from the cockpit and ran for the German plane. Shortly afterwards, to my immense relief, he got inside it. Now all he had to do was get it off the ground.

We were still circling, and in the distance, I could see a large number of army trucks approaching the airfield, not to mention soldiers now streaming from the main building. Jerry had finally got their act together.

Arjun swooped down and let loose a barrage. The soldiers dived for cover.

"Come on, Jonty, come on!" I said, knowing he could not hear me.

The longer we stayed there, the more likely all of us were going to die. If he was going to steal the plane after all, then he needed to get airborne for all our sakes.

The propeller of the Focke-Wulf started to turn, and then it sprang to life. Jonty had done it.

Thankfully he started taxiing out to the runway. The Focke-Wulf gathered speed and then its wheels left the ground. It was a relief, but Jonty had given us another problem.

"Shoot the Spitfire," I said. We had to do that before we left. We couldn't leave it there intact for the Germans.

We flew back again and fired some bursts across the airfield. I hit Jonty's Spitfire and it exploded. Then tracers started to fly across my canopy. There was another ack-ack and it had opened up. I glanced over to check that Jonty was away. We had no time to lose.

"Blackbirds, let's get out of here," I said.

I wanted to get as far away from the flak as possible. We were getting shot at from all directions, but by some miracle, none of us was hit.

"Form up around Blackbird Two," I told the others.

This part at least was in the original plan to protect the Focke-Wulf and get it back to Blighty.

Jonty let us catch him up, and I flew in front of him. Willie and Arjun took one side each, with Tomas to the rear. In this fashion, I set a course for the English coast.

"Otters, we're heading home. Keep them peeled for bandits," I said.

"Wilco, Blackbird Leader. That was quite a show you put on there."

"Tell me about it," I replied.

I couldn't talk to Jonty as he wasn't on our radio frequency. Although I could cheerfully have throttled him, I couldn't believe we'd actually made it away with a Focke-Wulf. Now we just had to keep it.

One thing I had learned was never to count your chickens. I checked the skies anxiously, looking for Jerry planes. There would surely be a response. The last thing they would want is us getting away with one of their precious aircraft.

CHAPTER FOURTEEN

It was a shortish hop back to England, and I really hoped we would get there in one piece. A second Hurricane squadron met us halfway across the Channel.

"This is Greyhound Leader, joining you for the ride," said the Flight Leader of the newcomers.

"Good to have you," I said. "We've got the package."

"So I see. Greyhounds, take up escort position."

The new squadron of Hurricanes split up and settled on either side of our wings. The Otters were flying above us and, surely, we would be safe enough. One thing I could count on was that Jonty would at least keep his plane on track and not try to join in the fight if there was one.

We had flown directly north, and I could make out the land which came out to a point at Dungeness. A few minutes more and we should be clean away.

Almost right on cue, we were attacked.

"Bandits at three o'clock," said Otter Leader.

"Break, break, let's intercept," said Greyhound Leader in response.

"Stay on track, Blackbird Leader. We've got this. This is our show now — get the package home," said Otter Leader to me.

"Wilco," I responded. "Blackbirds, we keep going, no matter what."

The incoming planes were Focke-Wulfs, and it looked like one squadron if not more. They weren't going to let us steal their plane that easily after all.

The Hurricanes peeled off and headed for the fray. Soon enough the air was thick with chatter and gunfire.

"To your right, your right."

"I've got him. I'm on him."

"I'm hit, going down."

It was hard to hear this without joining in, but we had one goal and that was to get the Focke-Wulf back to Banley. We crossed the coastline, leaving the fight behind us. At least one of the Hurricanes had already been lost.

I could see Ashford over on the right, and the distance between us and the Germans was increasing at every moment. I began to hope we would make it. Just then, Tomas shouted in alarm.

"One of the bandits is breaking away. He's coming after us."

Sure enough, a Focke-Wulf was racing towards us, having left the main dogfight. This was all we needed; there was no doubt as to his intention.

"Damn it," I said. "Do you have ammo?"

"I think so, yes."

"Then take him," I told Tomas.

"Roger."

Tomas peeled off and headed for the Focke-Wulf. I hoped he would keep him occupied long enough for us to get clear. I scanned the ground but abandoned the idea of landing; it would make us more vulnerable in any case. We could only communicate with Jonty via hand signals, so that also made it awkward.

I glanced back to see how Tomas was faring. He had fired at the Focke-Wulf, but it evaded him and sped away. It was still heading for us.

"He's getting away from me!" said Tomas.

"Permission to attack," said Willie at once.

"Yes, go, and take Blackbird Four with you," I said.

This left me and Jonty on our own, but it couldn't be helped. It was clear who the Focke-Wulf's target was. Willie and Arjun turned to meet the oncoming plane. However, the Jerry was quicker. They fired more than once, but he easily flicked his plane this way and that, dodging them.

"Don't waste your ammo," I said, knowing we'd all be low.

Somehow the Jerry slipped past both of them, now closer still. There was nothing for it. I went on the attack too.

For a split second as I turned, the Jerry was in my sights. I fired a burst, and he simply flipped to the side. My shots went wide. I was also out of position, and now Jonty's plane was open to him.

Jonty must have seen what was happening. He pulled a tight turn and headed for the incoming Focke-Wulf. He fired, and the Jerry dodged it just in time.

"Stay clear," I said to the others. "We don't know which is which."

We were helpless, watching the fight play out. We had no idea which one was Jonty anymore, and it would be impossible for us to take a shot safely. It was all up to Jonty.

Jonty was an expert pilot, that much I knew, and so he had every chance of winning the encounter. Besides, now he was also in a Focke-Wulf it was almost an even match. Except he had no real experience in the plane.

The two Focke-Wulfs dived and weaved in a dance of death. Bursts were exchanged and missed each time. First one would climb and loop over, then the other. It would have been a fantastic aerial combat display had it not been a matter of life and death. Then suddenly one Focke-Wulf got in a lucky shot and the other pitched and yawed before recovering, but something vital had been hit. The manoeuvrability was severely impaired. But which one was it?

The undamaged Focke-Wulf turned and fired again. Smoke started pouring from the engine of the other.

"Is that Jonty? Has he won?" said Arjun.

The smoking Focke-Wulf started to head towards the ground, and the canopy flew off. I saw the pilot bailing out. As his chute opened, he gave me a thumbs-up. It could only be one person.

"It's Jonty," I said. "Jonty's had to bail!"

"Damn him to hell! Why does he have to do this?" growled Willie, gunning his plane towards the other Focke-Wulf which seemed to be going in for the kill.

The Jerry was preoccupied and so never saw the bullets coming. Willie emptied his guns into the German plane, and it exploded. Almost at the same time, the Focke-Wulf Jonty had been flying blew up. Pieces of metal were flying everywhere. We banked away to avoid being hit.

"Well, that's torn it," said Arjun.

"Let's see Jonty safely down," I said. "Then let's go home."

Jonty landed without incident — we'd have to go and fetch him later. The four of us flew disconsolately to Banley. Now we had to face the music.

We landed and as expected, Angelica, Bentley, Audrey and the Marx Brothers were waiting. They would know by now what had happened, as I radioed it in to Control. In any case, Angelica would have gleaned the gist of it from the comms.

She detached herself from the group and ran to me. I caught her up in my arms, glad to feel her embrace. It was comforting, particularly after the disaster of our mission.

"Never mind," she whispered. "You're home — that's all that matters to me."

She kissed me and I kissed her back. It was almost as if she breathed life back into me. When our lips parted I felt so much better.

We walked hand in hand alongside the others, up to where Bentley was waiting. He was smoking his pipe and looking inscrutable.

"What happened out there?" he said.

I related the events in brief while he and the Marx Brothers listened impassively.

"It's a damned shame," he said afterwards. "Anyway, win or lose, we've got some food laid on, so let's repair to the mission room rather than standing out here."

It was a muted celebration all told. Out of all of us, Angelica was the happiest, but only because I'd come back unscathed.

Bentley came over to me once we'd eaten our fill. He was smoking his pipe as usual and seemed, thankfully, quite mellow. I felt it incumbent upon me to try to mitigate what felt like a disaster.

"We did our best, sir, all of us," I said.

He took a few more puffs on his pipe before speaking.

"I know you did, but once again that idiot Butterworth decided to go off script! Disobeying orders and pulling some half-baked stunt. If I hadn't had enough of court-martials, I would damn well have him hauled up in front of one!" said Bentley, firing up.

Jonty's antics rankled with him, and this simply added fuel to the fire.

I'd had time to think about Jonty's actions on the way back, and I also remembered something Bentley had said to me when I asked him why he'd picked me as mission leader.

"Didn't you once say, sir, that sometimes these things call for extraordinary acts of courage — decisive spur-of-the-moment decisions which can turn a failure into a success?"

Bentley eyed me with annoyance at being reminded of his own words.

"Hmph, did I say *that*? Well ... I might have said acts of courage, but not the bloody foolhardy nonsense that damn fool pilot of yours gets up to."

"Supposing he'd brought the plane back, though; wouldn't we be hailing him as a hero?" I persisted.

"Harrumph, hmm, well ... we'll talk about this later, yes indeed," said Bentley. "In the meantime, I suppose you'd better go and get him back here."

"Yes, sir," I said.

"Rotten luck," said Harpo, coming up to me.

"Yes, fortunes of war and all that," said Chico.

They seemed astonishingly phlegmatic about the whole thing.

"Aren't you upset we didn't get the Focke-Wulf after all?" I demanded.

"Yes ... and no," said Chico.

"To be honest, we only rated it a fifty per cent chance of success," said Harpo.

"What!"

Needless to say, I wasn't happy with this callous assessment of our chances.

"Lots of unpredictable factors, as you said," Chico added.

"The two of you were more than just optimistic about it before we did it!" I protested.

"Ah, of course, we always are, but that's life... It doesn't always come up roses." Harpo shrugged.

"You still shot up another lot of Focke-Wulfs, so there's that," said Chico.

"Small consolation when we lost the bigger prize."

"Ah well, don't take it too hard, old chap," said Harpo.

"Onwards and upwards," said Chico.

"I suppose so…"

I wasn't mollified by this, but it was the Marx Brothers all over. They moved seamlessly on to the next thing, and in their line of work there were probably as many failures as successes.

Later that day, Gordon drove me and Angelica down to retrieve Jonty. He was apparently resting up at a farmhouse near to where he had bailed out.

The Marx Brothers drove down too. They wanted to see if there was anything salvageable from the Focke-Wulf, so we went to inspect the crash site first.

The debris from the two Focke-Wulfs was spread far and wide. The explosions had ripped them apart and shredded them like confetti.

"Well, that's that then," said Harpo, surveying the scene.

"Is there nothing of use to the engineers? I mean, some of the pieces?" I ventured.

"Has it not escaped your notice that the remains, or should I say shards, are scattered all over the field?" said Chico.

"Well, yes…" I admitted. It really didn't look as if there was anything intact at all.

"If even the engine had stayed in one piece, it would have been of some use," said Harpo. "But as it stands, it's not good, I'm afraid."

"Blast," I said.

Harpo lit up a cigarette and took a drag. He looked at me with a speculative expression.

"We could always try again…"

"Oh no! No, I'm not doing it a second time," I said, turning to walk away.

"He's definitely not!" said Angelica hotly.

"We're joking, Flying Officer," said Chico, accepting the offer of a cigarette from his colleague.

"Well, it's damn well not funny," I told him.

Chico took a puff. "*C'est la vie*! We will just have to steal the plans instead."

"Oh, really? You couldn't have thought of that in the first place?" I said, unable to stop the tinge of acidity creeping into my voice.

"We did, but this was so much more exciting, don't you think?" said Harpo with a grin.

"Exciting for whom?"

"Where's your sense of adventure, Flying Officer?" said Chico.

"I think I left it in France that time I got shot down, or maybe in the Channel!" I replied.

"We think a lot of you, Flying Officer, and your fiancée here," said Harpo. "We know we're not your favourite people, but you've done more than your fair share in service to this country. We admire that."

"Even if you did shoot the spies we didn't want shot," added Chico.

I shook my head. They were irrepressible. Perhaps it was a feature of their profession.

"Cheer up, Flying Officer," said Harpo. "There's always next time."

"There won't be a next time," I told him.

"Never say never," said Chico.

Unfortunately, I knew he was right. Somehow, these two appeared to be a permanent feature in my existence as long as the war lasted. We left them at the field and went to collect Jonty.

"What-ho, Skipper," he said, looking pleased to see us.

We thanked the farmer, who Jonty designated as 'salt of the earth' and made our way back to Banley.

"How's old Bentley?" asked Jonty a little apprehensively as we drove.

"You'll find out soon enough," I said.

"Oh dear," said Jonty. "It's what Matron used to say before we got sent to see the beak."

"Yes, well, he's not happy, let's put it that way," I told him.

"She used to say that too…"

Bentley wasn't best pleased with Jonty and insisted on seeing him as soon as we arrived.

Jonty and I stood in his office while Bentley tended to his pipe. I was actually quite thankful for this, since it usually put him in a reasonable mood. He puffed on it for a few moments. The fact that we were left standing didn't augur well. Audrey had her head down at her desk, but she had shot Jonty a sympathetic smile when we entered the office.

"You're a bloody fool, Butterworth," Bentley started somewhat mildly.

"Yes, sir."

I wasn't fooled by Bentley's tone; he seemed able to become irascible in very short order. His next utterance bore testament to this.

"Yes, sir? Yes, sir — is that all you have to say? After yet another one of your blasted escapades?"

"No, sir," said Jonty. "I mean, yes, sir."

He looked flustered. Bentley got out of his seat and paced the room.

"I was in two minds about putting you on a charge," he said. "Disobeying orders, yet again! Endangering the lives of the other members of your flight. Committing one of the biggest acts of folly you've managed to date."

"Yes, sir," said Jonty, not knowing what else to say.

"Don't you think we've had enough court-martials in this squadron? Do you think I need another one?" Bentley continued, building up a head of steam.

"Yes, sir. I mean, no, sir."

Bentley puffed on his pipe for a few moments. He was calmer when he spoke again.

"You're a damn fool, Butterworth, and if you weren't such a good pilot, I'd have your guts for garters. We could have lost five of my best pilots all down to your desire to be a hero."

"Yes, sir. I'm sorry, I didn't think…"

"Exactly," said Bentley. "You don't think. That's the trouble. If you tried using your brain once in a blue moon, then maybe you'd actually stop acting like a bloody clown!"

"Yes, sir, I am truly sorry."

Bentley looked at him sceptically. "No, you're not, and I'm sure you'd do the same thing again, given half a chance. But if you could just try contemplating the consequences of your actions before you do something stupid, I'd be grateful."

"Yes, sir," said Jonty.

"All right, get out of here. Dismissed," said Bentley wearily.

"Phew," said Jonty as we left the main building. "It wasn't as bad as I thought it would be."

"Perhaps you could try to take his advice on board," I remarked wryly.

Willie joined us and put his arm around Jonty's shoulders.

"Got another carpeting?" he said.

"Not a bad one, but yes," said Jonty.

"Come and have a cup of tea."

I watched them go and made my way to the bench. Angelica was waiting for me. She smiled up at me as I sat down beside her. Her hand slipped into the crook of my arm.

"Poor Jonty. Did he get a terrible dressing down?"

"Not as bad as some he's had," I said, smiling back.

"You'd have done what he did yourself, given half a chance! Admit it," she said, chiding me gently.

"I thought about it, but only for a split second."

She laughed. "Perhaps I will have to marry you after all, just to make sure you never do anything as stupid as Jonty."

I looked at her to see if she was joking, but she seemed quite serious.

"If that's what it takes," I quipped.

"But I'm not going to be the little wife!"

"I promise never to call you that."

She sighed and her eyes began to twinkle. "It's a shame they don't have a female squadron. I've heard tales of the Night Witches. It's an all-female bomber combat unit in Russia, apparently."

"How on earth do you know *that*?" I asked her.

"I'm not privy to top security intelligence for nothing," she said with a mischievous grin.

"Well, thank God they haven't got one here, because that's exactly what you would go and do."

She giggled at my serious tone. "I don't want to fly, so you're safe enough ... but I'm not staying at home all day being a housewife, if that's what you think!"

I took her in my arms. "I think you should do what you want, and I'd prefer to stay in the RAF if they'll keep me."

"Then so will I, or perhaps I could go and work for the Marx Brothers," she said, teasing me.

"Don't you dare!"

Her lips formed a provocative pout.

"Oh? And how will you stop me?"

"I'll show you exactly how."

I kissed her and she responded fervently. For a few moments, nothing was said. Then our lips parted momentarily.

"Show me again," she whispered. "Never stop showing me…"

A slight breeze was blowing across the airfield. It was a warm, sunny afternoon, and now I was in her arms once more, I was glad to be alive.

A NOTE TO THE READER

Dear Reader,

I hope that you enjoyed the latest in the Mavericks series. Authors get attached to their characters, just as much as readers. I am certainly very fond of my Mavericks crew with all their foibles. I naturally have my favourites. Thank you very much for reading my book.

During my research for this book I came across the intelligence that an audacious raid had actually been planned by the allies to snatch a Focke-Wulf from the Germans, something along the lines of my fictionalised version. For various reasons the raid never took place but I wondered what would have happened if it had. Thus the main plot was born… the plot to steal a Wulf. As they say, truth is often stranger than fiction but I hope I've done it justice and spun a gripping yarn.

I would be very grateful if you could spare the time to write a review on **Amazon** and **Goodreads**. As an author, these reviews are hugely important, and always appreciated.

You can connect with me in other ways too, via my **website**, **Facebook**, **Twitter**, **Instagram**, and a special **Spitfire Mavericks Page**.

I very much hope you were entertained enough to read the next book in the Mavericks series.

Warmest regards,

D. R. Bailey

Sapere Books is an exciting new publisher of brilliant fiction and popular history.

To find out more about our latest releases and our monthly bargain books visit our website: **saperebooks.com**

Printed in Great Britain
by Amazon

44196087R00155